size doesn't Matter

THE BENNETT'S BASTARDS SERIES

JENNIE KEW

SIZE DOESN'T MATTER

ISBN: 978-0-6488899-5-3

Copyright © 2023 by Jennie Kew
Published by Wooden Key Press
Proofread by Hot Tree Editing
Cover design by Mayhem Cover Creations

For my readers,
Thank you for sticking by me
and for sticking around.
I know, this one took a while,
but's it's finally fucking here.
Let's do this!!

The Viking Blues – Heart Award 2021 (2022)
Erotic Romance – Winner

The Viking Blues – Passionate Plume Award 2022
Short Contemporary Romance – Finalist

The Viking Blues – Stiletto Award 2022
Erotic Romance – Finalist

His Own Heaven – Passionate Plume Award 2021
BDSM Romance – Winner

His Own Heaven – Stiletto Award 2021
Long Romance – Finalist

This Time Around – Koru Award of Excellence 2020
Short Romance – 2nd Place

This Time Around – Stiletto Award 2020
Mid-length Romance – Finalist

Third Time Lucky – Passionate Plume Award 2019
BDSM Romance – Finalist

Third Time Lucky – Stiletto Award 2019
Erotic/BDSM Romance – Finalist

"Be prepared to be taken along on a wonderful,
sexy, heartwarming, sometimes tear
inducing, slightly kinky joy ride!"
Review for *Third Time Lucky*

1

"He'll be here."

Sophie Bennett gritted her teeth against the thumping strains of the dance music vibrating through the floor of the ballroom and into her feet, working their way through her body until they reached her brain and shook it, slamming it against the front of her skull, contributing to the dull ache that had formed there before she'd even arrived at the stupid party.

She was distracted, and while she'd heard Anna speak, her brain was having trouble comprehending what she'd said. "What?"

"I said, he'll be here."

Glancing at her phone for the tenth time in as many minutes, Sophie sighed wearily, her shoulders slumping with resignation. "It's a quarter to twelve, Anna," she said, raising her voice against the music. "He's *not* coming, and I'm tired of waiting. Besides, my feet are killing me. I'm going to bed."

Anna tilted her head to one side and lifted a brow. "How could your feet possibly be sore? You're wearing ballet flats.

Unlike me who stupidly wore *these* monstrosities." She stuck out her foot, showing off her gold leather ankle boots with the lattice detailing and deadly four-inch stiletto heel.

Sophie had always loved those boots, even if she could never wear them herself. "But they're very cute monstrosities," she said, trying not to laugh at her friend's pained expression.

And yeah, okay, so her feet weren't killing her, not when compared to Anna's, but usually when she said some body part or other was hurting, Anna put up less of a fight and let Sophie go without argument. But the way her best friend was eyeing her with obvious mistrust meant she wasn't getting away with it this time.

With both feet firmly back on the floor, she said, "Nope. Nice try, babe, but you can't go yet."

"Anna, I really am tired," Sophie groaned. "And I have that video conference with my agent tomorrow. I need my beauty sleep."

Her friend snorted. "You're already beautiful, babe, and that meeting isn't until after lunch. You could sleep the morning away and still show up on time. Bonus, you don't even have to wear pants."

Sophie pressed her lips together, flattening them into a thin line in the hopes of repressing her heavy sigh. "I don't even know why I'm here."

"Because it's New Year's Eve, and we're here to have fun."

That wasn't even remotely what Sophie had meant, but explaining to her best friend that the on-again, off-again fling she'd been having with Australia's premier playboy was heading towards off again took more energy than she could muster.

"Come on, Soph," Anna pleaded, taking her hands in

hers and giving them a light squeeze. "Ethan is probably just waiting to make a grand entrance at the last minute. You know that's his signature move."

"Last minute," she muttered. "Like an afterthought."

Her friend stared at her, concern swirling in her pale green eyes. "Please stay. It's almost midnight. And hey, if you're worried about not having someone to kiss when the clock counts down," she added, waggling her eyebrows and grinning, "I've got you covered."

Sophie pursed her lips but couldn't restrain the laughter that bubbled out of her. "Fine," she said, shaking her head at Anna's antics. "I'll give him five more minutes."

Anna grinned and grabbed two fresh drinks from a passing waiter, handing one to Sophie. "That's the spirit."

"But I'm not making any promises, Anna, kiss or no kiss. If Ethan doesn't get here soon, I'm leaving."

"Fair enough. But... you'll see," she said, distracted by whatever it was she saw over Sophie's shoulder. "Something wonderful is going to happen tonight. I can feel it."

Following Anna's gaze, Sophie turned to watch a young man rip his shirt off, revealing a body of washboard abs and a plethora of tattoos to a crowd of squealing women.

Ten years ago, she would have been one of those women. Hell, ten years ago she would have been the one ripping *her* shirt off.

Now she just rolled her eyes and refocussed her attention on her friend, one eyebrow cocked and a small grin lifting her lips. "Wonderful." When Anna didn't say anything else, she added, "A little young for you, isn't he?"

Anna's taste in men usually ran to the more mature variety.

Her bestie grinned back. "A little. He's pretty to look at,

though." She sipped her drink. "What was I saying? Oh yeah. No way is Ethan missing his own party."

Sophie's grin slipped into a forced smile. She didn't blame Anna for thinking the best of Ethan. The man was adept at making people see only what he wanted them to. But Sophie knew better. She'd seen the man behind the curtain, had seen the mess he hid from the world.

Which begged the question, why was she still entertaining the idea of being with such a self-absorbed arsehole?

She wasn't that lonely.

Was she?

Sighing quietly, she handed her untouched champagne back to Anna and said, "Yeah, no. I'm leaving."

"No! Wait. Why don't you just, I don't know—" She looked around, almost franticly. "—go outside and get some fresh air," she said, waving the champagne flute at the balcony. When Sophie threw her a dubious look, she pleaded, "Please, Soph? Just until midnight. It's New Year's Eve."

Sighing again, she let her shoulders slump in defeat. "Fine. You go drool over your pretty boy and I'll get some fresh air."

Pushing through the heated crush of party people, Sophie slipped out through the balcony doors, letting them shut behind her. The noise instantly receded. The temperature, not so much. Oh, the joy of summer in tropical North Queensland—if the heat didn't kill you, the humidity would. Even at almost midnight, it was still stinking hot outside, and Sophie was glad she'd decided to wear her hair up for the night, even if it didn't frame her face in a perfect Insta-ready fashion.

She breathed deeply, her lungs filling with the intoxicating scent of frangipanis and ocean spray, and the continual rolling *shush* of the waves brushing against the sand helped settle her fractious mind.

She and Ethan had been enjoying their fling for the better part of a year. Okay, maybe *enjoying* wasn't exactly the right term—Ethan didn't do exclusive—but she couldn't deny he was fun.

Especially in the bedroom.

The man was obsessed with her curves, and as stupid as it sounded for a professional model to admit, he made her feel pretty.

As successful as she was, as famous as she was becoming, sometimes Sophie still felt like the fat kid she'd been in school. The one who was teased and bullied and lacked the confidence to stand up for herself.

Obviously, she'd grown since then, both in size and attitude, but along the way, she'd also come to realise that what the world thought of as fat actually wasn't.

By industry standards, yes, Sophie and others like her were the proverbial elephants in the room. In reality she was only a size 16. Not that big at all, really. But standing at six feet one, most people found her intimidating regardless of the size of her waistline.

Which was another thing Ethan had going for him. Even though he was the same height as her, he'd never once made her feel like she took up too much space in the world, never made her feel unfeminine just for being big. And when they were together, his attention was absolute.

But the gaps between their time together had been widening recently, to the point that she rarely saw him at all anymore, and his invitations had begun to feel obligatory.

Sophie was certain Ethan had only invited her to ring in

the new year with him as an afterthought. She was someone he could hook up with at the end of the night, someone familiar who didn't require all the little games and banter necessary for luring someone new into bed.

Not that Ethan had that problem. The scent of money to some women was like the scent of blood to a shark. Drop a billionaire's heir in the hot tub and watch the gold-digging predators circle.

Which was why he liked Sophie. She'd grown up with money and didn't give two shits about it or the status that came along with it. Not that her family's wealth rivalled Ethan's—not even close—but it was enough for her to know better than most that money didn't maketh man.

Manners did.

And Ethan's manners were sorely lacking.

Take this party, for instance. The man had gone to all the trouble of renting out an entire beachside hotel for this shindig, filled it to the brim with acquaintances, friends, and sycophants, then didn't even have the decency to show up.

Typical.

She wasn't even sure why she was surprised anymore. The man had practically made a career out of living an excessive lifestyle with little to no consequences for his actions.

Sophie lifted her gaze to the heavens, took in the silky black of the night sky, and sighed wearily as she realised she no longer much cared about Ethan or his lack of manners.

She hadn't done for a while. Not in any meaningful romantic way, at least.

Just then her phone buzzed with an incoming alert.

After tapping in the passcode and opening the app, she chuckled at the picture that sprang to life on the screen.

Anna had posted a selfie on Instagram, a photo of herself wrapped around the shirtless, tattooed guy while he grabbed her arse and licked her neck.

Getting my New Year's on, bitches! #NYE #partyon #cougar #bemyvalentine

Then her phone dinged with another alert, a video this time. But one that made her smile slip, her face flush, and her stomach drop so fucking fast she felt physically ill.

Someone had tagged Ethan in a video of him at a completely different party, half naked with a very obvious erection tenting his limited-edition Levi's, and with not one but *two* women taking turns shoving their tongues down his throat and their hands down his pants.

Ringing in the #NewYear with my bestie and her beau #bff #threesome #bigdickenergy #cumgetsome @EthanMartinOfficial @Britney-Boo-Boo-Bunnie

"Britney Boo Boo Bunnie? What in the actual *fuck*...?"

Sophie didn't know if she wanted to laugh, cry, or hurl her phone over the railing so she no longer had to suffer staring at the image on her screen. One thing she knew for sure was that she and Ethan Martin were definitely *off* again.

Permanently.

In the end, she settled for laughing as her incredulity at Ethan's disregard for her feelings hit an all-time high.

She didn't care that he wasn't with her.

She didn't care that he wanted to fuck other women.

They'd both known what they had together had a limited shelf life.

What Sophie did take offence to was the fact that Ethan had deliberately invited her to spend the evening with him, then summarily dismissed her out of hand in favour of Britney fucking Boo Boo and her BFF.

She'd been publicly discarded. Deemed unneeded. Unnecessary.

Unwanted.

She was superfluous pussy.

And the thought that she'd been desperate enough for his attention to even show up in the first place made her so goddamn mad.

Because she'd be lying if she didn't admit—at least to herself—that there just might be a grain of truth in it.

She'd been desperate.

Ethan was a selfish fuckboy and an emotional minefield of a man, but he'd made her feel good about herself, had boosted her self-esteem when she'd needed it most. She'd felt less alone in the world.

And that wasn't to say she couldn't be alone for any length of time and not be content, because she could and did. Quite often. But everyone needs to feel a connection sometimes, with someone other than their family or even their best friend.

Sometimes Sophie wanted—*needed*—a man.

Sometimes she needed to be touched and kissed, needed the weight of another human body on top of her. Thrusting between her thighs. Pushing her into the mattress. Or the wall or the floor. Sometimes she needed to feel the heated breath of a lover brush over her skin, craved the touch of a man's hands on her body, adoring her, loving her, pinning her down and fucking her like an animal.

Even if it was only for one night.

Ethan had given her that. And now he'd taken it away.

Whatever. What was done was done. Whatever they'd shared was finished. Time to move on. But on to... what?

More men?

More work?

More... cats?

Ugh. Clicking her phone off, Sophie squeezed it in her fist. "What the hell am I even doing here?" she muttered, not expecting an answer but getting one anyway.

"Same as me, I expect."

The smooth, silky voice coming from the other end of the balcony made Sophie jump, her hand clutching at her wildly beating heart. "Oh my God," she gasped, her breath sawing in and out of her lungs. "What the hell?"

"Sorry," the stranger said, smirking as he stepped out of the shadows.

"I didn't mean to startle you."

"I thought...." Her words faded to nothing as she took in her unexpected interloper, her breath catching in her throat as he moved towards her.

Struck by how graceful his gait was as he strode across the space, Sophie almost missed the way the moonlight caressed his face, highlighting his straight nose, strong jaw, and the flawless five-o'clock shadow that covered it.

Considering the shock she'd just experienced seeing Ethan with another woman—other *women*—she would have thought it impossible to find another man so damn attractive so quickly, but apparently her lady parts didn't give a crap about her emotional needs.

They saw, they wanted.

Simple as that.

As the handsome stranger drew closer, it was difficult to find fault with their reasoning. "And you are?"

"Jack," he said, extending his hand in greeting.

"Sophie," she replied. A tiny zing of electricity flickered along her fingers as she shook his proffered hand, and she almost yanked it away, but then he tightened his grip, preventing her retreat, and the warmth of his palm melted into hers. Melted her disquiet.

"Yes, I know who you are."

"Really?" she asked, surprised by the tone of pleasure in her voice. She was used to people recognising her, so why did the thought of this man knowing who she was make her heart beat a little faster, a little wilder? Jack nodded, and the zing in her fingers faded, morphed into something else, something more enticing than electricity and heat. "I thought I was alone out here," she added, suddenly breathless.

Jack's palm was soft, no calloused skin or scars to indicate he worked with his hands. But his grip was strong and firm, his fingers curling around hers in a show of authority and command. Then he dropped her hand, and Sophie forced down a needy whimper at the loss of his touch.

What the hell is wrong with me?

"Sorry about that," he said, confusing her for a moment until she realised he was apologising for stealing her solitude, not for depriving her of his magic fingers. "I just needed a break from the noise inside." He thumbed over his shoulder at the shadowy corner he'd emerged from. "Seemed like a good place to hide."

Relaxing a little at his admission, she smiled and asked, "And who were you hiding from?"

"No one," he said. Then his mouth kicked up in one corner. "And everyone."

She laughed, unable to repress the flirty undertone. "I guess that makes two of us."

"And what brings you here tonight, Sophie?" Jack asked, moving closer. "Was it a person or the promise of fireworks?"

Sophie liked the way he said her name, the way it slipped off his tongue like warmed honey. The whisper of a grin playing around the corners of his mouth made his suggestion of fireworks seem almost obscene, and when Jack rested his hand on the balcony railing right beside her waist, his thumb achingly close to her body, she was tempted to close the minuscule distance and lean into it just to see what he would do or say next.

Screw it. Closing the distance, she leaned against the railing, trapping his thumb between the warmth of her body and the cold steel. "I didn't think they were having fireworks this year."

Jack didn't disappoint. He stroked his thumb against the soft flesh at her waist, the pressure of the digit against her body firm and sure. The heat of the gesture slowly burned a hole through her formfitting dress, adding another layer of suggestion to his words.

"I guess that depends on your definition of fireworks, doesn't it?"

2

The light spilling from the party inside highlighted the blush colouring Sophie's cheeks and the straight white teeth sinking into her plush bottom lip. Her body's innocent reaction to Jack's thinly veiled innuendo made his cock twitch, and his need to touch her more thoroughly had him sliding his hand more fully against her generous hip.

Her gaze dipped for a moment, and her ample chest heaved as she sucked in a breath. When her dark brown eyes met his again, he saw her hesitation.

"In truth," she said, sighing softly, "I *was* supposed to meet someone tonight."

"Oh?"

"Yeah." She glanced away as though embarrassed. "But he ditched me for greener pastures."

My brother is an idiot. "Greener pastures, huh?" Jack grinned, hiding his displeasure at Ethan's callous stupidity. "That's funny."

Sophie's brow scrunched, and a little crease appeared

just above her nose, but she sounded more curious than offended when she asked, "How is that funny?"

"Greener pastures," he repeated, his grin broadening. "It sounds like one of those wordplays. You know, tell me your ex's new woman is a cow without telling me she's a cow?"

Curiosity turned into delight as laughter exploded out of her, a throaty, sultry sound that coiled itself around him, drawing him closer. Or maybe that was him, slipping his free hand over her other hip and tugging her closer, gripping her tighter and sinking his fingers into all that softness and warmth.

Pressing their bodies together in all the best places.

"I've never thought of it that way before," she said, smiling and suddenly breathless, "but you're right. It does kinda sound that way, doesn't it?" Then her smile faded, and she dropped her gaze again, pursing her lips as an odd combination of irritation and resignation clouded her pretty face. "And it was new *women*. Plural."

Jack's jaw clenched at the reminder of his brother's thoughtless actions. If Ethan had no intention of spending the night with Sophie, why didn't he just man the fuck up and tell her? That would have been 100 percent better than brazenly splashing his disregard for her all over social media for everyone to see.

But the look of consternation on Sophie's face forced Jack to relax, made him want to make her laugh again and forget all about the dumb twat who'd stood her up. "So, a herd of cows, then?"

Her expression softened into something resembling relief, and one corner of her mouth lifted in a rueful smile. "I guess so."

She tilted her head slightly and stared at him, her lovely eyes considering, skating over his features and studying him in a way most people didn't dare to. Looked at him as if he was more than Hugh Martin's youngest son, more than the uncompromising businessman he'd been groomed to be.

More than Ethan Martin's grim-faced younger brother.

"You're funny," she said with a decisive nod, as though she'd made up her mind about him.

Jack laughed at her observation, letting loose a rumbling chuckle he almost didn't recognise as his. "That's not something I'm often accused of."

She cocked one brow and grinned at him. "No?"

He shook his head. "Afraid not. And for the record," he said, leaning in to whisper in her ear, "I've always found the grass is greener where you water it."

Pulling back to stare at her, he noticed her breathing grow heavy, wanton, stuttering in and out of her lungs as her gaze dropped to his mouth and back again. As she stared at him with those dark, penetrating eyes. "A wise philosophy," she murmured.

Taking a chance, Jack angled his mouth over hers and leaned closer, loving how her height matched his, how well they fit against each other, and he wondered not for the first time how she'd feel stretched out beneath him, all her soft curves and silky skin his to touch and devour. His to brand with his teeth and lips and the sharp sting of his palm. His fingers curled into her hips, eager, wanting. "God, you're beautiful."

But his words didn't have the effect he'd anticipated, and Sophie pulled away slightly, her lips pressed together in a thin smile. "Oh, Jack, and we were off to such a good start," she said, her sigh slightly exaggerated as she straightened his collar.

Jack's eyes narrowed, his curiosity piqued. "Did I say something wrong?"

She shook her head. "Not really, no." When he cocked one brow in silent question, she elaborated. "It's just that you're the twenty-seventh man tonight to tell me I'm beautiful."

"Oh," he said, confused by her statement. Confusion wasn't a state of being Jack enjoyed. He had to know things. "And that's a *bad* thing?" He was going to need clarification on that point.

"When you know the only reason they're saying it is because they think you're a bobble-headed idiot and flattery is the quickest way to get in your pants, then yes, it's a *very* bad thing."

"I see your point," Jack said, nodding sagely. "And in that case, I take it back. You're hideous." He shuddered and made a gagging noise. "Ugly as sin."

The look of shock on Sophie's face was thankfully followed by another burst of laughter, the sound vibrant and wonderful. "I told you you were funny." Then she inclined her head and grinned at him and his odd compliment. "Thank you."

"You're welcome," he said, matching her smile with one of his own. The unfamiliar action was beginning to feel more natural the more he did it, as though his face had suddenly remembered how to do it and was determined to imprint the action into his muscle memory so he wouldn't forget again. His cheeks were going to hurt in the morning. "But tell me, do you always keep track of how many men tell you you're beautiful?"

"Not always." She lifted one shoulder in a small shrug. "Just when I'm with Anna."

"Anna Valentine?"

She smiled and nodded, then gave him an appraising look as though she was pleasantly surprised he'd bothered to take the time to learn her friend's surname. But of course he knew who Anna was. Not just because she was one of Australia's top models, but because she was Sophie Bennett's best friend. Which was common knowledge for anyone who didn't live under a rock, not at all weird or stalkery.

"Yes. We made a competition out of it years ago. Tally up how many times men tell us we're beautiful, highest score wins."

"Wins what?"

"Anything we want," she said, then added with a laugh, "up to a value of ten dollars."

"And what do buy with your ten dollars?"

Sophie cocked one brow. "You're assuming I've won?"

Jack stepped back and very deliberately slid his gaze from her lovely face and stunning eyes to the tips of her sensible yet fashionable shoes and back again, taking in every inch of her statuesque beauty, every luscious curve of her hourglass figure. Watched every staggered rise and fall of her ample chest as she awaited his answer.

"How could you lose?"

The way she suddenly dropped her gaze and sank her teeth into her bottom lip in a show of bashful pleasure was like catnip to a man like him, the submissive gesture combined with the pale blush staining her cheeks making his cock as hard as a steel pipe. Making him want to pull her even closer and steal her breath with a hard kiss.

But before he could pull her close again, tilt his head, and close the tiny distance that would bring his mouth crashing down on hers, a burst of excitement rose up from the party inside, and the sound of people chanting, counting down the seconds to midnight, filled the air.

And ruined the moment.

Sophie turned her head to glance inside the ballroom. "Sounds like it's time."

"Yes," he agreed, then lifted one hand from her hip to stroke his fingertips over her jaw, gently turning her to face him again. "May I kiss you, Sophie?"

Her attention focussed back on him, she smiled, seemingly surprised that he'd bothered to ask, then nodded. "Yes. Please."

Jack slid his hand from her face to the nape of her neck, pulled her close, and angled his mouth over hers. "Happy New Year, Sophie," he murmured.

"Happy New Year, Jack."

Inside, the revellers cried, "Happy New Year," and began singing a drunken rendition of "Auld Lang Syne", but when his lips met hers, all sound disappeared into the background, and there was only her. Only Sophie and the soft mewling she made as she pressed her body closer, slid her hands over his shoulders, and wrapped her arms around his neck. Clung to him as he parted her lips and tasted crisp champagne on her tongue.

He had no idea how long they stayed like that—it could have been years for all Jack knew or cared. Time ceased to exist, faded into the ether along with everything that wasn't her. Her warmth, her softness, the strong yet languid stroke of her silken tongue as it slid against his. These were the things that filled Jack's world now, that consumed it.

And him.

He wanted—*needed*—more of her.

He needed *all* of her.

Not just a single kiss on a balcony on New Year's Eve.

He wanted her in his bed, stretched out under his body as he took his pleasure in her and made her scream. Or maybe she would moan his name instead, her heated breath quiet and soft in his ear as she came.

He needed to know.

Jack tightened his grip on her neck, ensuring she couldn't escape him, then slid his other hand from her hip to her luscious arse and squeezed. Forced their bodies closer, pressed his aching erection against her soft belly.

Sophie's mewling turned to moaning, and her tongue lashed against his as their kiss grew more frenzied. Her fingers speared into the hair at his nape, her fingernails scoring his flesh. She tilted her hips and rocked her body against his, creating the most erotic friction. It was torture. Sweet, heavenly torture.

But it still wasn't enough.

Pulling his mouth away from hers, Jack dragged Sophie into the shadowy corner he'd occupied earlier, away from the lights and the noise of the party, cocooning them in cosy darkness. "More," he demanded, yanking her back into his arms as he leaned against the brick wall, protecting her from the rough surface as he thrust his knee between her legs, wedging them apart.

"Jack," she murmured, a desperate edge permeating her luscious voice. "Yes. More."

Their mouths collided in another violent ballet of passionate, blissful indulgence, until the balcony doors flew open and more people spilled from the ballroom, splashing champagne over the decking, laughing, and singing off key.

The interruption caused Sophie to break the kiss, snapping them both out of their tiny, intimate world full of endless possibility and back into the real world full of, well, reality. But no one said it had to stay that way.

The night was young.

The year was new.

Endless possibilities.

Wasn't that what New Year's was all about?

Jack watched, fascinated, as Sophie brought her finger-tips to the corners of her mouth, touching up her lipstick. He'd seen his mother do it often enough after his father had stolen a kiss to know that's what she was doing. Her dress had hitched up a few inches, too, the clingy red fabric barely covering that fantastic arse.

Leaning down, he straightened the hem, tugging it down to its usual midthigh length, then smoothed his hands over her hips. He let his gaze roam over her, making sure she looked as gorgeous and as unmolested as she had when she'd come out to the balcony—he checked his watch —*Jesus*, less than twenty minutes ago.

He'd never made out with a woman that fast before.

Seducing beautiful women within minutes of meeting them was Ethan's domain, not his. The thought of which had him wincing, realising he'd just taken advantage of a vulnerable woman.

But when his eyes met hers again she was smiling. And laughing, her body shaking with barely there tremors as she reached out to straighten his shirt collar and smooth her hands over his shoulders and down his chest.

"This was fun," she said, her eyes bright with light reflected from inside the ballroom. Then she lowered her gaze, and her smile grew shy. "Thank you."

She was thanking him. For what? For kissing her? For mauling her like a wild animal who hadn't gotten laid in months?

For rescuing her from a night of solitude and loneliness? Because that's what she'd done for him.

As it was, he still found it hard to believe she was even there, in his arms.

Sophie Bennett—his celebrity crush—had willingly and eagerly kissed him.

It was ridiculous. He was a grown man, for fuck's sake. Known for his ruthlessness in the boardroom and, for those who knew him more intimately, his dominance in the bedroom. He'd outgrown crushing on girls a long time ago. Yet here he was, staring at the most beautiful woman he'd ever laid eyes on, the urge to say something stupid like "You're welcome" heavy on the tip of his tongue.

Gripping her hips tighter, he pulled her close again—close enough to let her feel his still-rampant erection—then swallowed down his disbelief and said, "Thank you for what?"

Lifting her face, she pinched her lush bottom lip between her teeth before letting it slip free, gifting him with another one of those coy little smiles. "For the fireworks."

Jack couldn't restrain his grin as he stared at Sophie. Her words, simple as they were, made him feel ten feet tall and bulletproof. Invincible.

Bold.

"May I walk you back to your room?" he asked, the devil on his shoulder filling him with hope.

Sophie's eyes widened, and one corner of her mouth hitched up, transforming her smile into a lopsided grin, as though she wasn't sure if she was pleased by his question or not. Jack didn't often ask questions he didn't already know the answer to, so the fact that she didn't answer him immediately made his teeth itch.

He hated uncertainty. Especially when it looked like things might not go his way.

But then Sophie wriggled against him and leaned in close. Close enough that he could feel the heat of her lips brush over his. "No," she said decisively, crushing his newfound hope. Then she cupped his cheek in one hand and his aching balls in the other. "But you can take me back to yours."

3

Jack turned his suddenly grinning face against Sophie's hand and kissed her palm, then grabbed her wrist in his vicelike grip and dragged her back inside. It seemed he was fond of dragging her around. Like a caveman. A very sexy, well-dressed caveman who smelled like expensive cologne and tasted like the smoothest bourbon.

They made their way across the crowded ballroom, dodging dancing couples and waitstaff alike, and a small group of very enthusiastic exhibitionists who either didn't realise they were drawing an audience or simply didn't care. Nothing out of the ordinary for one of Ethan's parties.

But Sophie couldn't see Anna anywhere.

As they cut a swathe across the room, she checked her phone for messages or missed calls, but there were neither. *Where is she?*

Yanking on Jack's hand to slow him down, she threw him an apologetic look and raised her voice against the noise of the party. "I need to call Anna. To tell her where I'm going."

He nodded. "Let's get out of here first. It'll be quieter in the hallway."

As soon as they exited the ballroom and the doors clicked shut behind them, the noise died down to a dull roar, and Sophie hit the speed dial for Anna's phone number. Her friend picked up almost immediately. "Hey, babe! Happy New Year!"

Sophie sighed in relief. "Happy New Year. Where are you?"

"Ah, I just got back to our room. Why?" A male voice muttered something in the background, and Anna laughed, the sound sultry and low. "Where are you?" she asked, the tone in her voice searching, making Sophie's lips quirk and her eyes roll.

"I'm outside the ballroom. I'm just calling to let you know I won't be back to the room tonight."

"See?" Anna said, the word drowning in smugness. "I told you Ethan would show up eventually."

"*Yeeeah*," Sophie said, dragging the word out as she flicked her gaze to Jack and quickly found herself caught in his intoxicating stare. If she'd thought he was handsome out on the balcony where the lighting was iffy at best, it was nothing compared to what the man looked like in a well-lit hallway. He was gorgeous. Ovaries exploding, pussy running the show, power to make a girl stupid gorgeous. Her breath caught in her chest. "I'm not with Ethan."

"You're not with...? What happened to Ethan?"

Her gaze darted away from Jack's, embarrassment heating her cheeks. "Check your Instagram," she replied drily, her lips thinning as the memory of her on-again, off-again lover with someone else's tongue down his throat for all the world to see threatened to ruin what was shaping up to be a rather enjoyable evening, despite Ethan's betrayal.

Then Jack slid his hands over her hips and pulled her closer, nuzzled the sweet spot just below her ear, and chased the dark thoughts away. Sophie bit her lip to rein in her moan, but her voice still came out breathy when she said, "I have to go."

"Yeah, okay," Anna said, sounding as distracted as Sophie felt. "Name and room number?"

"His name is Jack, and he's in room...?" She pushed him back far enough to catch his gaze again and raised her eyebrows in question.

He grinned. "702."

"Room 702."

"Jack, 702. Got it. And Soph?"

She licked her lips, flicking her gaze between Jack's sapphire-blue eyes and the sensual curve of his mouth, only half listening to Anna when she replied, "Yeah?"

Anna paused the way she always did when she wasn't sure she should say something. "Don't overthink it, okay?" Sophie frowned at the comment, but before she could ask Anna what she meant by it, her friend added, her tone only slightly pleading, "Just have fun."

Oh. That's what she meant. Her gaze snagged again on Jack's penetrating stare. "I'll see you tomorrow," Sophie said, suddenly breathless again. "Be safe."

"You too."

After disconnecting the call, she fisted her hand around her phone. *Just have fun.* She wasn't sure she knew what fun was anymore, only that it wasn't what she'd been having for a long time.

"I like that," Jack said, interrupting her thoughts. "That you check in with each other. It's sensible."

Sophie didn't know if she should roll her eyes again or

groan. In the end, she snorted. "Yeah, because nothing says sexy like *sensible*."

He tugged her closer, pressed his warm lips against the shell of her ear, and purred, "I'm an accountant. I think sensible is *very* sexy."

Her body bouncing with quiet laughter, Sophie had the overwhelming urge to melt into Jack, to bury her nose in the crook of his neck and inhale more of his enticing scent. If sensible was sexy, a good sense of humour was sublime. "An accountant, huh?"

"Mm-hmm." His lips buzzed against her ear. But then the warmth of his body was gone, and Sophie was left staggering, weak-kneed at the loss of Jack's touch, his scent. He stepped away and pressed the call button for the lift, then turned slowly, his bottom lip pinched between his teeth and a slight frown pulling at his brow.

Sudden wariness stabbed at her, replacing her anticipation with something akin to dread. "Is everything okay?"

His expression smoothing out, Jack took Sophie's hand and faced them both towards the lift. "Yes." He paused. "Maybe."

"That doesn't sound promising," she muttered and tried removing her hand from his, but his grip tightened, locking her fingers between his.

She wasn't going anywhere.

The knowledge sent a little thrill through her veins, heating her blood and quickening her heartbeat. She liked it, his subtle display of dominance.

"Before we get to my room, I need to tell you something." Gently, he squeezed her fingers. "It's important."

The lift pinged, and the doors slid open. A group of laughing partygoers spilled from inside the mirror-lined box, almost knocking Sophie over, but Jack moved like lightning, locking a strong arm around her waist and shifting her out of harm's way.

"Thanks," she said, pressing her hand against her stomach in a bid to quell the butterflies fighting to free themselves from her belly.

Jack's seriousness had her old friends Anxiety and Insecurity fighting for dominance inside her brain. Why the sudden change in mood? Had he changed his mind? Was he going to reject her now?

She couldn't go back to her room if he did, not with Anna and her new plaything sexing it up. And she wasn't going back to the party to be hit on by drunken arseholes again.

Even she wasn't that pathetic.

As Jack guided her into the empty lift, the heat of his palm warmed her, chasing away the goose bumps her nerves had incited, but it wasn't enough to melt away all her unease.

"This thing you need to tell me," she said, lifting her chin in a show of confidence she didn't quite feel, "is it more important than, say, getting naked and enjoying a night of enthusiastic and imaginative sex?"

The sound that escaped Jack was half chuckle, half pained groan, and the last of her nerves settled as she regained control of herself. "I'm afraid so," he said.

Turning in his arms, Sophie slid her hands over his chest and nuzzled against his jaw, then nipped at the sensitive skin just below his earlobe and smiled when she felt him shiver. "And it can't wait until tomorrow?"

Jack sighed and extricated himself from her embrace, holding her hands in his. "Once I tell you what I need to tell you, there might not be a tomorrow."

Brow scrunched and eyes narrowed, she asked, "What's that supposed to mean?"

His jaw tightened, and his mouth twisted into a grimace. "It's about Ethan."

Resisting the urge to yank her hands away and fold her arms across her chest to barricade herself against whatever he was about to say, Sophie said, "Then you definitely shouldn't tell me."

The last thing she wanted to do was talk about Ethan.

She wanted to lose herself in Jack, to enjoy more of his sensual kisses and heated looks and strong hands on her skin.

She didn't want to think.

She wanted to fuck.

She wanted to let go, to forget, to just... *have fun.*

Jack's smile was bashful, almost grateful, before his mouth fell back into its former tight line and he raked one hand through his hair. "That's not really an option at this point." He cleared his throat and looked away, smoothing his hand down his shirtfront.

What could possibly make a grown man so nervous?

When the lift doors opened on the seventh floor, Jack again slid his hand to the small of Sophie's back and guided her into the hallway. "I'm up this way," he said, indicating the door to the far left.

The décor was a lot more lavish than the hallway on the third floor, where her modest room was situated. The carpet was plush, the wall sconces handmade, the artwork not mass-produced. And that was when she remembered the hotel only had seven floors. Her gaze slid sideways, her eyes wide as she took in the man beside her. Jack was staying in one of the penthouses.

Who is this guy? And what is he to Ethan?

As if reading her mind, Jack said, "Did Ethan ever talk to you about his family?"

Steeling herself for whatever bomb Jack was about to drop, Sophie said, "Talking about anything was never really high on Ethan's list of priorities, but yes, he did."

"What did he tell you?" Jack's tone was conversational, but his hand flexed against her lower back as he guided her to his door, as if he'd felt the sudden stiffness in her spine.

What had she gotten herself into? "No offence, but until I know who you are to Ethan, I'm not telling you anything that was told to me in private."

Jack chuckled and smiled broadly, transforming his expression into something almost boyish. "Beautiful, sensible, and trustworthy." Then that smile turned wry. "My brother is a fucking idiot."

"Brother?" Sophie stopped walking and stared at the back of Jack's head as he continued marching towards his room. He stopped when their hands began to pull apart and looked back over his shoulder, that wry grin of his coupled with a searching gaze. "Ethan's brother is called Jonathon," she said, the words barely squeezing past the lump in her throat.

Shaking his head, Jack said, "I hate it when he calls me that." Then he sighed and added, "Which is probably why he does it."

Wait. What? Every fibre of Sophie's body froze, her mouth ran dry, and she swallowed hard, almost choking on her incredulity. "I'm sorry, but it sounded like you said you're Ethan's brother."

He inclined his head. "That's exactly what I said."

She took a step back, and this time he let her, their fingers untwining, their hands falling apart. But the more she stared at him and let her gaze travel over his slim yet well-built frame, his long legs and trim waist, strong chest, stubbled chin and tousled hair, the more her eyes narrowed with suspicion. "You look nothing like him."

Jack bit back a laugh. "Look closer," he said, pointing to his eyes.

Almost squinting to see, Sophie stared into his eyes, but the muted hallway lighting wasn't ideal. Finding the torch app on her phone, she shone a light in Jack's eyes, making him wince and scowl, but she saw what he was talking about. His eyes were a very particular shade of sapphire blue. The exact same shade of blue as Ethan's.

"Oh my God," she groaned. "You're Ethan's brother."

4

"Jack Martin, at your service," Jack said with a slight bow. Then he took in Sophie's wide eyes and slack jaw and sighed quietly.

His perfect evening had come to a screeching halt.

"So let me get this straight," she said, pinching the bridge of her nose. "Not only did Ethan invite me to and then ditch me at his own party, but he made a spectacle of himself on social media ensuring I would *never* fuck him again, and then he set me up with his brother to what... soften the blow?"

"This isn't a set-up, Sophie."

"Really?" She stared at him like he was a complete idiot. "Because it feels very much like a set-up to me."

Jack scrubbed his hand across his jaw, frowning as he remembered Ethan's insistence that he attend the party, knowing full well how much Jack loathed parties and that he would probably end up slinking off to a quiet corner somewhere to wait until it was all over and then go to bed alone. As usual. "Hmm. It does, doesn't it?"

"That bloody coward," Sophie snarled through a

clenched jaw, then made the most adorable growl of frustration Jack had ever heard. "And you know what? No. I want to see some ID. I want proof you are who you say you are and not some twat wearing contact lenses."

Biting back a smile, he reached into his back pocket for his wallet and produced his driver's licence for her perusal, revealing another secret only a very select few knew about.

Sophie stared at his licence for a full minute before lifting her gaze to his, her eyes wide and her grin broad. "Your middle name is Aloysius?"

Jack scowled. "Yes. My father named me Jonathon after his father. My mother named me Aloysius after a teddy bear in a book."

A snort of laughter escaped his companion as she handed the ID back to him. "Fine. You are who you say you are. No one's going to admit to a name like that unless they have to." Her smile slipped, and her back straightened. "But this still feels like a set-up."

He had to agree. Taking in Sophie's stiff posture and look of annoyance, he sighed again and said, "I'll walk you back to your room."

She levelled a glare at him that would have felled lesser men, then cocked one brow. "Why?" she demanded. "As far as I'm concerned, Ethan's the one who screwed up here, not us. Why should we punish ourselves for *his* stupidity?"

Jack stared at Sophie with a combination of shock and awe, even as one corner of his mouth lifted in a satisfied grin. Of all the things she could have said, that was not the answer he'd been expecting. "Are you saying you'd still like to come in?"

"Will there be more kissing?" she asked, her glare softening, her gaze darting away, submissive once more.

He stroked her cheek and lifted her chin, let her see the

depth of his desire for her in his eyes. "Yes, there will be a lot more kissing."

"Then yes. I'd like to come in."

"In that case...." He pulled his room key from his pocket and held the card against the sensor until the lock clicked open. "Shall we?"

Holding the door open, he slid his palm to the small of Sophie's back and ushered her in ahead of him, enjoying the sway of her shapely hips and spectacular arse as she walked farther into the room. That curve-hugging dress was playing havoc with his control. It was going to kill him if she didn't lose it soon.

"Would you like a drink?" he asked, following her into the well-appointed living area of his suite.

Sophie glanced at him as she walked to the balcony and opened the doors, letting in the warm sea air and the sound of the waves brushing against the sand. "Sure. What have you got?"

Jack moved into the kitchen, opened the fridge, and chuckled, shaking his head and wondering if every party guest had been the recipient of his brother's generosity or if it was just him. Knowing Ethan, it was probably everyone. A ridiculously expensive bottle of champagne, a plate of chocolate-covered strawberries, and a charcuterie board filled with shaved meats, fresh fruit, and a selection of gourmet cheeses awaited them. A half dozen bottles of Italian spring water filled the fridge door.

"Champagne or water?" he called over his shoulder, doing a double take when he saw her standing directly behind him. He hadn't heard her cross the room, but he didn't miss the hungry look in her eyes or the way her pretty pink tongue flicked across her bottom lip. A sense of satisfaction flowed through him knowing she was looking at him that way.

"Water, please. I'm not much of a drinker these days." Then that hungry gaze shifted to the interior of the fridge and intensified. "And is that cheese? I'm starving."

Jack bit back a laugh at his presumptive thoughts—was this woman ever going to do or say anything he expected? —and handed Sophie two bottles of water. Grabbing the snacks, he kicked the fridge door shut. "How about we sit on the balcony?" he suggested, pleased when she nodded and held back the filmy curtains so he could walk through the doors unimpeded.

The view from the penthouse balconies was beautiful. Unlike the one from the first-floor ballroom, Jack's from the seventh floor wasn't obstructed by palm trees and frangipanis, although the heavy scent of the pink-and-yellow blooms did reach them on the thick tropical air. As he set the food on the table, he smiled to himself, watching Sophie close her eyes and breathe deeply, inhaling the perfumed air.

"Your view is a lot nicer than mine," she said, twisting the tops off the water bottles and setting them on the table. Reaching down, she tugged off her shoes and wiggled her toes, drawing Jack's attention to her brightly coloured toenails. *Cute.* "My room overlooks the pool," she continued, leaning on the railing and staring out at the water, "and call me old-fashioned, but moonlight looks so much prettier dancing across the Pacific Ocean instead of a chlorinated cesspit of bodily fluids."

Laughter exploded out of Jack, shaking his whole body with the effort and snapping his attention away from his languid perusal of her shapely figure towards her pretty face and the sassy grin that decorated it. "Come here," he said, pulling her closer.

She didn't resist, leaning into him eagerly and letting him take her mouth, letting him continue his languid perusal of her body on a more intimate level.

She felt so soft, not just the fabric of her dress but her— her hips, her arse, her breasts, her mouth. Everywhere he touched was soft and warm, but he needed more. He needed to feel her skin against his. Needed to touch *her*.

Sliding his fingers into her hair, he found the pins holding her updo in place and gently pulled them free, letting the long, dark strands cascade down her back and giving him something he could bury his fist in as he plundered her mouth once more. Sophie mewled against his lips, the little sound so perfectly feminine it made the semi-hardness he'd been sporting in his trousers since before they got in the elevator suddenly harden again, lengthen, beg for her attention.

"Jack." Sophie moaned against his mouth and tugged his shirt free of his pants. "Need to touch you," she said, sliding her hands under his shirt and over his stomach, electrifying his skin and making his muscles clench in response to her featherlight touch. Then she grabbed the waistband of his pants and tugged him closer.

But it still wasn't close enough.

"Strip," he demanded, twisting his fist in her hair. "Take the dress off. Now."

Sophie's eyelids shuttered, and her hot little mouth lifted in the smallest of smiles. He released her and she turned her back on him, sweeping her hair over one shoulder and revealing the zipper of her dress. "I'll need some help with that," she said, her voice soft and breathy.

So fucking sexy.

Jack slid one hand over her shoulder, then gently wrapped it around her throat, holding her still as he used his other hand to draw the zipper down. Inch by inch he revealed Sophie's back to his lustful gaze, felt her pulse tick faster, heard her breathing grow more laboured. If her panties weren't soaked by the time the zipper reached its end, he'd eat his own shirt.

Sophie slid the straps of her dress off her shoulders, then wriggled the clingy red fabric down over her bountiful curves until it pooled around her ankles.

"Fuck me," he growled, not knowing where to look as he tried to take in the vision of all of her at once.

"I thought that was the idea," she said over her shoulder, another one of those cheeky grins lifting the corners of her so-very-kissable mouth.

Jack caught her gaze, saw his own need reflected back at him in her rich, brown eyes. "Face me," he murmured, letting his hand trail from her neck to her shoulder and down her arm until he held her hand in his.

If he thought she was stunning with the dress on, it was nothing to how he felt now that she was almost naked. He'd seen photos of her in lingerie before, but nothing could have prepared him for the sight of her actually standing before him dressed like that. Her body wrapped in satin and lace, the delicate black fabric designed to drive a man wild.

And it did.

Sophie Bennett was his fantasy come to life.

"You're so beautiful."

Instead of sighing and pulling away as she'd done earlier, scolding him for saying something so clichéd, her smile grew shy, and her gaze dropped away from his. "Thank you," she said softly.

"Are you still hungry?"

She glanced up at him from under her lashes and nodded. "Famished," she said. "But before we eat... may I?" She tugged at the top button of his shirt.

Jack nodded. "You may."

Sophie popped the buttons open one after the other, her fingertips brushing against his chest with each torturously slow movement. Gritting his teeth, he fought back his need to laugh at her ticklish touches, and by the time she reached the last button, he was ready to rip his fucking shirt off and toss it over the balcony.

Jack wanted her hands on him, but not like this. He wanted her to explore his body, searing his flesh with her delicate fingers. He wanted to know exactly how her soft palm felt wrapped around his cock, how her lips and teeth and tongue felt as she swallowed him down her throat. He wanted her body under his, restrained and at his mercy as he took his pleasure in her.

Fuck.

He just wanted *her*.

Period.

But any man worth his salt knows his woman's needs come first, and Sophie needed to eat. As soon as his shirt hit the decking, he said, "Come here." Taking a seat at the table, he tugged her down onto his lap, groaning as her hip pressed against his erection.

"I like it when you make that sound," she said, picking through the selections on the charcuterie board.

He wrapped an arm around her waist to hold her steady as his other hand settled on her warm thigh. "You like making me groan in sexual frustration?"

"Absolutely."

"Why?" he asked, surprised to find he actually wanted to know her answer.

When was the last time he'd wanted to simply talk with a woman? With anyone, for that matter? He'd spent so much of the last few years alone that even his family were surprised when he showed up to events. Even more so when he actually engaged someone in conversation.

"Because... you want sex but you're not pushing me for it. You're willing to sit here, obviously uncomfortable physically, and wait for me to eat and drink, wait for me to become comfortable enough with you to let you fuck me." She grabbed a slice of watermelon and topped it with a small slice of brie. "And also...."

Jack smiled as she hedged around whatever she was about to say, her gaze dropping like it had before, her grin growing shy, and a blush staining her cheeks. "What?"

She glanced at him sideways, then pressed the snack to his lips. He greedily accepted it and swallowed it down, then grabbed her wrist to stop her retreat and sucked her fingertips into his mouth, licking clean the sticky sweet melon juice. He enjoyed the way her throat bobbed when she swallowed hard, her burning gaze now glued to his mouth.

She licked her lips, then shook herself, presumably to refocus on whatever it was she was about to say before he derailed her thoughts. "Ah, your groan, it wasn't an 'oh my God, you're too fat and heavy for my weak little matchstick legs' groan."

His mouth twitched at the corners again. "No?"

"No." She smiled. "It was a good groan. A sexy groan." She popped a wedge of cheese in her mouth, then wriggled her arse against his thighs, brushing against his rock-hard cock and making him groan again. "And I'm gunna go out on a limb here and say you never miss leg day, do you?" She wriggled again, and it took all his restraint to stay still and let her torture him. "Your thighs are freaking impressive."

Jack's body shook with his amusement. "Thank you. And you are correct. I never miss leg day." He grabbed her hand again and held it against his chest, his smile growing as Sophie began exploring his body on her own, stroking her fingers over the muscles he'd spent years cultivating in the gym. Leaving those fiery little trails he craved in her wake. "I never miss any day."

Her eyes narrowed playfully. "Gym junkie, eh?"

Jack shrugged. "I'm single. I have to burn off my excess energy somehow."

Her gaze turned contemplative, and he had a hunch she was comparing him to his brother. Ethan had a very different way of burning off energy, and it didn't involve suicide sprints.

Before he could internalise that thought and let it eat at him, Sophie wriggled her arse again and grinned.

"I bet we could sit like this all night, and you wouldn't complain, would you?" She popped another piece of brie in her mouth. "I bet these tree trunks you call thighs could withstand pretty much anything. Hell, I'm more likely to end up with a sore arse from sitting on rock-hard muscle before you tell me to get off your lap."

"Hmm, let me think about that one," Jack said, biting back his amusement while pretending for all of three seconds to contemplate her words. "Complain about a beautiful woman sitting in my lap half naked, feeding me snacks and making me laugh more in the past few minutes than I have in the past few years?" He nodded slowly. "Yeah, I think I'm okay with that. As for the other thing...."

"Yes?"

"The second you say you're done," he growled, nodding

at the food, "I'm ripping that lingerie from your body and using the scraps to tie you up." His grip tightened on her thigh until she whimpered. "Then I'm going to give you something else rock-hard to sit on, and by the time I'm done with you, you will *definitely* end up with a sore arse."

Sophie sucked back another sudden breath, her breasts heaved, and her hand fluttered to the base of her throat. She moved to lower her face again, but Jack caught her chin and made her meet his gaze, revelled in the fire he saw staring back at him. The wanting, the need that flooded her dark eyes was like a siren's call, willing him to close the gap between them and take her.

But she beat him to it when she leaned into him, her mouth hovering over his, and whispered, "I'm done."

5

Sophie's hunger for food was forgotten as her hunger for Jack took over. She'd wanted cheese, and what he'd said to her was pretty damn cheesy, but *fuck* if it wasn't sexy too.

The moment she said she was done, his mouth crashed against hers, hot and demanding. Forcing her lips apart, his tongue slipped inside her mouth, and the second it met hers, she moaned, long and unashamed.

His kisses were near perfection, able to drive every irrelevant thought from her mind. Probably a few relevant ones too. Thoughts like *Am I really going to do this? Am I really going to sleep with my ex-hook-up's brother?* And *What does that say about me as a person? As a professional?*

But then Jack squeezed her thigh again and hauled her closer to his insanely tight body, and the strength required for him to do that wiped her brain clean of pretty much every thought she'd ever had.

Everything other than *I want this man. Now.*

She whimpered when he pulled back from their kiss but

forgave the rude interruption when he said, "Should we take this inside?"

Her head seemed to nod of its own accord, and Sophie readily agreed. "Yes."

Jack slid his hand into her hair and pulled her back for one more searing kiss before slapping her arse and urging her to her feet. Her pussy throbbed, his dominant actions speaking to her on a level she'd never been able to deny, and if he hadn't figured it out yet, he soon would.

Sophie was a sexual submissive.

She liked it hard and she liked it rough and she really hoped Jack could deliver.

Taking her hand, he led her back inside, then shut the door and closed the curtains. She appreciated his caution. Ethan would have left them open, daring people to watch them and listen to them, even *film* them. That man had so many sex tapes on the internet he could start his own porn channel. And while he'd assured Sophie more than once that he'd never discovered one with her in it, there was always a niggling doubt at the back of her mind. It was definitely possible that someone had caught them together at some point and filmed the event for posterity.

Jack came up behind her, and the feel of his warm hands sliding over her hips distracted her wayward thoughts, especially when he pulled her back against him and nestled his thick erection against her arse. "The bedroom is through here," he murmured against the side of her neck before nipping her flesh between his teeth. She shivered at the erotic contact and let him direct her towards the door on the other side of the living area.

Sophie loved the way Jack touched her as they moved. His large hands were gentle against her skin, yet his grip was strong, eliciting a feeling of assuredness, of safety. It was a rare gift. One she was discovering she appreciated more and more because of its rarity.

"I can feel you thinking about something." His lips brushed against the shell of her ear as they entered the bedroom. He turned her to face him, stroked his knuckles over her cheek. "We can stop whenever you want to."

Her curiosity piqued, she asked, "What do you mean, you could feel me thinking?"

"You stiffened as we walked in here, as though maybe you'd changed your mind. And it's okay if you have," he said, his hands settling on her hips again, his thumbs stroking her skin like he had outside the ballroom, the action deliberate and sure. Confident. "We don't have to do anything you don't want to do."

Sophie felt like she'd entered the twilight zone. Who was this man with his non-grabby, non-pushy, non-arse-holey ways?

Since transitioning from makeup artist to model, she thought she'd given up all rights to personal space and the right to say no to people.

Especially men.

At least that's what people—again, mostly men—would have her believe.

Thankfully, her parents had both been models in their day, and occasionally she'd attended fashion shows and photo shoots with them, so the arseholery in the industry wasn't a total surprise to her. It was one of the main reasons she'd decided *not* to follow in their footsteps... until five years ago, when Anna had dragged her kicking and screaming to her first tryout.

"Stand your ground," she'd said as they'd sat in the

waiting area. "Project confidence. You're the daughter of Paul Bennett and Sofia fucking Montini. You're a legacy. A legend in the making."

It was at that point that Sophie had rolled her eyes. "Laying it on a bit thick, don't you think?"

"Just trying to get you pumped up."

"You're making me nervous." Sophie remembered her belly filling with butterflies, and not the good kind. Her butterflies had razor-tipped wings that had sliced at her insides until she'd felt like vomiting. "I think I'm going to be sick."

"You'll be fine," Anna had reassured her, squeezing her hand. "Just don't let them take advantage of you. Don't be afraid to say no to them. And if they won't take no for an answer, flip them off and walk the fuck out."

Sophie had never flipped anyone off in her life, but she had walked out a couple times in the past five years and earned herself a reputation as someone not to be underestimated in the process.

The fact that Jack made her feel like doing anything other than walking out spoke volumes.

That didn't mean she wouldn't test the waters, though. "You'd be okay with that? If I changed my mind?"

"Of course," he said, looking slightly offended that she would even think otherwise, then narrowed his eyes under a stern brow. His grip tightened on her hips. "Are you saying you've been with men who *weren't* okay with it?"

The fierceness in Jack's voice soothed away any remnants of doubt that lingered in the back of her mind. "I can handle myself," she replied, knowing her smile held an edge of viciousness. There were several ball sacs and at least one nose in the fashion world that would never be the same again after their owners "weren't okay with it".

Even if she couldn't handle things herself, she had a family full of overprotective uncles who would quite literally crush her enemies for her. Not to mention what her dad would do to anyone who dared to hurt his one and only child. The man often came off as cold and aloof, and they hadn't always gotten along, but he would burn down the world for those he loved.

Jack's frown deepened. "That doesn't answer my question, Sophie."

She slid her hands over his chest, enjoying the feel of his warm skin and hard muscles. "Of course there have been men who weren't okay with it. There are always men who aren't okay with it, but I can take care of myself," she assured him, then shrugged. "Most men who try that shit are cowards, and one of the upsides to being my size is I tend to intimidate cowards." She smiled again but with less edge. "Besides, my dad taught me how to box. We spar at least once a week."

"How did I not know this about you?" he said, one corner of his mouth tipping up in a lopsided smile.

Sophie frowned. "Why *would* you know that about me?"

Jack's smile went from bewildered to bashful in the blink of an eye. "I have a confession to make."

"Another one?"

His last confession had come as a shock, and she could understand his reluctance to tell her, all things considered. She could only guess at what he was going to say this time, but she had a hunch it wouldn't be anything as shocking as admitting to being Ethan's brother. Nevertheless, nervous energy had her hands fisting, then flexing at her sides.

Jack rubbed the back of his neck. "When I told you earlier that I knew who you were...." His gaze flicked back to hers, as though gauging her reaction.

"Yes?" she said, drawing the word out as she watched him more closely.

"What I meant was I've followed you on social media for a long, *long* time," he said, then sighed and shoved his fingers through his hair, obviously embarrassed by the admission.

She found his discomfort charming. "You have?" Her hands relaxed by her sides, and her body let go of the tension she hadn't realised she was holding on to.

Jack was a fan?

"Yes. In fact, I think it would be fair to say I've maybe had a bit of a crush on you for a while. Even before you started dating Ethan."

Sophie's eyes widened at his admission, and her mouth opened and closed several times before her words squeaked out. "A crush?" She pointed at her own chest, disbelief flavouring her tone even as it went up an octave. "On me?"

"A little one," he said, holding up his hand, his fingers pinching the air.

Her eyes narrowed. "Did Ethan know?"

That lopsided smile reappeared, making Jack look almost boyish. "I never told him outright, but he caught me looking through your Instagram account more than once. Contrary to popular opinion, Ethan is a smart man. It wouldn't have taken him long to figure it out."

Stunned into silence, Sophie's mind whirled. This new information only added to her theory that Ethan had set them up, and she didn't know if she wanted to slap the bloody idiot sideways for his deviousness or kiss him.

When she continued not saying anything, Jack's smile faded, and his frown returned. "Is that okay? That I kind of, maybe stalked you online?" Caution laced his words.

"Yes!" she wanted to shout, but the word stayed jammed behind the lump in her throat, unable to escape, so she nodded instead. At least her body knew what she wanted from Jack, even if her brain couldn't keep up.

He cupped her face in both hands so she couldn't look away. "I need to hear you say the word, angel," he said softly, the endearment sounding sincere, which only added to the jumble of thoughts and emotions swirling through her body and mind. Usually the word was uttered with a hard edge of condescension or contempt. Then again, the men usually saying it generally weren't as respectful or as... *nice* as Jack.

And how sad was it that she had come to expect the worst of men and yet she was still willing to be alone with one?

Was she really that lonely?

"Yes."

Jack's smile returned, and his shoulders relaxed, and Sophie realised he hadn't been sure she wouldn't change her mind.

The thought made her smile too.

For a dominant man he really was very sweet.

Her confidence bolstered by his reaction, she leaned into him and said, "So, I'm pretty sure I heard you promise to rip my underwear off and tie me up with it, or was that all just a bit of male posturing?"

Instead of replying, Jack dropped to his knees and began inspecting her panties, running his fingers over the lace, slipping them under the waistband and testing the elastic. His touch was so light it almost tickled, and her stomach clenched, her muscles practically dancing at the feel of his skin skating over hers.

"Sadly, I think these are too well made for me to keep my promise," he said with an exaggerated sigh, then levered to his feet. Then his hands went to his belt, and he slowly unbuckled it. His smile was pure wickedness. "I guess I'll just have to find another way to tie you up."

6

The sound of Jack's belt ripping through the loops of his trousers made the air still in Sophie's lungs. *Holy shit!* He'd just dialled the heat up to eleven, and yet she still shivered at his statement.

"G-Golden," she stuttered, earning her a cocked brow from Jack. "My safe word is golden," she said, answering his silent question. "It used to be golden retriever, but it was too much of a mouthful when I needed it."

Jack smiled at her rambling and folded his belt in half, then dangled the loop of leather from one hand and lifted the other to stroke her cheek again. "Good to know," he said, then slid that hand down to circle her throat and lightly brushed his lips over hers.

His grip was gentle, but Sophie wasn't naive enough to think it would stay that way. Jack had already demonstrated his dominant nature, and judging by the strength he'd displayed earlier, he could squeeze the life out of her as easily as he could blink.

The thought was an arousing one, and yes, she knew her way of thinking was a little left of centre. Not many people would be turned on by the thought of a man literally holding their life in his hands, but many people didn't understand.

Most didn't even want to.

Jack might be physically stronger than her, might be dominant and wish to control her, but there was strength in surrendering that control. In trusting someone enough to take care of her when she was at her most vulnerable. He'd told her they could stop whenever she wanted, and she knew it would only take one word.

Golden.

One word, *her* word, would shut everything down.

That power was hers and hers alone.

"Since this is our first time together," Jack said, "we'll take things slow. I don't know your limits, and you don't know me well enough to let me test them."

His words made a lot of sense, and yet Sophie struggled to force down her disappointment. "Does that mean you're *not* going to tie me up?"

He grinned and tightened his grip around her neck, just enough to focus her attention solely on him. "I'll still tie you up, angel—a promise is a promise—but only your wrists this time, not your legs."

"This time?" she asked, her eyes widening and her heart racing at his implication. Her mouth twitched into an eager smile. "There will be other times?"

Jack moved into her personal space, disturbing the air around her and sending a shiver of awareness skittering over her skin. "Only if I'm very lucky."

Only if *he* was very lucky? *Jesus, this man.* This gentle, quiet, humble man was the total opposite of his brother and—

No.

She had to stop comparing Jack to Ethan.

Obviously there would be differences between them—no doubt there would be similarities too—and she would discover them all soon enough, especially if they continued seeing each other as Jack had insinuated. Until then, she would take him and everything he had to offer as he came.

One moment at a time.

"I guess you'd better make this good, then," Sophie said, sliding her hands over his broad shoulders and spearing her fingers through his hair, tugging his mouth closer to hers in a show of defiance, leaning into the strong grip still circling her throat. "You know, if you want to get lucky."

He stared at her for a moment, his blue eyes almost twinkling with mischief as his grin grew devilish again, and then he kissed her, hard. His lips pressed flat against hers before slowly parting and taking her bottom lip between them. Sophie closed her eyes, lost to the sensation of his mouth playing with hers, gently plucking at one lip, then the other before her eyes snapped open and her breath escaped her on a pained gasp—her bottom lip pinched between Jack's teeth.

He growled at her—literally *growled*—then slowly let her lip slip free of his bite. When he spoke again, all mirth was gone from his rich voice, replaced with a tone of command that made her knees weak and her pussy ache to be filled. "Keep your eyes open," he said. "And keep them on me. I want you to remember exactly who's fucking you tonight."

Sophie stilled, her breath caught in her throat. Was it possible she wasn't the only one who'd been making comparisons between Jack and his brother? Or had he simply guessed where her mind had been a moment ago?

The heat of shame flushed her cheeks, but before she

could give any sort of response, Jack released her neck, removed the constant pressure that had kept her steady on her feet, and trailed his hand down her chest, distracting her from the apology dancing on the tip of her tongue.

Tracing his fingers along the lacy edge of her bra, he followed the swell of her breasts and teased her flesh until goose bumps appeared, causing her to shiver. "So soft," he said, the words so quiet it was as if he'd spoken them for his ears alone, then added more gruffly, "Turn around."

Sophie did as she was told and turned away from Jack, letting him continue his gentle exploration over her shoulder and down her back, all the way to the top of her panties. His touch was so light it made her giggle and squirm. "That tickles."

He chuckled and swept her hair aside, pressed what felt like smiling lips to her shoulder, then continued torturing her with his featherlight touch. "Payback's a bitch," he said, his humour evident in his tone. Then he singlehandedly unfastened her bra and flicked the straps off her shoulders, causing her large breasts to sag in their lacy prison.

Payback? What is he talking about? But before she could voice her question out loud, Jack went down to his knees again and began caressing her arse, stroking her skin where it met the lace of her panties. Slipping his fingers underneath and exploring the bountiful curves of her arse. Torturing her. Teasing her. *Tickling* her.

Then it hit her, and she tried to bite back her smile, even as she giggled and wriggled again.

His shirt.

When she'd unbuttoned his shirt, she'd taken her sweet time, had wanted to savour the moment and enjoy his hard chest, his smooth skin. His heat and his strength, his scent. His all-consuming maleness. She must have tickled him, and now he was taking his revenge. She would have laughed at the realisation had he not chosen that exact moment to slap the leather belt against her arse.

The smack was light and playful and accompanied by Jack's growly voice. "Fuck. I intend to worship this arse tonight." Then she felt his fingers hook under the waistband of her panties again, felt the scratch of lace as he dragged them down her legs, then urged her to step out of them and kick them away. A moment later, he was standing behind her again, pushing the hardness of his erection between her buttocks while pressing another soft kiss to her shoulder. "Face me."

Sophie had to fold her arms under her breasts to stop her bra from falling clean off her, the heavy weight of the large globes rendering the garment useless in its unfastened state. Jack smirked and stared at her chest, then hooked one finger between her breasts and tugged on the little lacy panel that held the cups together.

"Arms down, beautiful," he said, tapping his belt against her elbow.

She pursed her lips and shot him a mock glare at the endearment but did as he asked and lowered her arms, letting him drag her bra off her and cast it away to join her panties on the floor.

Jack's gaze slid over her naked body like a caress, starting with her face and ending at her feet, his tongue peeking out occasionally to moisten his lips, his hands flexing on her hips. The leather belt he still held dug into her soft flesh, pinching her, distracting her from the intensity of his perusal.

From the urge to cover herself.

An urge that was almost foreign to Sophie now.

Five years ago, when she'd first started modelling, it

was an everyday occurrence. It had been intimidating, having all those people poking and prodding at her like a slab of meat. But slowly she'd learned that her body, with all of its wobbly bits and stretchmarks and cellulite, was nothing to be ashamed of at all.

Popular media had spent years teaching her everything that was wrong with her, when in fact it was all her "flaws" that made her so bankable. An instant sensation, both with audiences and designers alike. She'd had to unlearn years of false negativity and embrace her new truth.

Sophie was desirable.

Sexy.

Sensual.

Wanted.

Now *she* was the intimidating one.

But standing there in front of Jack and his piercing blue gaze, letting him visibly devour every inch of her, letting him judge her, was... *terrifying*, but she fought the urge to cover herself and let him look his fill.

"I know you don't like the word, angel," he said after a solid nerve-racking minute of silence, "but I can't think of another one more appropriate right now." He cupped her cheek and pinned her with his electric gaze. "You are so fucking beautiful."

Her lips quirked up at the corners of her mouth, and a nervous yet relieved laugh huffed out of her. Sophie didn't like that word, but hearing it fall from Jack's very kissable lips, hearing the sincerity in his rich, velvety timbre, made it a lot easier to bear.

To believe.

She bit her lip to hold in a whimper of need, but she could do nothing about the way her heart raced or how her chest heaved with every breath. She wanted him to kiss her again, wanted to feel his silken tongue wrestle with hers. Wanted to feel his fingers on her naked breasts, between her legs, inside her pussy. Wanted to hear the command in his voice as he whispered in her ear, wanted to know the strength of his body as he held her down and fucked his way inside her.

Suddenly, wanting wasn't enough.

Sophie *needed* these things.

Needed *him*.

"Jack," she whispered, her eyelids fluttering as she leaned closer and tilted her head, angling for another kiss, but he held a finger to her lips, silencing her. Pushing her back.

Putting her in her place.

"You will call me 'sir'," he said, cocking that brow at her again, waiting for her response.

"Yes, sir," she replied, the submissive action settling low in her belly, relaxing her and releasing the last of her tension. Grounding her in the moment.

Jack smiled, pleased. "Good girl," he said quietly. "Now, give me your wrists."

7

"One on top of the other."

Sophie nodded and held out her wrists as instructed. "Yes, sir," she said, her voice soft yet eager.

Jack's mouth twitched into another barely there smile, her simple submission stirring something inside him he'd long since thought dead. "Good girl," he said again, enjoying the way her chin dropped, her cheeks flushed, and her gaze sought out his.

Seeking his approval.

The urge to grab her, to throw her down on the bed and take her, was near overwhelming, but he wanted to savour the moment. Wanted to enjoy every second he spent with Sophie in case the inevitable happened and he never saw her again.

In the past, that wouldn't have bothered him, his infrequent trysts serving a purely biological need. He didn't care if he never saw those women again, and neither did they. But this tryst was different. This *woman* was different, and not just because he had a crush on her.

Sophie Bennett was every wet dream Jack had ever had rolled into one delectable woman and brought to life—his very own Galatea—and the fact that she was standing in front of him, staring at him with those deep, dark eyes, smiling at him, for him... the pleasure he felt deep in his gut was indescribable.

Wrapping the belt around her wrists, he made sure not to bind the leather too tightly. He hadn't tied anyone up in a long time—years—and wanted to ensure he didn't hurt her. At least not yet. And not like this.

She would feel pain at his hands, and soon, but it would be controlled, dished out bit by bit as he edged her closer and closer to his end goal.

Sophie screaming his name in pleasure.

As soon as he buckled the belt in place, he ran his finger under the leather and made sure she had some wiggle room. He didn't want to leave any permanent marks on her body, and seeing as this was their first time together, he didn't want to frighten her. His belt around her wrists was more of a gesture than an actual restraint.

He nodded towards the bed. "Lie on your back."

"Yes, sir," Sophie said, the words falling from her pretty mouth with such ease it made Jack's balls tighten and his cock twitch.

Fuck. He had to take this slow or he'd blow his load before he had the chance to blow her mind.

His playmate crawled onto the bed, the swaying of her hips and arse exaggerated by the fact that she was forced to navigate the soft bedding with her wrists bound. Jack couldn't wait to sink his teeth into that spectacular arse. He'd always been a sucker for a woman with curves. He loved to see large soft breasts and a rounded tummy, and a set of shapely hips swaying from side to side as a woman walked away from him was one of his all-time favourite things to watch.

But a nice arse?

A nice, soft, spankable arse that jiggled and rippled when his hand smacked hard against it was the sexiest thing in the world. That, and seeing his handprint marked in red against her alabaster skin.

He sucked his bottom lip between his teeth but bit down too late to stifle his appreciative groan.

Sophie turned her head and glanced over her shoulder at him, her dark eyes bright with mischief, her luscious lips curled in a sexy smile, but when she turned over and lay down on her back as he'd instructed, her smile softened, and she shuttered her gaze. Looked away from him, almost shy. Bashful.

Her submissiveness was subtle but so very alluring, and Jack had to hold himself back. Had to stop himself from going to her—running to her—and taking her without any further ado. But if he did that, if he acted that impulsively, he would hurt her. And he'd promised both of them he wouldn't do that.

He would be gentle.

Well, as gentle as a man who wanted nothing more than to tie up a gorgeous woman, spank her perfect arse until it shone with a beautiful red glow, then fuck her into oblivion could be.

"Jack," Sophie whispered, the sound of her sweet yet sultry voice loud in the quiet of the bedroom, stirring him from his thoughts. "Sir."

She held her hands in front of her, her arms bent, her bound wrists pressed against her breasts, blocking them from view, and suddenly he was very aware of her nakedness.

More accurately, he was very aware that he was *not* naked, and that his not-nakedness was preventing him from enjoying Sophie to the fullest.

Dropping his hands to the button at his waist, he made quick work of it and the zipper, shucking his pants while toeing off his shoes and socks.

A moan from the bed made him lift his head.

Sophie was staring at him, wide-eyed, her pretty pink tongue slipping along her bottom lip before a row of perfect teeth sank into the lush little pillow, turning it a deep red.

He knew that look.

Hunger.

Hunger for *him*.

The feeling was mutual as he stalked to the foot of the bed, then crawled onto it. He stared deep into her sultry eyes as he slowly covered her body with his.

Grabbing the belt, he used it to force her hands over her head, then held them there, pinned to the pillow beneath her. His grip was tight, and she let out another little moan as she wriggled against him. "I want to hurt you, Sophie," he whispered against the shell of her ear. "I want to spank you so hard you'll feel it for days. I want to leave my marks on your body so every time you see them you remember this night. And I want to fuck you so goddamn hard you won't be able to walk straight tomorrow." He paused to nuzzle against her neck, to breathe in her delicious scent. He loosened his grip on her wrists. "But I won't. Not yet. Not tonight."

He felt a rush of satisfaction when she made a sound of displeasure, then pulled back so he could enjoy watching her emotions play out on her face.

She didn't disappoint and narrowed her eyes at him. "I can understand not wanting to bruise me, but I won't lie," she said, cocking one perfectly sculpted brow. "I was kinda looking forward to not walking straight tomorrow."

Jack's laughter burst out of him, Sophie's sass catching him off-guard again, her quick and sudden grin testing his resolve to go easy on her.

"I like your laugh," she said, smiling up at him, her cheekiness replaced with a look of genuine approval that warmed him more than the tropical summer heat. "It's so open and free."

"Another thing I'm not often accused of," he replied, his laugh simmering to a chuckle.

"Which one? Open or free?"

Jack stared down at her and traced his fingertips along her jaw, learned the shape of her face, admired the softness of her skin. "Both."

His pulse kicked up a notch when she closed her eyes and leaned into his touch.

"You're obviously not hanging out with the right people."

She wasn't wrong. Not only was Jack not hanging out with the right people, but he rarely if ever hung out with anyone anymore. What little spare time he had was reserved for sleeping or hitting the gym or family commitments. And since his family commitments were usually tied into his work commitments, he felt like he never got a damn day off. A situation that would only become worse in the coming weeks and months.

But that was a problem for another day.

Right now he had a willing woman in his bed, a dick so hard it could hammer nails, and nowhere to be in the morning.

The recipe for a perfect night.

"Pretty sure I'm with the right person tonight," Jack said quietly.

Sophie's eyes fluttered open, and she smiled up at him again. "Yes, sir," she whispered, her breath hitching, causing her breasts to swell against his chest. "Definitely the right person."

Angling his head, he lowered his mouth over hers and kissed her, slowly, deliberately, pushing his tongue inside her sweet mouth the way he intended to push it inside her hot pussy. When he felt her arms lower and her hands touch against his hair, he pulled back with a snarl, grabbed her wrists, and forced them back over her head. He held them there with one hand while the other curled around her throat once more.

"Leave your hands where I put them, Sophie," he said. "Naughty girls get punished."

Sophie tugged against his hold, and her mouth twisted with mischief, and he realised something.

She'd done it on purpose. She'd wanted to provoke a response out of him.

"I was kinda looking forward to not walking straight tomorrow."

Tilting his head to one side, Jack narrowed his gaze and studied the woman beneath him, observed the defiance in her features, the jutting of her chin, that one boldly cocked brow daring him to do his worst.

And that was when he realised the woman in his bed wasn't just submissive.

She was a *brat*.

He bit back the urge to laugh as she tested his hold on her again, rubbed her pretty little nipples against his firm chest, as if that would make him move.

Neither of them was going anywhere.

But maybe he *was* being overly cautious.

His infrequent conquests over the past couple of years had served a purely biological function, not a kinky one, so it was possible he had misjudged the situation by erring on the side of caution.

Maybe he'd gone so long without a truly submissive partner that he'd forgotten what it was like to be with someone who not only wanted what he was offering but actually craved it.

Deciding to test his theory, he tightened his grip on her wrists and gave her throat a gentle squeeze, careful not to close off her airway. "Is that what you want, Sophie? Do you want me to punish you?"

"I want you to do what you said you weren't going to do," she said, frustration bleeding through her words as she tugged at her wrists again.

Jack smiled slowly, wickedly as he eased his grip on her hands and throat and pushed himself up so he was straddling Sophie's hips, his rock-hard cock on blatant display between them. "You want me to spank you?"

She shifted as if she was about to reach for him again, but a quick glare down at her saw her stiffen and keep her hands where he'd put them.

Good. She was a fast learner.

"Yes, please," she said, her tone of frustration replaced by an eagerness he liked very much.

"And you wouldn't mind me leaving marks on your skin?"

Her gaze dropped, and her teeth worried at her bottom lip. "What kind of marks? I'm not into knife play or anything extreme like that."

Stroking his hand over her hair, Jack said, "Neither am I. But I would love to see my handprint painted across your arse, or the stripe of my belt around your thighs. Maybe even the tip of my whip on your tits." He cupped her breasts and squeezed them tightly, loving her sultry moan and how her soft flesh bulged between his spread fingers. "It's been a very long time since I decorated a body as beautiful as yours." He released one breast to pluck at her nipple, relished her whimper when he pinched it hard. "Would you be okay with those types of marks?"

"Yes, sir." Sophie nodded excitedly, and Jack let go of the breath he didn't realise he'd been holding.

He wanted this woman so damn much.

He wasn't sure what he would have done if she'd said no.

"Good girl," he said, stroking his hands down over her belly to grip at her waist. "But like I said earlier, you don't know me well enough to let me do all of that to you. Not yet." He smiled as she pouted. "So how about we start with a spanking and work our way up from there?"

8

The enthusiasm in Sophie's eyes was like a shot of pure adrenaline straight up Jack's spine.

"Yes. Please, Jack."

Yeah, I am definitely with the right person tonight.

Leaning down, he brushed his mouth over hers again, then trailed his lips along her jaw and down her throat, across her shoulder and over her breast, stopping to take her nipple between his teeth and give it a playful nip.

Her back arched, forcing more of her breast against his smiling lips, but her moan morphed into a frustrated whimper when he continued his journey south over her belly and detoured across to her hip.

"Jack?" The breathy way Sophie said his name made his cock twitch.

I want to be inside her.

"Yes, angel?"

But as desperate as he was to sink inside her sweet heat and feel her softness wrapped around him as he slaked his thirst for her, he was just as frantic to know how she tasted on his tongue. He wanted to hear her sultry moans and soft cries as he made her dance to his tune. He wanted to feel her body grip his fingers, wanted to watch her pretty eyes as she came apart for him.

Wanted to erase his brother from her brain by blowing her mind with pleasure.

Was it petty? Probably.

Did he care? Nope.

If Jack had his way, he'd brand the word *Mine* onto Sophie's luscious arse and never let her out of his sight again.

The thought pulled him up short. He'd always enjoyed being in control, but he'd never considered himself a control freak.

He'd never felt *possessive* of someone before.

It felt... good.

Scary, but good.

"I thought you were going to spank me," Sophie said, pouting slightly even as her eyes shone with playful intentions.

Jack's hand itched to slap her thigh, but at this point, it would only serve as a reward for bad behaviour, and that was not how he played the game. Allowing another sly grin to decorate his face, he slowed his descent towards her pussy, taking his sweet time to kiss and lick every inch of available flesh. "Good things come to those who wait, Sophie."

Her eyes narrowed, and her pout twisted into a grimace. "I hate waiting."

He chuckled. "Good to know."

In the past, when a playmate had offered up such delicious information, he would have dragged out her pleasure even more just to prove a point: he was in charge. As it was, he'd already teased Sophie for far longer than he'd intended, and it had been so long since Jack had sex he wasn't sure how much longer he could hold out before making a fool of himself on the bedsheets.

As he slid farther back on the bed and lowered himself between her thighs, his cock brushed against her leg, and he groaned at the exquisite agony. "*Fuuuck.*" Then he re-exerted his self-control, forced down his own physical desires, and focussed on the pretty little cunt laid out in front of him.

Like a feast for one.

Sophie, like many models, was completely bare between her legs, and while it wasn't something he'd ever given much thought to before, Jack had to admit it was sexy as fuck. He especially liked how sensitive her skin was there, how she shivered and squirmed at the lightest touch of his fingertips.

When he followed his fingers with the tip of his tongue and licked along the crease where her inner thigh met her body, her stomach clenched, and she tried to slam her legs shut.

"That tickles!"

Chuckling again, Jack gripped her thighs and shoved them open, then slowly parted the soft folds of her pussy and looked his fill. Only when his lover started to squirm under his intense stare did he lower his head and stroke his tongue over her clit.

And the moment he licked that hard little nub, her hips bucked off the bed, and she made the sexiest sound he'd ever heard come out of a woman—a sort of gasping, needy whimper.

Desperate and lustful.

"Oh God. Yes, Jack," she said. "More. Please."

"More, *sir,*" he reminded her before nuzzling into her

and inhaling deeply, taking her sweet feminine scent deep into his lungs before teasing her further, blowing warm breath over her clit and making her shiver.

Only when he heard her say, "More, sir. Please more," did he give his full attention to his task and begin eating her pussy like a man starved for air.

Sophie bucked and writhed beneath him as he licked and nipped at her, then slid two fingers inside her wet, warm pussy and imagined how good she would feel around wrapped his cock. He tortured her sensitive little nub and coaxed it out from under its hood, brushed his stubbled chin over and around it, and within minutes she was begging for release.

Begging him to let her come.

"Please, sir. Please. I need to come. Please, Jack. Sir. Oh God."

Jack kept slowly thrusting his fingers in and out of her dripping wet cunt, kept her teetering on the edge without letting her slip over, then gently rubbed his stubble over her clit again, eliciting another cry. He lifted his gaze to look at Sophie's face, to see her bound hands. There was nothing for her to grip at the head of the bed, so the fact that she still kept them where he'd put them—despite her lower half thrashing around as if she were possessed by a demon —made him swell with pride.

"Such a good girl," he murmured against her naked mound, then pressed a kiss there. But he wanted to push her further. Wanted to see how she'd react to something unexpected. "You're going to feel a little pressure now, angel."

Reaching below her pussy, he brushed the pad of his thumb over her arsehole, unsurprised to find her juices had slipped down and lubricated the area.

She was fantastically wet.

Sophie bucked her hips at the intimate touch, but when they came down, Jack used her momentum to press into her, to breach that tight little ring of muscle.

"Sir?" Her cry was questioning but not angry, or worse, afraid.

"You're doing so well, baby," he cooed at her, wriggling his thumb, pushing it deeper in her arse while still thrusting his fingers slowly into her pussy.

Her cries quickly slipped into moans. Her moans slipped into panting. And when she started begging him again, pleading with him to let her come, he knew it was time.

"Don't come until I say you can, Sophie, or the spanking you get will not be the one you want."

Her delicate hands clenched and flexed as if seeking something to hang on to, to anchor her to the bed, or possibly in the moment, but with nothing else available, she had to rely on the strength of her own will to obey his command.

"Yes, sir," she said, her voice husky, shaky with lust and need.

"Good girl," he said, then lowered his mouth over her clit.

The sounds Sophie made as he fucked both her holes at once while he licked and sucked on her clit were the best ones he'd ever heard. Better than any music he could imagine, either natural or invented. Her voice rose and fell in time with his thrusts, and when he changed it up and switched his rhythm, her cries became animalistic.

With a quick glance up, he saw her hands clenched in the bedding above her head. She was trying so hard to be good for him. Trying so hard to be his good girl.

It was time to reward her obedience.

"Come for me, baby. Let me taste you."

A second later she came.

Screaming.

Wailing.

Body shaking, thighs clenching.

Sobbing.

"Sir," she cried. "Oh God, Jack!"

He didn't relent, didn't stop licking her, didn't stop fingering her, couldn't stop sucking on her clit until he'd wrung every last drop of her pleasure from her.

She flooded his mouth with that pleasure, a sweet, salty liquor he'd been dying to taste for what felt like forever.

Slowly he pulled away, eased his fingers from her pussy and arse, and placed one last soft kiss on her mound, just above her clit. Then he shifted to a kneeling position again and took in the breathtaking sight before him.

Sophie's eyes were closed, but her mouth was open, the corners hitched up in a very satisfied grin. Her dark hair was a unruly mess strewn across the pillow. Her chest heaved as she sucked in lungful after lungful of air, and a thin sheen of sweat clung to her breasts. Her nipples tightened into rosy peaks as the air conditioning cooled her sweat and goose bumps broke out all over her, causing her to shiver.

And still she didn't lower her hands.

Still she obeyed him.

Something inside him settled, something he hadn't felt in so long he'd forgotten how good it could feel.

It wasn't just satisfaction for a job well done.

It was *contentment.*

"You can put your hands down now," he said quietly, rubbing his own back and forth along her thighs, enjoying the feel of her silky skin, warm against his palms.

"Okay," she replied. Her voice sounded off, distant. She didn't move.

Jack frowned. "Are you? Okay?"

Her eyelids fluttered open, and she stared back at him, her rich brown eyes looking languorous under the veil of her thick black lashes. Her mouth stretched in a broad smile, and she took a deep breath to slow her breathing. "Better than okay. That was the most intense orgasm I've had in a long, *long* time."

"Is that a fact?" he drawled, his smile broadening to match Sophie's, his ego swelling with pride. "How long are we talking, angel? Weeks? Months?"

How long had it been since she'd last slept with Ethan? Because Jack knew his brother took great pride in his pussy-eating skills. Not that he saw this night as a contest, but it kinda was. And Sophie was his prize.

One he was determined to claim at any cost.

"Years," she sighed, stretching her limbs like a contented cat before finally lowering her arms.

Mine!

The thought screamed inside Jack's head, triumphant and proud.

Possessive.

Sophie was his now, and if Ethan thought for even one second that he could steal her back, he had another think coming.

Jack stared at his woman and his cock twitched, eager and urgent, but it wasn't just the sight of her naked and spread out before him that drove his lust. He'd wanted her for years, had followed her social media accounts, lusted after her from afar. But in doing so, he'd also seen her kindness and generosity, her humour and intelligence.

She was beautiful both inside and out.

Yes, he was a rich man, and she was a model. Yes, he could have manufactured a reason to force an introduction between them, especially with his connections, but Jack had been hurt before and in the worst way possible. It had been easier to leave the billionaire playboy clichés up to his brother while he buried himself in work and rendered himself invisible to the fairer sex. Even if it meant denying himself a chance at happiness.

Now he knew he'd been a fool.

A total fucking idiot.

Sophie was everything he'd dreamt she'd be, and in that moment, she was all his.

Hmm. Maybe branding her isn't such a crazy idea after all.

9

Sophie yawned loudly as Jack unfastened the belt from around her wrists and tossed it on the floor, then gently checked her over to make sure she was okay. The little gesture screamed volumes about him as a man, even more so as a Dom.

Her wrists were a little irritated from being bound, but as she suspected, there were no bruises, no broken skin. She tugged one hand free and covered her mouth in a vain attempt to stifle another yawn.

What time is it, anyway?

He chuckled quietly, the warmth of the sound doing strange things to her heart rate. "You're not going to fall asleep on me, are you, beautiful?"

"It's your fault if I do," she said, biting back her smile.

Jack slowly crawled over the top of her and pinned her wrists to the bed on either side of her shoulders. His face was stern, one brow cocked. "Oh?"

An involuntary shiver rippled through her body at the gravelly growl that had issued that one-word challenge. And it *was* a challenge. One she accepted. "Orgasms make me sleepy," she said, dropping her gaze for a moment before looking up at him from under her lashes in feigned innocence.

"I see," he said, nodding sagely, playing her game. Then his expression turned curious. "I wonder how many orgasms you can endure before you pass out completely?" His mouth twitched into another devastating smile. "Want to find out?"

Sophie nodded enthusiastically. "Yes, please."

His grip tightened on her wrists. "Yes, *sir*," he growled.

She lowered her gaze as another frisson of excitement buzzed through her veins. "Yes, sir," she whispered, feigning nothing that time.

Her submission was real.

"I think you need a reminder of who's in charge, beautiful," Jack said, using that word again. The word that had—for now, at least—ceased to be so annoying.

In a move that left her breathless with wanting, he flipped her onto her stomach, hooked his hands under her hips, then hauled her up onto her hands and knees. His big hand pressed between her shoulder blades, shoving her upper body down so she rested on her elbows, forcing her arse high in the air.

Presenting her to him.

Allowing him access to everything.

Not for the first time that night, she felt vulnerable, as though Jack could do whatever he wanted to her and there wouldn't be a damn thing she could do to prevent it.

And just like every other time that night, her pussy grew wet just thinking about it.

A light chuckle sounded behind her, and suddenly his hands were smoothing over her arse, stroking her. Almost petting her. "You like this, don't you, baby? Being open to me. Helpless to stop me." His fingers slipped between her legs again and easily slid inside her soaking-wet pussy. "I can't wait to fuck you here," he said, his voice so deep and dark, so commanding that she pushed her body back towards him, desperate to have more of him inside her.

But then he brushed the pad of his thumb over her arse-hole again and she clenched up, determined to keep the digit out of there. Not that what he'd done earlier had been unpleasant, she just wasn't used to it.

It felt... weird.

"Has anyone ever fucked you here?" he asked, pressing harder against her puckered hole.

She shivered at his question as much as she did his crude touch.

Sophie shook her head. "No. Never."

"Not even with a toy?" She heard the frown in his voice.

"No, sir."

"Sophie, look at me." She turned her head to obey and was met by kind eyes, full of need and understanding. "Was tonight the first time anyone has breached this perfect little hole?"

Her embarrassment flooded through her, and she felt her whole body flush with the emotion. Sure she must be bright red all over, she bit her lip and nodded. "Yes, sir."

Jack's mouth twisted with an odd combination of excitement and disappointment. "Hmm, something to explore more thoroughly next time, then," he said, his hint not at all subtle as he pushed his thumb harder against her. Not hard enough to violate the tight little pucker again but enough to make her gasp in panic that he might.

"There you go again, sir," Sophie said, trying to breathe through her discomfort. "Making plans for the future with your 'next times' and—" She gasped as he poked at her again. "—your kinky ways."

Jack's chuckle floated around her, wrapped her in the warmth of his good humour. "I think you like my kinky ways."

"What makes you say that?"

His chuckle deepened into something more sinister. "Because your pussy gets wetter every time I do this," he said, pushing harder, the tip of his thumb stretching her arse open.

"Oh God." Sophie groaned as the discomfort in her arse morphed into something less unsettling, something hot and... almost pleasurable. She swallowed hard and tried to focus. "Your point?" she asked, purely to be bratty.

A sharp slap fell across her arse, stinging her skin and jiggling her flesh, ringing another moan from her and another chuckle from Jack. "My point is, the *next time* we meet, I'm going to start training you to take my cock in your gorgeous virgin arse until you either beg for mercy or beg for more." He punctuated his statement by pushing his thumb deeper inside her arsehole and making her moan again, his slow and deliberate invasion giving her body time to adjust, time to... *enjoy* was the wrong word, but begin to *appreciate* what he was doing to her. An act she never in a million years thought she'd ever agree to. "And I have a feeling I know which one you'll choose."

Slowly, he eased his thumb out of her, leaving her feeling empty, even as he pushed a third finger inside her pussy.

"No," she cried out. Jack froze until she mumbled, "Could you, um... put it back? Please."

"Please, what?"

"Sir. Please, sir."

"Good girl," he purred behind her and slowly pushed his thumb back in.

Sophie squirmed on his fingers as he alternated his thrusts, slowly sliding his thumb into her arse as he pulled his fingers out of her pussy. Driving her mad with wanting and a fierce need to come. But his measured movements wouldn't allow her that release.

Eventually her arms collapsed beneath her, pressing her upper body flat against the bed and forcing her arse even higher into the air. Jack growled behind her, the sound one of approval and appreciation, and his pace quickened, his fingers sliding in and out of her body with a crazy sort of rhythm designed to drive her wild. And it did.

Especially when he spanked her again.

She had no idea how he was managing to alternate his thrusting digits while stinging her arse with his other hand, and she didn't really care, but it was a talent she appreciated more and more as her belly tightened with heat and need and her pussy clenched around his fingers.

She was so close.

Jack's voice was a rough rumble of masculinity behind her. "Don't you dare come until I say so, Sophie. Understand?"

Biting her lip, she nodded frantically, her climax building and winding itself tighter within her. "Yes, sir. I understand."

He made another sound of approval. "You really are such a good girl," he said, spanking her harder with each word he uttered. "And good girls get rewarded."

"Thank you, sir," Sophie said, concentrating so hard on controlling her body's response to Jack that she practically panted the words.

Concentrating so hard she almost missed the fact that

he'd switched from spanking her arse to stroking her clit, circling the overly sensitised nub with such a sure, firm touch it was going to send her over the edge at any moment.

But then Jack whispered, "Come for me, baby," and her whole world flew apart, only to reform and fly apart again as a second wave of bliss steamrolled over the first, leaving her a shaky, sobbing wreck, her hands fisted in the bedding so tightly her fingers ached with the effort and her brain so far gone to la-la land that she didn't notice he had left the bed until he returned.

"On your back, angel," he said, gently nudging her where she lay sprawled across the bed.

Sophie took a moment to gather her strength, then rolled onto her back, wincing slightly as her reddened arse cheeks scraped against the cotton bedding. Jack sat beside her with a damp washcloth in his hand.

"Spread your legs."

Again, she did as he commanded, then closed her eyes and sighed contentedly as he gently washed between her thighs and dipped down to brush the soft cloth over her freshly abused arsehole.

When she opened her eyes again, she met his gaze and blushed at the intense desire she saw there. Jack had already rocked her world—twice—but she still craved his touch. Needed more of him to satisfy her own hunger. Of course, the fact that he had yet to fuck her could have had something to do with that. Maybe, also, the sight of his above-average cock still standing proud between his thighs might have had something to do with her libido refusing to back down.

"Jack," she murmured, her voice soft, breathless.

Pleading.

He pulled out the top drawer of the bedside table and took out a box of condoms. Carefully, he opened one and rolled it over his thick erection, then lay with Sophie and began kissing her again. Touching her. Caressing her. Exploring her body and learning her secrets, like how she was ticklish beneath her breasts, or how the feel of his fingers digging into her thigh as he wrapped her leg around his waist made her so freaking horny for him that she was going to cry if he didn't fuck her soon.

"Ready?" he whispered against the shell of her ear, his rich voice making her shiver.

It was all Sophie could do to stop the needy whimper that was clawing its way up her throat from escaping. "Yes, sir," she said, proud of herself for keeping her voice steady. Until he nipped her soft earlobe between his teeth and made her moan. The tiny bite of pain caused her pelvis to tilt, and a moment later, Jack was buried balls deep inside her.

"Oh, Jesus, fuck," he growled, his eyes sealed shut as he pressed his hips hard against hers. "You're so fucking tight." His eyes snapped open, and he frowned down at her. "Am I hurting you?"

Sophie shook her head. "No, sir. Not hurting." To prove her point, she rocked her pelvis and tried to make him move, thrusting her hips and wriggling beneath him. He wasn't hurting her one little bit, and the only reason she was tight was because she hadn't gotten laid in months. And she'd doubled down on the number of Pilates classes she'd been attending. And Jack was hung like an ancient fertility god.

He pressed a kiss against her neck, and she felt his smile. "Okay, angel," he murmured. "If you're sure."

When Jack pulled back to look in her eyes again, Sophie

almost swooned. The desire was still there, the lust and the need, but laced through it all was a tenderness she didn't know what to do with. This was sex. They'd only just met. And, well... he was a guy.

So where was that look coming from?

Then she remembered what he'd said about stalking her online, and her breath stalled in her lungs.

But before her mind could run away with the disturbing thought, he slid his cock almost all the way out of her, then slammed it back in. Her eyes rolled back in her head, and a groan of intense pleasure escaped her gaping mouth.

Jack buried his face in the crook of her neck. "Wrap yourself around me, baby, and hold on tight."

She did exactly that. And he started fucking her exactly how she'd hoped he would.

Hard, fast, and dirty.

After two orgasms already, Sophie was primed to pop, but she held back as best she could, determined to wait until Jack gave her permission to come. When he pushed up on his powerful arms and stared down at her, the look of determination written across his face was mesmerising. All traces of tenderness she thought she'd seen were gone.

His hips slammed into hers again and again, his long, thick cock stretching her wide and hitting so deep inside her it made her teeth rattle.

It was glorious.

Jack was glorious.

And when he smashed his lips down on hers, when he pushed his tongue inside her mouth and stole her breath away, she knew the time had come.

She couldn't wait for his permission.

She had to beg for it.

"Please? Oh fuck," she said, closing her eyes as she tried to hold back the wave of bliss building in her gut.

"Please, what?" he growled, sounding just as desperate to come as she was.

"Please, I need to come," she said, embarrassed by the whining undertone in her voice. "Please, sir. Please let me come."

Jack's expression turned wicked. "What will you do if I say no?"

Sophie did whimper that time and shook her head. He wouldn't be that cruel. Would he? Unsure how to answer him, it was pure frustration that had her digging her fingernails into his shoulders and dragging him closer so she could sink her teeth into the side of his neck.

Her lover laughed out loud, seemingly unbothered by her attack. "Feisty," he murmured, then kissed her again, hard and fast. "Now, ask me nicely."

Sophie wanted to scowl and make *him* ask nicely, but she couldn't hold it back any longer. Even felt the tell tale signs of her orgasm starting to crest as she opened her mouth to ask, "Please, sir, may I come?"

"Yes."

Her back arched, and her mouth fell open in a silent scream, his permission the final catalyst she needed to let the cresting wave of ecstasy break over her, through her, surround her. She'd held out for so long, and now she was going to drown in her abandon, shaking, shivering. Clinging to Jack like a life buoy.

And when he came, too, and pressed his hips into her, held still over her as he emptied himself inside her quivering body, a quiet sob escaped her.

She'd thought her previous orgasm was the best she'd felt in years, but it paled in comparison. She was in Heaven.

Soft kisses rained down on her, dashing away her tears. Then they were rolling, and she found herself tucked in tight to Jack's side, his strong arms around her, his commanding voice telling her what a good girl she was. How proud he was of her.

He pressed a gentle yet lingering kiss to her mouth. "I'll be back in a sec," he said, staring down at her with that tender look again before leaving to dispose of the condom. "Are you all right?" he said when he returned. "Would you like some water?"

Sophie nodded, and he disappeared into the other room. She took the opportunity to go to the bathroom and freshen up. When she returned, she found the bedding turned down and Jack propped up against the pillows in the middle of the bed, sipping water. He'd placed another bottle on the bedside table closest to her, so she grabbed it and took a drink.

She hadn't had a one-night stand in a very long time and was unsure of the protocols involved, but she figured it was time to leave. Before things got awkward. The thought made her sad. She'd had fun with Jack. And not just because the man was a certifiable sex god.

He was sweet, and she didn't want to leave.

But what if he didn't want her to stay?

Just then he tapped the mattress beside him. "Get over here."

Her heart raced, and she had to tamp down her immediate reaction to leap onto the bed and snuggle into him.

Her hesitation made him frown. "Unless you'd rather go?"

Shaking her head, Sophie smiled shyly. "No, sir. I don't want to go."

"Good, because the only place you're going tonight is over my lap."

Her eyes widened, and she bit her lip to rein in her smile, then crawled over the bed and knelt beside him. "You still have the energy for that?"

Jack chuckled and tugged her forwards, encouraged her to lie across his lap, then grabbed her arse in both hands and squeezed hard. "I told you, beautiful," he said, his voice a warm purr. "I intend to worship this arse tonight."

10

Sophie slowly blinked her eyes open only to squint them shut again and block out the sunlight flooding the bedroom. Rolling onto her back, she dragged her hands through her hair and tugged at the inevitable knots, then swiped the back of her hand over her mouth.

"Morning, sleepyhead."

Oh God.

Squeezing her eyes even more tightly shut, Sophie prayed Jack had not just been witness to her daily morning ritual of removing the drool from her face, but the humour in his voice suggested otherwise.

Fighting with the sheets that were twisted around her, she managed to sit up and face Jack where he sat in the chair at the side of the bed. The intensity in his bright blue eyes made her drag the sheet higher until all of her wobbly bits were hidden. When he frowned at her, she doubled down, scrunching the sheet in her fist. If he tried to pull it away now, he'd have a fight on his hands.

"Morning," she mumbled, quickly shoving her free

hand through the wreckage of her hair again, wincing when it got caught on a particularly heinous knot. "Ouch."

Jack rose from the chair and moved to the bed. His hair was dishevelled, as though he'd recently rolled out of bed, and he wore a fresh pair of boxer briefs that hugged his strong thighs and showcased his erection perfectly.

But....

She frowned. "Were you watching me sleep?"

"Yes," he said, his tone completely lacking remorse.

Her eyes narrowed. "For how long?"

"Long enough," he said, shrugging. "You're very cute when you snore, by the way," he added, grinning.

Sophie felt the heat of her embarrassment stain her face and neck.

Jack leaned down and whispered by her ear, "You're even cuter when you blush."

The intoxicating cocktail of his smooth, rich voice mixed with whatever the hell was in that sexy-as-fuck cologne commandeered the last of her good sense and turned her brain to mush.

She was helpless to resist him.

"Let go of the sheet, angel."

Her grip loosened for a moment, then clenched around the sheet where she held it bunched beneath her chin. Staring up at Jack, she watched his face for any hint of disgust, any sign that he was mocking her, but all she found was a serene smile and desirous eyes. Swallowing hard, she let go of the soft cotton barrier and let it fall back into her lap.

Jack's sharp intake of breath was followed by a slow exhale, and then he pulled his bottom lip between his teeth and swore softly.

"You really are so very beautiful," he said, staring down

at her like she was the answer to all his questions. Precious to him somehow. Which was completely crazy. They barely knew each other. Then his lips quirked in that cheeky grin that made him look ten years younger and he said, "And you know that's not just lip service, because I've already gotten in your pants."

She snorted and shook her head at the reminder of her words outside the ballroom, but she still wasn't quite willing to believe him. No man had ever wanted her with the same passion the morning after the night before. All of them—even Ethan—had looked at her with varying degrees of regret.

"You're not disappointed?" she hedged. "Waking up to —" She waved a hand down her body. "—this?"

His smile vanished and his brow furrowed, as though she'd said something offensive. "What do you mean?"

"I mean me," she said, huffing out a resigned sigh. "The *real* me with the smudged make-up and my hair a mess and drool on my face. No space-age underwear holding back the muffin rolls. No gravity-defying push-up bra." She shook her head again. "You're saying you're okay with this? With... *just* me?"

In an instant she was under him again, his weight pushing down on her, pinning her to the bed. His strong hands encircled her wrists, his powerful hips spread her thighs apart, and his rock-hard erection pressed against her core, making her gasp, making her buck against him. Sharp spikes of arousal flared in her clit as she rubbed herself on his thick cock, the friction making her moan.

A deep, rumbling growl emanated from the back of Jack's throat, and the expression on his face....

Wolves could take lessons from Jack Martin on how to ensnare their prey.

His eyes were liquid blue need, his smile predatory yet completely disarming at the same time. And his voice... his voice was dark velvet.

Soft, luxurious, alluring.

Sophie would happily be his prey.

"Until I woke up beside you this morning, I thought last night had all been a fantastic dream." He stared unflinchingly into her eyes. Into her very soul. "I watched you sleep because my tiny brain couldn't comprehend how the fuck I came to be so lucky as to wake up with you in my arms."

Her eyes widened and her mouth fell open on a gasp, but then she smiled. She couldn't help herself. Never in all of her life had a man said something so lovely to her, so romantic, or with such sincerity. "Thank you," she whispered, afraid if she said it any louder that he'd change his mind and take it all back.

It was a foolish thought—Jack had been nothing but a gentleman—but experience was a cruel mistress.

Before she could say anything else, Jack moved off the bed and hauled her up with him. He gripped her hip in one hand and slid the other to her nape, then pulled her close and kissed her.

The moment his lips touched hers, she moaned and melted against him, let him deepen their kiss until her pussy was clenching, wanting him inside her, and she was practically panting with need.

But then he pulled away, smirking at her eagerness, and she realised she'd somehow straddled one of his thighs. Heat flamed her cheeks again. She'd been humping his leg like a bitch in heat.

She tried to pull away, but Jack's grip tightened on her body and he held her fast. "Don't even think about running away from me, angel," he growled. "You're perfect exactly as you are."

Sophie stared at Jack in amazement and smiled. No wonder Ethan had never introduced them. She probably would have jumped ship within ten minutes of meeting him, especially if he'd spoken to her like he just had.

Leaning in for another kiss, their lips were just about to touch when someone started knocking on their door. Banging was more accurate. They both turned towards the interruption and sighed. Then Jack stroked her hair back from her face and placed a quick kiss on the tip of her nose, making her blush again.

This man....

"Why don't you hop in the shower, and I'll get rid of whomever is out there and then order us some brunch."

"You don't want to shower with me?" she asked, the mischief in her tone belying her over-the-top pout.

Jack chuckled, then slid his hand to the front of her throat and squeezed lightly. "Baby, if I get in the shower with you, I'll just make you all dirty again."

Sophie shrugged. "So? I don't mind getting dirty with you."

His eyes narrowed, and a devilish smile twisted his lips. In an instant, he spun her around and pulled her against him so her back nestled against his muscled chest. Then he murmured in her ear, his voice pure gravel, "Give me five minutes."

He released her with a soft kiss on her shoulder and a hard swat on her arse, and she grinned through her entire morning routine. The hot water hitting her skin felt amazing, relaxing muscles she hadn't realised she'd used, and the body wash smelled like coconuts and lime, perfect for the tropical summer heat that awaited her outside. But it wasn't until she'd finished washing her hair—and Jack was still a no-show—that she started to worry.

Where was he?

Who exactly had been at their door?

Drying herself as quickly as possible, she exited the bathroom to find all of her clothes on the bed, and the bedroom door was shut.

This can't be good.

Her chest constricted and her breaths came fast as panic threatened to overcome her, but she closed her eyes and counted to ten.

Jack wasn't hiding her away. He was giving her privacy.

She had to believe that.

After yanking her dress on, she frowned, realising she couldn't fasten the zipper beyond her waist. She'd need to be a contortionist to get it all the way to the top. Anna had helped her into the dress the night before, and Jack had helped her out of it.

Sophie grinned. Maybe he would help her out of it again?

Pulling her hair up into a messy bun, she crossed the room and tentatively opened the bedroom door. Sticking her head out, she looked around. "Jack?"

"I'm here, angel."

She crossed the penthouse to the dining table and found her lover standing there, his arms folded across his chest and a look of stern concentration on his handsome face. Unfolding his arms as she approached, he held one out and beckoned her to him. That's when she saw Ethan sitting at the table, scowling at his phone, and Anna standing behind him, reading over his shoulder while chewing her bottom lip and shaking her head.

"You!" Sophie snarled at Ethan, striding forward to

stand with Jack. He'd put his trousers back on but nothing else, and she took comfort in his warm body as he wrapped a strong arm around her waist and snuggled her against his side.

The faint smell of sex still clung to his skin, and it took all of her willpower not to bury her face in the crook of his neck and lick him.

Ethan lifted his gaze from his device and grinned—fucking *grinned*—at her as she snuggled against his brother. "Hmm... truce?"

"I ought to kick your arse for the stunt you pulled last night," she growled at her former playmate.

"You may still get the chance," Jack said, glaring at his brother.

"Why? What's happened?" She looked to her best friend. "Anna?"

"Hey, babe," Anna said quietly but didn't elaborate further.

Sophie narrowed her gaze and stared at each of them in turn. "What's going on?"

"Morning, Sophie."

She frowned at the phone in the middle of the table, the one with the screen filled with the bleary-eyed face of Danielle Kay. "And why is my agent on the phone?" she said, adding a belated "Morning, Dan."

Jack, Ethan, and Anna all exchanged a look before Jack nodded and sighed heavily. "Show her," he said, then pulled out a chair. "You'd better sit down."

The blood drained from Sophie's face and her knees gave way, causing her to fall onto the chair. "Oh God," she whispered. "Who died?" She clutched at the sudden stabbing sensation in her chest. "Is my dad okay?"

All eyes turned to her, a combination of shock and

surprise, until Anna hurriedly assured her, "Oh, honey, no. No one died. And Paul is fine. I promise."

Sophie processed that and took a much-needed breath, then frowned. "Then why is everyone acting so serious? What in the bloody hell is going on?"

Ethan slid his phone across the table. "Read that," he said, pointing to the screen, all evidence of his earlier grin replaced with another scowl.

Her frown deepened as she picked up the device and began reading, unsurprised to find it was an online gossip column masquerading as a news article. A photograph of her and Jack kissing on the ballroom balcony at midnight sat front and centre under a headline that read *"New Year, New Lovers!"*

Celebrity couple Ethan Martin and Sophie Bennett have split (again), only this time it seems to be sticking! Sources confirmed that even though the on-again, off-again pair stayed at the same luxury hotel in North Queensland for the big night, Martin and Bennett spent New Year's Eve partying with other people. When the clock struck twelve, some eagle-eyed partygoers were shocked to see Sophie Bennett ringing in the New Year with Martin's younger brother, the notoriously reclusive Jonathon "Jack" Martin, and all evidence points to their interaction being anything but platonic.

Martin's wife—

Wait. What? Martin's wife? Sophie's breath seized in her lungs, her heart practically stopped in her chest and her brain stalled, snagged on that one tiny word.

Tiny, but significant.

Wife.

Jack had a wife?

A feeling of dread slithered over her skin, and her palms grew clammy. Her throat bobbed as she audibly swallowed, as she tried to quell the shock, the hurt, the urge to hit something—or some*one*. Her hand clenched around Ethan's phone until she heard the device creak in protest.

"Soph?" Ethan said slowly, his deep voice edged with caution. "Are you okay?"

Closing her eyes for a moment, she sucked down a much-needed breath, then lifted her gaze to his, smiled, and said, "I'm fine."

She was far from fine, but she also had an audience, including the man she'd allegedly had an affair with. It was not the time to freak out or make a scene, so she kept reading.

Martin's wife, Sydney socialite Lisa Bancroft, with whom he is currently in the midst of a lengthy and acrimonious divorce, stated that she wasn't surprised by her husband's behaviour, insinuating that his marital indiscretions were the cause of their split three years ago.

Industry insiders say it's highly likely Mr Martin will soon be named CEO of Martin Cosmetics after his mother, founder of the company and current CEO, Sienna Martin, announced her retirement just before Christmas.

Those same insiders say Sophie Bennett has spent the last few months aggressively campaigning to be named the new face for the Martin Cosmetics all-natural product line, and that her blind ambition caused the tension that saw Ethan Martin distancing himself from her in recent days.

With this new relationship coming to light, the question

must be asked: If Ms Bennett succeeds in her campaign, will it be because of what she knows or who she knows? Only time will tell.

Ms Bennett is the daughter of former fashion model turned photographer Paul Bennett and the late Italian fashion icon Sofia Montini, sometimes known in social circles as Sofia Martini due to her partying lifestyle. Ms Montini passed away ten years ago from an accidental drug overdose.

Neither Ethan Martin nor Jack Martin was available for comment.

"What. In the actual. Fuck?" she murmured, scrolling back through the article to stare at the photograph of her and Jack kissing outside the ballroom.

From the angle of the photo, she could tell it had been taken from inside the ballroom, and that it was from before Jack had dragged her to the shadowy corner. Just enough light had fallen over them to show their faces, to show their lips locked and their bodies pressed together in a very non-platonic way.

Her hands were pulling him closer. His hands were curled around her hips, holding her against his erection. Not that anyone could have seen *that*. But she'd certainly felt it. Like an iron bar stabbing into her.

A thick, heavy iron bar.

An involuntary shiver gripped her at the memory, and at the sight of Jack's big hands clutching her to him, at the memory of them touching her, stroking over her heated skin, slipping easily inside her willing body.

Was it crazy that even now, after everything she'd just discovered, she still wanted to crawl into his lap and let him soothe her? That the thought of being in his arms again made her heart race and her pussy wet?

Absolutely.

On both counts.

Jack Martin didn't deserve to touch her. He'd lied to her. Tricked her. And now her reputation was being called into question. A reputation she'd worked so hard to cultivate. She'd never slept with anyone for a job, and she certainly didn't sleep with married men. She wasn't her mother and never would be.

The urge to hit something flooded through her again, but again she counted to ten and took a deep breath. Violence never solved anything.

Nobody else said a word as she sat there, thinking. Silently imploding. It was as if they understood she needed the silence to unpack and absorb the volume of information that had just been dumped in her lap. So much to unpack, but out of everything, she kept going back to that one tiny titbit. The one thing that stood out more than the rest.

Shoving down her hurt, she turned in her seat and glared up at Jack, then snarled, "You're married?"

11

"You didn't tell her you were still married?"

Jack closed his eyes and pinched the bridge of his nose, ignoring the censure in his older brother's tone as he took a second to control his temper. "Not helping, Ethan," he said, opening his eyes and glaring at his sibling.

Sophie started to laugh, only it wasn't the sweet, shy giggling or the riotous, unabashed laughter he'd heard the night before. This sound was darker. Sadder.

Lonelier.

He understood that sound more than he'd ever want to admit, and it broke his heart to hear it emanate from his woman. "Baby, I—"

"Don't," she snapped at him, rising to her feet as she said it. "Don't call me baby. Or angel. And don't you dare make excuses."

Jack shoved his hand through his hair, his frustration gnawing at his insides, making him sick to his stomach. "I'm not going to make excuses," he said, forcing himself to be calm, "but I'd appreciate the chance to explain myself."

She shook her head and laughed again, that heart-wrenching sound that tightened his gut with guilt. As she pushed in her chair, he noticed the zipper of her dress was only partially fastened. Stepping forward, he grabbed the back of her dress and tugged at the zipper.

She tried to move away from him. "Don't—"

"Be still," he said firmly, sighing with relief when she obeyed his command. "I never cheated on my wife, Sophie," he murmured as he fastened her dress. "Even after...."

Her zipper fully closed, Sophie attempted to step away again, and this time Jack let her. "Even after what?"

He flicked a glance at his brother and Ethan nodded, indicating he could trust Sophie with the truth. He just wasn't sure he was ready to share it yet. Not all of it. Not when she wasn't ready to hear it.

Sensing his hesitation, his brother spoke up instead. "Lisa was the one who cheated on Jack," he said, folding his arms. "And that wasn't even the worst of what she did to him."

Sophie's gaze met his and he nodded, hoping she could see the sincerity in his eyes. "It's true. She cheated on me the whole time we were together, but when your family owns one of the largest media empires in the southern hemisphere, you can put a spin on pretty much anything and get away with it. In fact, I'd bet good money that she's behind this nonsense," he said, waving dismissively at the article. "Trying to sway public opinion in her favour."

Sophie seemed to consider that for a moment, then shook her head again and narrowed her eyes. "But you still lied to me, Jack," she said, her voice strong even though her hands were shaking. "You told me you were single."

He wanted to take her hands in his and hold them steady, wanted to assure her he was a good guy and not the scumbag the article made him out to be. "I've been separated for three years and have zero interest in reconciling with my ex. She's the one dragging out the divorce, not me. I *am* single."

The muscle in her cheek ticked as she spoke through gritted teeth. "You also said you're an *accountant*, not the freaking CEO of Martin Cosmetics."

"Technically, I'm not CEO yet. Nothing's been made official."

"Technically?" She scoffed. "Technically, you're not single either," she said, glaring at him again, her hands now firmly planted on her hips. "Not making things official seems to be a bad habit with you."

Ethan snorted loudly, then covered his stupidly grinning face with his hand. When Jack continued glaring at him, he said, "What? It was funny. And she makes a very good point."

"You're an arsehole."

"As interesting as this all is, can we get back to the main issue, please?" Sophie's agent spoke through the phone on the table, her tone impatient. "And how this whole debacle is affecting Sophie's career?"

Sophie's skin paled as she dropped her hands from her hips and began wringing them together, twisting her fingers until they looked like they would snap. "How bad is it?"

Danielle sighed, the heavy sound crackling through the phone. "I got a phone call from Maxine Anderson, the head of marketing, this morning. The fact that she felt the need to call me on a public holiday is generally not a good sign. You were at the top of their short list, but now they have... concerns. Apparently they weren't worried about your relationship with Ethan because he's not directly involved with company operations. But Jack is. He was head of accounting, and it's all but assured that he'll be the new CEO come Monday, so they're worried about how it will look if they award you the contract."

"I literally met Jack less than twelve hours ago," Sophie said, throwing her hands in the air. "I didn't even know he worked for Martin Cosmetics, let alone ran the whole freaking company."

"It's all about the optics," Danielle said. "They don't want it to look like they're playing favourites."

"Of course we play favourites," Ethan said, his tone clearly annoyed. "It's a family company. Nepotism is what we do."

"It's true," Anna agreed. "My future in my mother's company is all mapped out, and as much as I hate to agree with Ethan, he's right. We're legacies. It's what we do."

"It might be what we do, but it's not what *Sophie* does," Jack said quietly, watching for her every reaction. "That's why she avoided modelling for so long, so people couldn't compare her to her parents. That's why she chose to become a make-up artist instead, to forge her own path. It's also why she's perfect for the advertising campaign." Her features softened and her eyes widened, a small smile lifted her lips. A smile he returned before adding, "I've followed your Instagram for years, even before you turned to modelling. You always touted Martin Cosmetics as the gold standard. Always gave sound advice. You were as well respected in the make-up industry as you are in the modelling community, and it would do the head of marketing well to remember that. One photograph of two people kissing at midnight on New Year's Eve is not as scandalous as some people would have us believe."

"Oh, I like you!" Danielle said. "When I call them back, can I quote you?"

A rueful smile tugged at Jack's mouth. "I wouldn't recommend it. I'm not exactly their favourite person right now."

"Why not?" Anna asked.

"In an attempt to rein in their overspending, I cut the department's budget last year. Maxine has been pissy with me ever since."

"Still, you make some very valid points," Danielle said. "I can work with that, even without dropping your name into the conversation. I'll talk to you tomorrow, hon, and let you know where we're at. In the meantime, lie low and get some rest." And then she hung up.

Sophie's mouth twisted to the side and she scowled at the now-blank phone screen. "Even if Danielle works her magic and I do win the contract, people are going to think I only got it because I slept with the boss." Then she hung her head and groaned. "And if I don't get it...."

Jack frowned. "What?"

"If she doesn't get it, people will think she's a dud lay," Ethan supplied.

"Huh?"

Sophie rolled her eyes at his obvious ignorance. "If I couldn't secure the contract after fucking the boss, then I must be completely useless in bed. Because if I was *good* in bed, then...." She left the statement hanging, her eyes widening as she waited for Jack to take the hint.

He closed his eyes and groaned as the hint smacked him in the face. "If you were good in bed, you would have won the contract." He pulled out a chair and sat down. "Fuck."

"Yeah, so it's not the photo of us kissing that's the problem so much as the whole infidelity thing," Sophie said, her anger resurfacing. "And the aggressively campaigning thing and the being accused of sleeping my way to the top thing."

Jack noticed Ethan and Anna share a look. "What was that?"

"What was what?" Ethan shrugged.

"That look between you two," he said, flicking his gaze from one to the other. "What aren't you telling us?"

Anna suddenly looked very guilty, gnawing at her bottom lip and constantly switching her weight from one foot to the other. "Ethan, we should tell them."

"Tell them what?" Sophie asked slowly, her voice dropping, her eyes narrowing under a stern brow. She looked fierce. Scary. Sexy.

"We set you up," Anna blurted.

"Anna," Ethan groaned, dropping his head forward.

"I'm so sorry, Soph. I really thought we were helping you."

"Helping me how?" Sophie said through gritted teeth.

"You've been so miserable lately, so quiet, and that's not like you. I could see how lonely you were," Anna explained, then shrugged. "You're not as good at hiding it as you think you are." She shook her head. "Listen, I knew you weren't happy with Ethan. You two are just too different. And between work and your family, you never seem to have the time to date anymore. So when Ethan came to me a few weeks ago with the same concerns, we hatched a plan to set you up with his brother." She waved her hand at him.

"Admit it," Ethan said, smiling at Sophie. "Jack's a much better fit for you than I ever was."

Jack fisted his hands on the table, the urge to beat his brother senseless nearly overwhelming. "Why the fuck didn't you just tell us?"

"Because you wouldn't have come," Ethan said, the unspoken *duh* hanging heavily in the air. "Neither of you would have shown up if you'd known what we were planning." He crossed his arms. "You're both as stubborn as mules when it comes to leaving your comfort zones." Then he looked directly at Jack, his gaze softening. "And you're just as bad as Sophie when it comes to the whole work-life balance thing. I see how lonely you are, Jonathon. You can't hide it from me."

"I hate it when you call me that," Jack said quietly, choosing to ignore his brother's insights into his personal life. He'd always hated how easily his big brother had been able to see right through him. The man wasn't as stupid as he would have people believe.

Looking up at Sophie, he saw the sheen of tears swimming in her dark eyes, her gaze unfocussed and distant. Her hands were bunched into fists by her sides, and her shoulders were rigid. But then she lifted her chin and all emotion melted away from her face.

He'd thought she'd looked scary before.

Standing before them now, she practically vibrated with fury.

"Sophie?" Anna said cautiously, inching towards her friend. "Babe... say something."

"What would you like me to say?" she said, halting Anna in her tracks. She looked at each of them in turn. "In the span of a single evening, my best friend lied to me, my ex humiliated me, and the man I actually—*stupidly*—thought I had a connection with has turned me into the one thing I swore I'd never be. My integrity has been called into question, and my dream modelling gig, the one I've worked my *arse* off to get," she said, her voice growing louder with every word, "the one I was so close to winning I could fucking taste it—" She shrugged, then threw her hands up in surrender. "—is gone. Buried in a shit heap of gossip and innuendo." Her bottom lip quivered before she pulled it between her teeth and bit down hard, turning the plush little pillow a deep red. "So I'm going to go now, before you three think up any more ways to screw me over."

"Soph, wait." Tears streaked down Anna's cheeks.

"No." She shook her head and backed away from the table, away from them. Away from him. "Last night was a mistake. All of it was a huge fucking mistake that I have no intention of repeating," she said, then turned on her heel, headed for the door.

A mistake? No. Jack didn't make mistakes.

Suddenly, his anger at his brother—and at himself—his disappointment and his desperation, and the sharp panic that he'd never see her again all collided in that moment, and he slammed his palm on the table. "Sophie, stop," he said, rising to his feet, the command whipping out of him before he could think better of it. His heart beat a little faster when she obeyed.

Good girl.

Stalking towards her, he stopped when his chest was only a hair's breadth from her back and the front of his trousers brushed against her shapely arse. Keeping his voice low as he spoke, he let his words caress the shell of her ear. "I know you don't mean what you said. You don't think we made a mistake any more than I do."

"You really don't want to know what I'm thinking right now," she snarled, turning slowly to face him once more, her beautiful eyes spitting fire, her proud chin thrust forward, leading the charge of her defiance.

He slid his hands over her hips, tightening his grip when she tried to escape him again. He was desperate to make her stay. "If you want that job so badly, I will make sure it's yours. I will—"

"You really don't get it, do you," she said, cutting him off. "Un-fucking-believable." That scoffing laugh bubbled out of her again as she looked at him like he was stupid. "And you know what?" she added, knocking his hands away from her and backing towards the door. "I *am* beginning to see the family resemblance." She waved a hand between him and Ethan. "You're both arseholes!"

Then she yanked open the door and disappeared through it, slamming it shut as she left.

Jack felt like he'd been punched in the chest.

Sophie was gone.

She was upset—*furious*—and she was gone.

Pinching the bridge of his nose, he swore, giving the word a lengthy life as he pushed out a long, slow breath. "*Fuuuck.*" Then he looked at his brother and his hand fell to his side, clenched in a fist. "I'm going to beat the shit out of you."

"Oh God. What have we done?" Anna said, her cheeks wet with tears and a shell-shocked expression on her face. "She's never going to speak to me again."

Ethan stood and pulled her into his arms, rubbed soothing circles on her back as she sobbed on his shoulder. "Shhh, come on now. It'll be all right. This is Sophie we're talking about," he said, pulling back and brushing his thumbs over her cheeks, wiping away her tears and giving her a sympathetic smile. "She's one of the most forgiving people I've ever known, and you're her best friend. Of course she'll talk to you again." Then he looked at Jack. "You want my advice?"

"Not really," he said drily, knowing his brother would ignore him.

Ethan smirked. "Give her a couple of days to unpack everything and work through her feelings, then give her a call and ask her out properly. She won't stay mad forever."

Jack hated that Ethan knew that about her, that he knew Sophie better than him, but before he could say anything, there was a knock at the door.

"Sophie." The tightness in his chest suddenly eased as he rushed to let her in. But instead of finding his lover, he was faced with a young man carrying several large brown paper bags with the hotel's restaurant logo printed on them.

"Room service for you, sir," he said with a smile, holding out the bags.

Sticking his head into the hallway and looking left and right, Jack bit back his disappointment.

Sophie was well and truly gone.

"Sir? You *did* order room service, didn't you?"

He'd intended to, but then Ethan and Anna had barged in and ruined his day. "No."

"Yes," his brother said, appearing beside him to take the bags. "I ordered food for everyone. Figured we might be here a while."

Jack left Ethan to deal with the food while he stalked back to the bathroom and shut himself away for a moment. He needed to think.

The woman who'd made his cold heart flicker to life again had left him floundering, wishing he'd never agreed to go to that damn party in the first place. He was a creature who lived in the shadows, and he never should have ventured into the light.

Staring into the mirror, Jack scrubbed a hand down his face. "What the fuck was I thinking?"

Sophie Bennett was pure sunshine.

Brilliant and blinding.

She didn't belong in the shadows any more than he belonged in the light.

But he had enjoyed his time with her. Spanking her luscious arse until she was a wriggling pile of lust and need, then holding her down and fucking her like an animal. Kissing her mouth, her body, drinking her in one glorious inch at a time. Making love to her, slowly, tenderly. Passionately. Then holding her in his arms as she'd slept, her lush body curled around his, warm and trusting.

A trust he'd broken with his own selfish need.

Yes, he was still married, but only because his greedy wife refused to sign the divorce papers until he gave her more money. But after what she did, she was lucky to get anything at all.

And she was well overdue a reminder of that fact.

Resolve straightened Jack's spine.

He would get Sophie back.

He had to.

He'd had a taste of sunshine, and he needed—*craved*—more.

But first he had to end his farce of a marriage once and for all.

"Where's my phone?" he demanded, striding back into the penthouse living area.

Ethan tossed him the device he'd left on the table earlier. "Who are you calling?"

"My solicitor."

His brother grinned. "It's about fucking time."

12

Jack shoved his hands in his pockets and stared out the floor-to-ceiling windows of his new corner office. The sheer amount of sunlight streaming into the expansive room seemed rather opulent compared to the fluorescent lighting he was used to in the accounting department, hidden away in the bowels of the building.

The view was nothing to sneeze at either. He'd take the morning sunshine bouncing off the water in Sydney Harbour over the greige walls and mass-produced artworks in accounting any day. He smiled as he remembered Sophie's comments on the subject on New Year's Eve, about her view of the swimming pool compared to his view of the moonlight on the ocean.

God, I miss her.

Checking his watch for the umpteenth time that morning, he twisted his mouth. He was irritated. He was waiting for his soon-to-be ex-wife to appear for their mid-morning meeting, and she was late. *As usual.* God forbid Lisa Bancroft adhere to any sort of schedule, her own or anybody else's. People might get the idea that she *wasn't* the free-spirited devil-may-care heiress she purported to be and was, in fact, the most manipulative, calculating, and mean-spirited woman he'd ever had the misfortune to know.

He checked his watch again and let loose an impatient sigh. She was almost an hour overdue. *Typical*. He sighed again. He couldn't wait for this to be over.

Turning back to his desk, he surveyed his growing mountain of work. He'd been CEO of Martin Cosmetics for one week, and already he needed a holiday. His life had been nothing but endless meetings, pointless memos, and an unrelentingly full email inbox.

Currently, he was going over the quarterly financial reports for each department and making sure they were staying within their budgets while still hitting their targets. As much as he tried not to, he couldn't help returning again and again to the marketing department's reports, specifically the modelling contracts. He grinned like an idiot.

They'd hired Sophie for the new advertising campaign.

Without his interference.

Not that the gossip columnists would believe it. They'd continued printing bullshit about them, including photos of Sophie sitting in Jack's lap on the penthouse balcony, clearly enjoying herself, feeding him cheese and fruit while wearing nothing but sexy lingerie.

The photos didn't paint a very flattering picture for his girl or her reputation, and he still wanted to know how the hell they'd even gotten them. They'd been sitting on the penthouse balcony, facing the ocean. There had been no vantage point for the paparazzi to exploit.

Probably used a fucking camera drone.

Jack had contemplated issuing a public statement denouncing the gossip being printed but had been warned against it. The company publicist told him it would only add fuel to the flames and that it was best to ignore the lies and let them die a natural death.

He rubbed the back of his neck. It grated against his nerves to sit back and do nothing, to leave his woman exposed to such degrading rumours. But Ethan had reluctantly agreed with the publicist, reminding him that he'd been through this situation more times than he could count and that a big part of Jack's new job was to let the experts do theirs.

Putting one report aside, he paused for a moment to stretch his neck, then picked up the next and continued reading. It was only when a gentle knock sounded on the frosted glass door that separated his office from the other executive suites that he stopped and looked up. Realising he'd gotten lost in his work, he checked the time and scowled.

"Come," he barked, more sharply than he'd intended.

The door swung open. "Sorry to interrupt you, Jack, but your... *wife* is here to see you."

He didn't miss the way his assistant's mouth twisted or how her voice dripped with disdain when she uttered the word *wife*. The sour expression on her face didn't suit the fastidiously professional woman either.

Bethany had worked for Jack for six years and knew his pending divorce was not an amicable one. Being the consummate professional she was, she kept her thoughts on her boss's private life to herself, but when she did see fit to express an opinion on the subject, it was brief and to the point. The woman could write a book about the efficiency of a well-timed eyeroll, and Jack almost smiled at the change his ex could affect in even the most pleasant of people.

"Did she tell you to call her that?"

She pursed her lips and nodded sharply. "She did."

Jack looked at his watch again. Lisa was more than two hours late. The urge to make her wait while he finished going over the stack of reports warred with his need to make her disappear from his life as soon as humanly possible. She'd dragged their separation out for long enough, and he was beyond sick of it.

It was time to end it once and for all.

Shifting the stack of work documents into the desk drawer, he pulled out the shiny new divorce agreement he'd had his solicitor draw up on New Year's Day. To say the man had been unimpressed by Jack's demands was an understatement, but he'd gotten the job done and been well compensated for his efforts.

Jack placed the papers front and centre on his desk. He even laid out his best fountain pen for the occasion.

"Show her in," he said and leaned back in his chair.

Bethany nodded and disappeared, and the next time the door opened, Lisa was standing there, looking as primped and picture-perfect as she always did.

Jack didn't bother to stand and greet her. He no longer felt the need to be polite to the woman. All he wanted was for her to sign the papers and go.

And this time he wasn't taking no for an answer.

"Jack, darling," she said, her lips curled in a tight smile. "I was summoned?"

Like the demon she is.

"Have a seat," Jack said, keeping his tone short as he indicated the chair in front of his desk.

Lisa folded her curvy little frame into the leather chair and crossed her legs. She had always had a lovely figure, and a pretty face to match. Unfortunately, she was also the personification of all that glitters not being gold. Her sexy façade hid a wealth of faults, the most prominent being greed, entitlement, and selfishness.

He'd married her for all the wrong reasons, he knew that, but it had still shocked him to his core to discover how callous, how cruel she truly was. But the facts had been hard to argue with. She'd used him, lied to him, cheated on him.

And worse.

The proof of her treachery had broken his heart, and until a few days ago, he'd thought it could never be healed. But then he'd met Sophie Bennett and his whole world had turned on its head.

He'd smiled again. Felt *happy* again. Hopeful.

I will get her back.

"I have a full schedule and you're late, so I'll keep this brief. Sign the papers, Lisa. No more of your games. This ends right here, right now."

Her eyes narrowed slightly, and her tight smile spread into something more sinister. "Are you really so eager to get rid of me, Jack?"

He didn't flinch. "Yes."

"Ouch," she said, pretending to pout. "Words hurt, Jonathon."

Jack simply stared at his ex, keeping his expression carefully neutral. "Sign the papers, Lisa."

"Now, hang on a moment." She leaned forward in her seat, drawing his gaze to her ample cleavage. That little movement combined with the glint of challenge in her eyes used to make him want her. Used to drive him crazy with a need to drag her over his knees and make her submit. But that was a long time ago.

Now it just pissed him off.

"Why now?" she asked. "You've been dragging this out for years—"

"I'm not the one dragging this out and you know it," he said, his calm mask in danger of slipping.

Lisa scoffed, all pretence gone from her demeanour. "If you had just given me what I wanted in the first place, then all of this would be over by now. So yes, you *are* the one dragging this out."

He cocked one brow. "Are you saying you won't sign the papers?"

"Are you giving me the twenty million I asked for?"

"No."

"Then no, I'm not signing the papers. Not until I get what I deserve."

Jack's smile was slow and purely self-indulgent. "*Two* million."

Lisa jerked back in her seat and stared at him in disbelief. "I beg your pardon?"

"Sign the papers now and you'll get two million dollars, to be deposited into any bank account of your choosing."

"But that's half what you offered me last time."

"Yes, it is. And if you don't sign today, I'll halve it again."

"You can't do that," she spat at him, her manicured talons digging into the armrests of the leather chair.

Jack smoothed his hand down his tie. "I can do whatever the fuck I want. Or maybe you've forgotten about the infidelity clause in our prenup? The one stating that if you cheat on me during our marriage, then you walk away with nothing more than a paltry fifty thousand dollars."

She scoffed. "Fifty thousand per year is nowhere near enough. That wouldn't even cover my rent."

"Then I suggest you downsize," he replied, a vicious smile spreading slowly across his face. "Because that's not an annual sum. Fifty thousand is the total amount payable."

Her outraged gasp was music to his ears. "You're insane if you think I'll settle for that!"

"Then take the two million," he said. "I told you, I'm done playing your games. I have proof, Lisa, and I'm not afraid to use it."

Her smile grew nasty. "By all means, tell the world how bad you are in bed. Because that's the spin I'll put on it when it hits the media. Why else would I have strayed from our marital bed? Or maybe I should just tell them about how you used to beat me during sex. I'm sure that would go down well with the board. You'll be the shortest-serving CEO in the history of Australia."

"Beat you." Jack chuckled, undisturbed by her threat. "You realise, of course, that I have photos of you being *beaten* by other men. From memory, there's a video, too, and judging by your screams for *more*, I think it'll be a hard sell to make people believe you were under any duress."

"You prick."

"Or maybe I should share why we really split up," he added, all humour gone from his expression. "I'm sure your father's competitors would find *that* story fascinating."

Lisa's eyes narrowed, and her grip on the chair turned her knuckles white. "You wouldn't."

"I wonder what sort of *spin* they'd put on that? 'Socialite kills baby for money.' It has a certain ring to it, don't you think?"

In an instant, his ex was out of the chair and slamming her hand on his desk, her eyes wild and her face red. "It was a foetus, you arsehole. *Not* a baby."

"Yes, because the public are so good at making that distinction," he snapped back, his lip curled in disgust.

Lisa's face blanched, and she sank heavily back in her seat. "You can't," she whispered. "My reputation...."

"*Your* reputation?" Of course she only cared about herself. He didn't know why he was even surprised. "What about Sophie's reputation? What about mine?" he demanded, holding up a hand to silence her when she opened her mouth. "Don't deny it. I know it's you stirring up the rumours in the gossip columns, Lisa. They have your stink all over them." Her cheeks reddened, and all traces of her fear evaporated in the heat of her glare. He let loose a bitter laugh. "Why should I care about *your* reputation after all the damage you've caused, all the heartache?"

"Jack—"

"You knew I wanted kids, knew I wanted to start a family of my own. You got pregnant on purpose, knowing I would marry you. And as soon as that ring was on your finger—" He bit off what he was going to say, the pain lancing through his heart as fresh as the day he'd discovered her treachery, the day he'd discovered her miscarriage wasn't all it seemed to be.

"Tell me why, Lisa," he said through gritted teeth. "You owe me that much. Was it for the expense accounts? The big house? The fancy cars? Because you had all of that *before* I married you. So tell. Me. Why."

Lisa stared at him for so long, remained silent for so long, that Jack thought she wasn't going to answer him. But then she lifted her chin and squared her shoulders, and any hint of remorse she might have felt, even if it was self-serving, vanished completely. "It was never going to work, Jack."

"Then why did you do what you did, knowing you would fall pregnant, knowing I would want to marry you?" he said, his impatience loud and clear in every word.

"You want the truth?"

"Yes." He needed to know, to hear her say it.

"Fine," she said and crossed her arms. "Because it seemed like a good idea at the time. Are you happy now?"

He pinched the bridge of his nose and let out a slow exhale, tried to quell his temper. "It seemed like a good idea at the time," he repeated slowly, trying to make sense of the words and failing. "Which part of any of this seemed like a good idea, Lisa?"

"Mostly, the part where I got away from my controlling-as-fuck father. How was I supposed to know you would be just as bad?"

"What are you talking about?"

"I'm talking about the doctor appointments, and the vitamins, and the yoga classes, and the parenting books, and the food restrictions. The never-ending stream of rules. I enjoyed your control in the bedroom, Jack, but your control outside of it was just too much to bear."

Jack stared at his ex, his brow furrowed and his jaw slack as he tried to understand what she was saying. "So, because I showed an interest in your health and wellbeing, and that of our unborn child, I was too controlling?"

"Yes."

"And instead of talking to me about it, you decided the best course of action was to have an abortion and try to pass it off as a miscarriage. Do I have that right?"

"Be glad I did, Jack," she said, flicking an invisible piece of lint off her skirt, "or this whole situation would have been a lot more complicated."

Jack bristled at her flippant attitude. How could she be so cold? So indifferent to the hurt she'd caused?

Closing his eyes, he counted to ten.

He only made it to four before his hurt morphed into

rage and he was out of his chair, leaning over his desk and glaring at his *wife* with every ounce of hatred he possessed. "Sign the papers, Lisa," he snapped. "I'm done. *This* is done. Take the two million and get the fuck out of my life. And if I have to ask you again, I will not be so polite."

Lisa stared at him for what felt like an age, then huffed out a sigh, the sound heavy and resigned. "Very well." Slowly, she pushed herself out of the leather chair, then took her time straightening her dress, until finally she picked up his fountain pen and flicked through the divorce papers, scribbling her signature next to all of the little yellow tabs. When she was done, she placed the pen on top of the pages, grabbed her handbag, and turned to leave, but not without uttering one more barb.

One more reminder of his failures.

"If I'm being completely honest," she said, tucking her bag under her arm, "I'm not even sure if the kid was yours."

"Get out," he snarled at her, then watched every step she took until she reached the door, until one final thought had him calling her name. "Lisa."

She didn't say anything, just glanced back over her shoulder, waiting for him to speak.

"I truly hope you get *everything* you deserve."

Her eyes narrowed and her mouth pinched, the subtle jibe hitting its mark. Then she yanked the door open and slammed it shut behind her for what he hoped would be the last time.

Picking up the document, Jack flicked through the pages and made sure everything was in order, then dropped them back on his desk. A heavy breath of relief shuddered out of him as he lowered himself back into his chair, but his relief was short-lived as another knock sounded on his door.

"What?" he barked.

The door cracked open. "Jack?" Ethan stuck his head through the gap. "I just saw the harpy getting in the lift," he said, his unasked question obvious in his expression.

"She signed them."

"Thank fuck," Ethan said, looking as relieved as Jack felt. "So, you up for a celebratory lunch?" He held up a takeaway bag from his favourite sushi restaurant and a cup tray with two chocolate shakes from his favourite retro cafe.

Jack forced a smile and nodded, but his brother knew him better than that.

"Are you okay?"

Pushing to his feet again, he directed his brother to the sitting area on the other side of the office. "I'm fine. I'm just glad it's finally over and done with." He nodded at the cup tray. "That milkshake better have whipped cream and cherries on top."

Ethan chuckled as he laid out their lunch on the coffee table.

"What's so funny?"

"Nothing," his brother said, grinning like a loon. "For a moment there you sounded exactly like a very sexy model we both know and love."

Jack's gaze snapped to his brother's. "Love?"

Ethan shrugged and handed him a pair of chopsticks. "You know what I mean."

"I don't know that I do," he said cautiously. "Do you... *love* Sophie?"

His brother laughed. "Yes, but not the way you do. I love her, sure, but I'm not *in* love with her. And before you try denying it, yes, you are. Not that I blame you," he said. "Sophie Bennett is a beautiful woman, inside and out. She's got a big heart and a lot of love to give." He sighed. "And if I were a better man, I never would have let her go. But I'm not, so I did."

Now it was Jack's turn to grin. He wasn't the only Martin with a secret crush. "And you not committing to any one woman in particular has absolutely *nothing* to do with you and a certain family friend we both know and *love*," he said, throwing his brother's words back at him, "turning forty this year, right?"

Ethan's eyes snapped to his. "No," he answered, a little too quickly, then lifted his chin. "Layla and I made that pact as a joke. When we were twelve." He resumed eating. "It means nothing. Besides, we were talking about your fucked-up relationship issues, not mine."

Turning his focus to his own lunch, Jack said, "Considering how we were raised, you'd think we'd be better at this."

"Not really. Our parents have set an impossible standard when it comes to love and marriage." Ethan shook his head. "How the fuck do you find a soulmate?"

"The better question is what the fuck are we supposed to do once we've found them?"

"That one is easy," his brother said, his expression suddenly fierce. "You fight for them."

13

Melville's Cross, The Forge, three weeks later

Sophie stood in front of the mirror and blinked slowly as she stared at her haggard expression. "What the hell did I eat last night?"

She'd been feeling unwell for a few days, but the night before, her stomach had decided to up the ante from unwell to "please, God, I want to die," and she'd been throwing up ever since, which was not an ideal situation to find herself in on the day of her uncle's wedding.

"Sophie, are you all right? Do you want me to call the doctor?" Her father's concerned voice filtered through the bathroom door.

"I'm all right," she called back, splashing water on her face. "Just food poisoning, I think." From eating the exact same food as everybody else in the house, food that had made exactly no one else sick. She swallowed thickly against the need to vomit again, then rushed to the toilet and fell to her knees.

The bathroom door flew open behind her, and suddenly there was a strong hand rubbing circles on her back and her father's voice telling her to breathe through her mouth. "You are *not* all right," he growled, helping her to her feet after she was sure she wouldn't vomit again. "And no one else is sick. This is not food related."

"Well, then maybe it's a tummy bug. I don't know." She returned her father's scowl. "I'm sure I'll feel better after I have a shower and wash my hair. Anyway, there's nothing left in my stomach to throw up."

Her dad continued glowering at her, his lips pinched together. The man never spoke unless he had something worth saying, and it was obvious he had something to say. But he also knew his daughter was as stubborn as he was and that whatever he wanted to say would fall on deaf ears, so he simply nodded and said, "Yell if you need anything."

Sophie locked the door behind her father, then let down her hair, stripped out of her pyjamas, and got in the shower. The hot water streamed over her as she just stood there and stared at the wall. She'd barely had the energy to get out of bed that morning, let alone lift her arms over her head and wash her hair, but eventually she did it. She made the effort and completed her morning routine. She had to. She was supposed to do everybody's make-up for the wedding, and she refused to let them down.

But by the time she'd gotten dressed and made her way to the kitchen, make-up seemed to be the last thing on anyone's minds.

All hell had broken loose.

Her father, Paul, was the second eldest of nine children, eight boys and one girl, and every single one of them was crammed inside the large kitchen, along with her three cousins, her uncle's bride, her aunt's fiancé, her grandfather, and the bride's next-door neighbour, a surprisingly feisty seventy-something-year-old woman with lavender-coloured hair.

And everyone was talking over top of each other.

From what she could decipher, the wedding chapel and town hall had been double-booked, so they no longer had a suitable place to get married, something had happened to the cake, and the white flowers her uncle had ordered for the bouquets and table arrangements had just arrived and were all various shades of hot pink.

The groom, Toby, looked ready to murder someone, while his bride-to-be, Lucy—an ex-firefighter and one of the strongest women Sophie had ever met—looked close to tears.

I guess everyone has their breaking point.

But then Mia Caldwell spoke up, and the room breathed a collective sigh of relief. She had a plan.

Mia was her uncle Ollie's girlfriend, and she'd recently moved back to Melville's Cross after almost twenty years serving in the Royal Australian Army. She walked with a cane, and her resting bitch face made her look like she'd happily shove that cane up someone's arse and ride them like a pogo stick if they even dared to look at her funny, but the way Ollie stared at her, as though he would move mountains just to breathe the same air as her, made a tiny pang of jealousy stab at Sophie's heart.

Nearly a month ago, Sophie thought she'd found someone who looked at her the same way, but it had all been a lie. A beautiful, tantalising lie that had made her scream in ecstasy more times than she could count, but it was still a lie.

Unfortunately, Jack Martin had taken up permanent residence inside her brain. Even more annoying was the fact that he had the audacity to star in a never-ending fantasy loop that made it difficult to focus on everyday things. How, for instance, was she supposed to remember to put her panties on the right way around when she had the memory of being bent over Jack's lap as he spanked her sizeable arse running through her mind?

She sighed quietly and shook her head to shoo away the memory, then made herself a cup of tea as Mia handed out assignments and got the wedding back on track.

Luckily, the woman had inherited her parents' house on the other side of town, an old Queenslander with magnificent views of the local mountain range. "I have troops incoming with marquees, tables, and seating," Mia said. "We can set up everything at Someday. I mean, we already cleaned up the yard for the photos anyway, so we may as well put it to good use. Rafe?"

"Yes?"

"Can you call the caterers, the band, and the celebrant and let them know about the change of venue? Then check on Jane and the cake?"

Her second-youngest uncle nodded. "On it," he said, shoving a piece of toast in his mouth.

"Toby?"

The groom didn't answer, just stared at her with one brow raised and a look of displeasure on his face.

"Are you sure you can't use those?" Mia asked, pointing to the collection of pink roses piled up beside the kitchen sink.

"Positive," he growled.

Mia nodded. "Then I want you and your brothers—not Crispin—to visit every resident in town who has white flowers growing in their yard and use your considerable Bennett charm to beg, borrow, steal, or swap them for those pink ones. I suggest starting with Mayor Rose and working your way down from there."

Sophie watched her uncle's tension melt away, pulling a half-smile from him as he tucked Lucy under his arm. "Yeah, we can do that."

"And what will I be doing?" Crispin asked from his spot at the kitchen table.

Grinning at the interior designer, Mia said, "You're coming with me to Someday. I need someone with your expertise to tell my soldiers where to set up the marquees to make the most of the space and the views."

Cris threw out a mock salute. "Lead the way."

"Uly?"

"Yes, sweetheart?"

"I need you to source as many boxes of white fairy lights as you can and bring them to Someday in two hours or less."

The old man smiled broadly. "I like a woman who knows what she wants. Consider it done."

Mia nodded her thanks. "Everyone else needs to help Lucy and her bridesmaids get ready, including getting to their beauty appointments on time, starting with their mani-pedis in forty-five minutes." She tucked her tablet under her arm, looking every bit the Army major she had been until a month ago. "Everyone know what they're doing?"

Everyone just sort of murmured, shrugged, and half nodded, their lack of urgency causing Mia's back to straighten, her chin to lift, and her voice to snap out, "I said does everyone know what they're doing?"

A roomful of startled people, including Sophie, blurted, "Yes."

"Good. Then let's get moving."

Forty-five minutes. She had a whole forty-five minutes to kill before their mani-pedi appointments, after which they'd get their hair done, and then it was back to The Forge, the Bennett family home, so Sophie could do everybody's make-up.

A whole forty-five minutes to try and not think about Jack Martin's strong hands. Or his big dick. Or all of the things he knew how to do with his strong hands and big dick—

"How are you feeling, poppet?"

Sophie startled at the sound of her grandfather's voice, like a naughty child caught doing something they shouldn't, then laughed as he gently bumped his shoulder into hers. "I'm okay. A bit tired, but I'll live."

"And how long have you been feeling a bit tired?"

She blew on her tea and shrugged. "A couple of weeks, I guess. Between selling my house in Brisbane, moving all of my stuff to Sydney, and starting my new contract with Martin Cosmetics, I feel like I never get enough sleep. And don't even get me started on the real estate market down there. Shopping for an apartment has been a nightmare."

Ulysses Bennett tilted his head and stared down at her in an unsettling way. "And the nausea? How long has that been going on?"

"What are you getting at, Grandad?" she asked, one brow cocked.

But the wily old man just shook his head and shrugged. "Nothing. I was just wondering if there was something you'd like me to pick up while I'm out."

He stared at her expectantly until her hand wandered to

her stomach and she realised what he meant. *Oh.* "Yes, please. Some antinausea medication would be awesome. Can't be throwing up while the happy couple says their 'I do's.' That would not make for a magical moment. For anyone involved."

Uly's lips quirked into a secretive little smile, and his old blue eyes practically twinkled with mischief. "That's all? Nothing else?"

Sophie frowned. "Nothing comes to mind." What was he up to?

Uly kissed her forehead, then chuckled as he walked away, and Sophie grabbed a vacant seat at the kitchen table. A few minutes later, her father and most of his brothers had divided up the mountain of pink flowers and were heading out to beg, borrow, steal, or swap them for white ones.

Before he left, her uncle Toby bent down to kiss Lucy slowly, passionately, and again she felt that pang of jealousy stab at her. In the past year, there had been a chain reaction of romances happening in their big family, and as much as she loved to see it happen, it also left her feeling even more alone.

First her aunt Abby—who was only two years older than Sophie—met her fiancé, Wolf. He'd caught her skinny-dipping in a creek, had decided to join her, and they'd been together ever since.

A few months later, her uncle Rafe had discovered Jane Melville, the undisputed love of his life, was pregnant with twins. After years of bad timing and worse decisions, they had *finally* tied the knot and were now sickeningly happy and eagerly awaiting the arrival of their babies.

Around the same time that was going on, Toby met and fell head over heels in love with Lucy. She'd interviewed for the position of office manager at his garden centre, and then he'd met her again a week later at a speed dating event. They'd gone home together, and the rest was history. He'd asked her to marry him on Christmas Day, the same day she'd told him she was pregnant.

And the most recent link in the love chain was Oliver and Mia, childhood best friends turned hot-and-heavy lovers. According to Abby, whom they were currently living with, the pair hadn't been able to keep their hands off each other since they'd reunited.

Staring at her tea as she sat in thought, she rotated the warm mug in her hands. When Sophie met Jack on New Year's Eve, when she'd felt that connection with him, felt so at ease with him, she'd thought maybe she'd be the next Bennett to fall in love. And judging by how frequently he invaded her thoughts, maybe she had been.

She'd hardly spoken to anyone in her family about what happened, but she knew they'd all seen the photographs that somehow kept appearing in the gossip rags. Someone was certainly going out of their way to make it look like she'd earned her job the old-fashioned way. She didn't know who, and she didn't really care. Their jealousy—or whatever it was that made them feel the need to tear Sophie down—was their issue to deal with, not hers.

The head of the advertising department, Maxine, had assured her at their first meeting that Jack had said and done absolutely nothing to win her the contract. That she'd always been their number one pick, and after talking to Sophie's agent, she knew she'd made the right choice.

Sophie was the perfect ambassador for Martin Cosmetics.

"Are you going to be all right, Sophie?" Lucy asked from her seat at the end of the table. "We can do our own make-up if you're not feeling up to it."

"I'll be fine," she said, smiling through another wave of nausea. "Uly is getting me some medication while he's out hunting for fairy lights."

"Are you sure?" Lucy asked, rubbing her hand in circles over her belly. "Trust me, I feel your pain. I think I've thrown up more during the first two months of my pregnancy than I ever have in all my life. I am so tired. Last week, I vowed to cut Toby's balls off if he even thought about knocking me up again, but everything seems to be settling down now. Hopefully for good," she added, crossing her fingers. "I do not want to spend my honeymoon throwing up."

Sophie sat there, listening to Lucy talk as she sipped her tea, but the more her future aunty-in-law explained about her pregnancy, the more unsettled she became. Tiredness and nausea. How long had she felt this way? How long had it been since her last period?

Ho. Ly. Shit.

Shock shot through her, straightening her back and stiffening her limbs. She swallowed hard and levered to her feet. "I need to call Uly," she said, interrupting the conversation. "There's something else I need him to buy."

"What's that?"

"A pregnancy test."

14

Sophie paced back and forth in the bathroom as she waited for the timer on her phone to go off and for the pregnancy test to be ready. Abby and Lucy waited with her, all of them dressed in their wedding finery.

By the time Uly had returned with the fairy lights and pregnancy test, they'd all had their nails and hair done, eaten a light lunch, and Sophie had thrown up again.

"It could just be stress, you know?" Abby said. "Your period has never been regular, and stress can exacerbate the problem."

She nodded, but she wasn't really paying attention. She was too busy freaking out over the fact that she might be pregnant. With Jack Martin's baby.

Jack Martin, who was married to another woman. Jack Martin, who every gossipmonger in the country thought she'd screwed for a job, because God forbid she earn it on her own merits and not on her back. Jack Martin, the man she still daydreamed about way more than was healthy for her, and wished things had been different with, and that she could have had her very own fairy-tale ending with, just like every other Bennett had recently.

The timer buzzed.

Sophie froze to the spot. "I can't look." She turned to Abby. "You do it."

"What? Why me? I don't want to touch your pee stick."

"Oh, for crying out loud, I'll do it," Lucy said, shaking her head at the pair of them, and picked up the test. She stared at it for a moment, then picked up the instruction leaflet. "Do you know what you're hoping for?"

Sophie swallowed again, barely choking down the air caught in her windpipe. "I don't know."

"I'm assuming you know who the father is?" Abby said.

"The whole bloody country knows who the father is," she grumbled.

Lucy looked at the test again, then the instructions again, then at Sophie and said, "It's positive."

Her knees went out from under her, and she sat heavily on the toilet seat as an emotional cocktail of confusion, need, and pure unadulterated joy overwhelmed her, then burst forth from her eyes and streamed down her cheeks. "I'm having a baby?"

In an instant, Abby was kneeling beside her, hugging her so tightly, she almost couldn't breathe. "Don't cry, sweetie. It'll be all right, you'll see. We'll help you with whatever you need."

Sophie sniffed loudly and swiped at her tears. "It makes no sense," she said, shaking her head. "A baby is the last thing I need in my life right now, especially with a man who's married to someone else—"

"He's separated, Soph. Has been for a couple of years, from what I can tell," Abby interjected. "That's not the same as married."

"It's not single either, which is what he told me. Even so, I—" Sophie looked up at Lucy and Abby. "I'm happy." She laughed, unable to hide the hint of hysteria, then sniffed again and reached for some toilet paper to blow her nose. "I'm having a baby! Although...."

"Although... what?" Lucy pressed.

"I don't know how it happened. We used protection. We used condoms. Every time."

Lucy's eyebrows shot up and she pinched her lips together as if holding in a laugh, then said, "*Every* time? How many times are we talking here?"

"Lucy!" Abby scolded her.

Lucy shrugged, her grin unrepentant. "Oh come on. Tell me you're not curious how many times is 'every time.'"

Sophie blushed. "A few," she hedged. "And we used protection every... time... oh no."

"What?" The other women stared at her expectantly.

"Well, there was one time, at the end of the night. Our last time. We'd run out of condoms."

"You ran out of condoms?" Lucy grinned like the sex fiend she was. "Go Jack!"

"Soph," Abby groaned. "It only takes one time. You know this."

"But we didn't have sex," she said, her eyes wide as she tried to explain. "We just fooled around until he, uh, you know, came *on* me. But I couldn't get pregnant from *that*... right?"

"*Where* on you?"

"Upper inner thigh." Sophie stared at each woman in turn, hoping they'd give her the answer she needed. "So, you know, *close* to my, uh...."

"Vagina?"

Sophie's blush deepened until her cheeks practically burned. "Yes. But no cigar. So to speak."

Lucy grabbed the box of pregnancy tests and thrust it towards her. "How about you do another test? If it comes back positive, too, then I'm gunna say yes, Jack coming on your upper inner thigh can make you pregnant."

She looked at Abby, but her aunty agreed. "Probably best to do all three tests, just to be sure."

"Yeah, and the next time you run out of condoms," Lucy added, trying—and failing—to hold in her laughter, "may I suggest you *smoke* the cigar instead?"

"Lucy!"

For the rest of the afternoon, Sophie felt like she was going through the motions. After confirming she was pregnant—twice—she did everybody's make-up, forcing herself to pay attention to what she was doing so she didn't make them all look like homicidal clowns. The fact that she was using Martin Cosmetics to complete her task kept her new situation front and centre in her mind.

Thankfully, the antinausea medication her grandfather had procured for her was doing the trick. She hadn't felt so much as queasy since taking it. Unfortunately, it did nothing to stop the near-constant wave of panic flowing through her.

She was pregnant.

With her boss's baby.

What the hell am I supposed to do now?

Obviously, she had to tell him, but would he even want to speak to her, given how she'd behaved in the weeks since they'd met?

Jack had tried reaching out to her several times since she'd stormed out of his hotel room, and she'd slapped back at him each and every time. First, he'd sent her three dozen Twilight Zone roses. She didn't know how he'd found out the deep purple blooms were her favourite, but clearly he had.

She'd sent them all back with their heads cut off.

Next, he'd sent her a box of her favourite handmade chocolates from a small boutique chocolatier hidden away in an obscure arcade off Hay Street Mall in Perth. She wasn't going to destroy those little bundles of deliciousness, so she put them in a Tupperware container and sent back the empty box with a note inside.

It simply read "No."

His last attempt to reach out had involved a special delivery of gourmet cheeses. Miniature bries, vintage cheddars, and blue veins were all mixed in with assorted artisan crackers, dried fruits, and honey-roasted nuts. The fact that he'd also included a large wedge of pepper jack did not go unnoticed.

She'd stared at the beautifully packaged shipment of goodies for what felt like an age, wondering not only *why* he was persisting in pursuing her but how? How did he know so much about all of her favourite things? She knew he followed her on Instagram, but none of these were things she'd shared with the world.

In the end, she'd given the delivery to her next-door neighbour, a parting gift before moving permanently to Sydney.

Now she was in Mia's backyard in Melville's Cross, sitting in a beautifully decorated chair surrounded by string upon string of fairy lights and masses of artfully arranged flowers, watching the sun set behind the mountains as she listened to the most stoic of her uncles declare his love for his bride.

And for the first time in a long time, she didn't feel alone.

Her hand drifted to her stomach.

She'd never be alone again.

The celebrant raised her voice. "Toby and Lucy have chosen to write their own vows," she said, then invited the big man to come forward as she stepped back and let the groom speak.

Toby stroked his knuckles over Lucy's scarred cheek and stared down at her like she'd hung the moon and the stars in the sky. As though he lived and died by her leave. "Lucy, I'd never believed in love at first sight until I met you. Everything about you called to me. The boldness of your gaze, the strength in your voice, the vulnerability in your touch. The sway of your arse in that damn pencil skirt." Everyone chuckled, and Lucy ducked her head to hide her laughter, but Toby hooked a knuckle under her chin and lifted her face back to his.

"Being with you, *loving* you, is the scariest, most complicated, and easiest thing I've ever done, and I will spend the rest of my life making sure you know exactly how much you mean to me. I love you, baby."

Lucy stared up at Toby, the tears welling in her eyes clear for all to see. But the wonder that shone through her expression as she stared up at the man she loved told everyone they were tears of joy. "Toby, words cannot express how happy I am to call you mine. From the moment we met, you have treated me with care and respect. You accept me—scars and all—without question. Your quiet leadership and gentle dominance show me every day that you are a man I can trust—" She grinned up at him. "—even when you're being pig-headed and bossy." Again, everyone chuckled, especially when Toby grunted in response. "You are my safe place. You are my home." Her fingers brushed over the heart-shaped pendant she wore around her neck, the silver collar he'd given her at Christmas. "You are my heart, and I can't wait to spend the rest of my life with you. I love you, Master."

Sophie sniffed quietly and accepted a tissue from her cousin Sally, who sat beside her.

The celebrant stepped forward again and asked for the rings, and Toby's twin brother, Charlie, held out his hand. A few more official-sounding words were spoken, rings were exchanged, and then the celebrant said the words everyone had showed up to hear.

"I now pronounce you husband and wife! Congratulations, you may kiss your bride."

Everyone stood and cheered and threw rose petals into the air, and as the sun slunk ever lower and the fairy lights twinkled against the twilit sky, Toby wrapped one big hand around Lucy's throat and growled, "Mine." Then he slammed his mouth to hers and kissed his wife long and deep.

Sophie watched the happy couple walk back down the aisle amid the cheers and well wishes of their family and friends, and she sighed contentedly to see people she cared about so happy in their situation. The pair was an excellent match and complemented each other perfectly.

Again her mind drifted back to the New Year's party—to Jack. To the man she'd stupidly thought might be her perfect match.

Fighting the sadness that tugged at her heartstrings, she ignored the little voice in the back of her mind, the one calling her an idiot for pushing him away and not fighting for what she wanted.

But how was she supposed to fight for someone who wasn't hers to begin with?

On paper, Jack ticked every one of her boxes. He was smart, witty, fun, hung, and dominant as fuck. And she'd *trusted* him. As stupid and as crazy as that sounded, she had trusted him, a man she'd never met before in her life. She never would have submitted to him if she hadn't.

But he'd turned out to be another selfish arsehole who'd taken what he'd wanted from her and damn the consequences. And as usual, those consequences were heavier for her, the woman, than they were for him, the man.

"Wow, who is *that*?"

Sophie turned to Sally, her brow scrunched. "Who?"

Her cousin pointed to a man standing near the dinner tent, talking to her father. "The hottie chatting with Paul."

Her eyes widened, and her heart picked up pace. "It can't be," she whispered. But then he turned slightly and looked right at her, confirming her suspicions. "Oh bloody hell, it is." When he started walking towards her, she turned to Sally, panic lacing her words. "Please don't leave me."

Sally shot another look at the man moving towards them, then back at her, eyes wide and her mouth tipped up in a grin. "That's him, isn't it? The guy from New Year's Eve."

"Yep, that's him. That's Jack."

Her billionaire baby daddy.

"He's shorter than I'd expected, but holy hell, the photos online do not do him justice." She bumped her shoulder against Sophie's. "Nicely done."

"Yeah, great, the man's a snack. Please don't leave me," she said again, grasping Sally's hands in hers.

But her cousin had zero sympathy for her dilemma and extricated herself from Sophie's grip. "Three's a crowd, cuz, and you two have some big talk ahead of you. Good luck," she whispered, then abandoned Sophie to her fate.

"Sally!" she whispered through gritted teeth, desperate for the woman to stay by her side and offer some small layer of protection between her and the man she apparently couldn't ignore even if she tried, but her cousin simply winked at her and walked away.

"Hello, Sophie."

The sound of her name in Jack's deep, melodious tone almost took her to her knees, and the expression on his face as he gazed at her with those gorgeous sea-blue eyes would have kept her there if she had.

"Jack," she said, her voice more breathy than she'd intended. Straightening her spine, she lifted her chin, tried to project an aura of indifference. "What are you doing here?"

His lips twitched up in one corner, but it did little to lessen the stern line of his mouth. "I would have sent more roses, but I figured you'd have a harder time cutting *my* head off."

"Well, I do enjoy a challenge," she bantered, annoyed at how quickly her inner brat came out to play.

Jack's laughter obliterated his severe expression. Stepping closer, he crowded Sophie's personal space, cupped her face in his warm hands, and gazed at her like she was his. "Fuck, I have missed you."

15

Jack stroked his thumbs along Sophie's jaw, happy just to be in the same space as her, let alone touching her soft skin, inhaling her sweet scent. He hadn't lied. Every damn day since they'd parted ways, he'd missed her.

Hungered for her.

Worked towards getting back to her.

"That doesn't answer my question," she said, scowling at him. "What are you doing here? And how did you even know where to find me?"

He'd decided before seeing her that he wasn't holding anything back anymore. He'd learned that lesson the hard way, knew if he wanted to earn back her trust, he was going to have to tell her everything she wanted to know about him, no matter how simple.

Or difficult.

"I knew where to find you the same way I knew where to find your favourite chocolates, and what your favourite rose is, and which cheeses you like best." He shrugged and told her the truth. "Anna told me."

Sophie's scowl deepened. "Oh, I am going to *kill* her."

"No, you won't," he said, grinning at her empty threat, then stroked her cheeks again, revelled in the peace he felt at the fact that she still hadn't pulled away from him. Hadn't yet rejected him. "And I'm here because I couldn't wait another day—another hour—to see you."

She looked less than impressed as she cocked one brow, sounding bored when she said, "Oh? And why is that?"

"Because I'm single, Sophie. Technically."

Her eyes widened and her lips parted on a silent gasp, his news obviously not what she'd been expecting him to say. Then she grabbed his hands and pulled them away from her face, but she didn't let them go.

"Can you repeat that, please?" she asked, the shock on her face mirrored in her tone.

"I'm single. My divorce was finalised this morning." Sophie continued to stare at him, her mouth opening and closing like a goldfish as a myriad of emotions flitted across her gorgeous face. Jack smiled at her response, a flicker of hope sparking to life in his chest. "It's been a long time coming, and I—" His smile faltered and he sighed, shoved a hand through his hair. The thing he was about to do, about to say was harder than he'd thought it would be. Jack had a reputation for being ruthless and unapologetic in all aspects of his life, but he was self-aware enough to know when he'd fucked up. Especially something as special as the night he'd spent with Sophie. "I'm sorry for not making my situation more clear to you when we met. I never meant to deceive you. That was selfish of me. It won't happen again."

But Sophie continued staring at him, her dark eyes slowly blinking, her sultry pout frozen in a kissable moue of confusion.

Was it too much to hope that she'd be receptive to him

just showing up and crashing her uncle's wedding? Her best friend had thought it a brilliant idea, had even roped in Sophie's father to help smooth the waters in case it all went to shit. Which was looking more and more probable the longer she remained silent.

Jack knew she wasn't a timid woman—she hadn't had any trouble telling him exactly what she thought the last time she'd seen him—so why hadn't she said anything yet? But then she closed her eyes for a moment, and when she opened them again, the myriad of emotions pinballing across her face had narrowed down to just two. The same two he'd felt since commandeering the family jet and flying off to find her.

Longing.

And fear.

But what was she afraid of?

He cupped her cheek again. "Sophie? Baby, talk to me."

"Yes," she whispered. "Baby." Her hands were shaking and she visibly swallowed, her throat undulating softly. "Jack, I... um...."

"What is it?" He took a breath. He'd never had such an awkward conversation in his life. Ethan was the one women usually got tongue-tied around, not him. And certainly not *after* he'd taken them to bed. "Do you—" He shoved his hand through his hair again. "—want me to leave?"

"No!" She practically shouted the word at him, her vehemence assuaging his uncertainty. "I...." She hung her head and took a deep breath, and when she lifted it again, she tilted her chin, stuck it out in defiance. He saw the determination in her dark gaze. "I'm... pregnant."

The summer sun was fading quickly, slipping behind the mountains in a beautiful display of pink and orange as the darkness of night chased it across the sky. It was a spectacular view, and one Jack usually appreciated, a promise at the end of a hard day that tomorrow would be better.

But as he stood there, surrounded by empty chairs and floral arrangements, he barely even registered it. His brain was shutting out everything, narrowing his field of consciousness down to the woman standing in front of him, telling him the one thing he never thought he'd hear again.

He was going to be a father.

Or was he?

He couldn't move.

His mouth, unfortunately, could.

"Not to sound indelicate," he began, then cleared his throat. "But I don't know when you and Ethan last... ah...." The sight of Sophie's lovely lips thinning in annoyance made the thought trail off. He scrubbed his hand against the back of his neck and grimaced. After berating him for lying to her, there was no way she'd do the same to him. Sophie wasn't Lisa. "I'm an idiot," he muttered.

To his surprise, Sophie laughed. Not so surprisingly, she agreed with him. "Yes, you are." An instant later, she threw her arms around his neck and sniffed. Her voice quavered, and her cheek felt wet as she pressed it against his and said, "But I'm really glad you're here."

Jack wrapped his arms around Sophie and held her shaking body tightly, stroked his hand in circles against her back, and listened to her breathing even out. Sucking down a lungful of air, he pulled her sweet scent deep into his lungs. He'd missed her smell, her touch, her voice. Her moans and screams of pleasure. And now to think—to *know* —he had her, held her and their *child*, was nirvana. *Bliss.*

He knew it was nuts—they barely knew each other— but he couldn't find the will to care. At long last he was going to be a father, going to have the family he craved. After years of watching from the shadows, watching his friends find the love he knew they deserved, it was finally his turn.

And he was finally free to pursue the life he wanted.

"Angel, there's nowhere else I'd rather be."

After a moment, she pulled back and used her knuckles to delicately wipe away her tears while trying not to mess up her make-up. "Why aren't you mad?" she asked, accepting the handkerchief Jack pulled from his pocket. "Most men would be freaking out if they'd just been told they'd knocked up their one-night stand."

"The most beautiful woman in the world just told me she's having my baby. Why the fuck would I be mad?" he said, then leaned closer, brushing his lips over the shell of her ear. "And if our one night together wasn't enough for you to understand that I'm not like other men, then we need to revisit a few things."

He gently nibbled her earlobe and revelled in the shiver that ran through her body, in the quiet gasp that caused the sudden rise and fall of her ample breasts as they pushed against his chest. He wanted to push her further. He wanted to ask if she was wet for him, wanted to push his fingers inside her hot body and find out for himself, and he might have if her father hadn't interrupted them.

"Is everything okay over here?"

Paul Bennett was an intimidating man. He stood a good few inches taller than Jack and carried himself with a quiet confidence that screamed "Don't fuck with me." If Jack had been a lesser man, he probably would have wet his pants under the intensity of the older man's stare, especially after the words they'd exchanged when he'd first arrived. Thankfully, he'd been raised by an intimidating man and was comfortable with intense stares and awkward questions. The familiarity of the situation was almost calming. But before he could assure Paul that everything was fine, Sophie spoke up.

"I think so," she said with a watery smile, using his handkerchief to dab at the corners of her eyes.

"Everything's perfect," Jack said, a feeling of contentment settling over him like a warm blanket as he returned her smile.

Paul cocked one brow, looked him up and down, then grunted. "Uh-huh." Turning his attention to his daughter, he added, "They're ready to serve up dinner," then headed back towards the party.

"I don't think he likes me," Jack said, taking Sophie's hand in his as they followed slowly behind.

She shrugged, undisturbed by her father's attitude. "When you spoke to him before, did he threaten you with bodily harm?"

He swallowed thickly as he watched Paul Bennett stalk away in front of them. "He might have mentioned something about siblings with flexible morals and easy access to a wood chipper."

His lover laughed so hard and so suddenly that she leaned into him for support, and his heart picked up pace when she pressed her palm against his chest, right over the racing organ. "You'll be fine," she said, grinning up at him. "They only threaten people they like."

"They?"

"My dad and his brothers."

"So I should be happy that they want to turn me into mulch?"

"Exactly. When they met Wolf, my aunt Abby's fiancé, they threatened to cut off his fingers one by one. They told him, and I quote, 'Abby has eight brothers, and you have eight fingers. You do the math,'" she said, deepening her voice to imitate her uncles. Jack frowned, not understanding how dismemberment could be worse than death by wood chipper. Sophie saw his confusion. "He's an author," she explained. "His ability to type is pretty high on his list of priorities." She indicated their seats at a long wooden table, dressed in more fairy lights and flowers. "Shall we?"

He looked around at all of the unfamiliar faces and scrubbed at his neck again. "Maybe I should go back to the hotel and wait for you there."

Sophie looked genuinely confused. And maybe a little hurt. "Why?"

He squeezed her hand. "Baby, I crashed your uncle's wedding."

"So?"

"So maybe they don't want a random stranger sharing their table."

Her confusion dissolved into laughter as she rolled her eyes, and this time she was the one to squeeze his hand. "Okay, the first thing you need to know about the Bennett family is this: there's always room for one more. And you're not a random stranger. You're my—" Her mouth silently opened and closed as she searched for the right word. Then she shrugged and smiled at him. "You're mine."

Jack couldn't have stopped the broad smile that spread across his face if he'd tried.

"You're mine."

Had anyone ever spoken truer words than those? He'd been hers from the moment they'd met, and he was determined to keep it that way. Leaning into her, he nuzzled against her cheek and whispered in her ear, "Thank you, Sophie."

"Don't thank me yet," she whispered back, her grin unmistakable against his cheek. "You still have to meet the rest of them."

16

ophie was impressed. Not many people experienced a Bennett family gathering first-hand and lived to tell the tale, but Jack seemed to take it all in stride, answering every question her family threw at him and asking several of his own.

She especially appreciated that he made a point of getting to know each person along the table, including her fourteen-year-old cousins, Josie and Diana, the latter of whom he had an in-depth discussion with regarding the inevitable zombie apocalypse and the importance of a proper survival readiness plan. When she chuckled at the silliness of their conversation, Jack turned his narrowed eyes to her and said, "Do *you* have a zombie survival plan?"

"Well, obviously," she scoffed. "Who do think taught Diana?"

"Is that true?" he asked her cousin.

Diana grinned at him in her own devilish way. "Yep," she said before leaning around him to speak to her. "I like him. I vote you should keep him." And then she left the table in search of her twin.

"I think you should keep me too," Jack said quietly, his melodious voice making her insides quiver with awareness and a wish to find somewhere private so they could explore exactly what keeping him would look like. Then he leaned in close and whispered, "I like your family. They're almost as weird as mine."

Her eyes widened as she stared at him. "Almost?"

No one's family was as weird as hers.

Jack grinned. "I come from a big family too. *Lots* of cousins. Family events generally involved a lack of adult supervision and a lot of mischief. Usually led by Ethan and our cousin Matt."

A delighted laugh burst out of her at this new information. Sophie had never dated anyone with a family as big as hers before. Except Ethan, of course, seeing as he was Jack's brother, but since they'd never been introduced to each other's families during all of their on-again, off-again bullshit, it didn't really count.

"Tell me everything," she said. "I want to know *everything*."

"All in good time, baby." Leaning in again, Jack planted a smiling kiss on her lips. It started soft and slow but quickly deepened, only ending when a disgruntled growl sounded from across the table.

Breaking the kiss, Sophie glared at her father. "What?" she demanded. Paul flicked his gaze to Jack and back again, then sighed but said nothing. She smiled, smug in the knowledge that her overprotective father wasn't getting involved. Until she felt a strong hand grip her thigh under the table and Jack's heated breath against her ear.

"Don't make me put you over my knee in front of your family, angel."

Her brow furrowed as she whispered back, "What did I do?"

"Your father only wants to protect you. He doesn't know me yet, doesn't know what type of person I am or how I'll treat his daughter. He has every right to be cautious. You don't get to snap at him for being wary." He pulled back far enough to stare her down. "Now apologise."

Sophie's eyes narrowed. "What?"

But Jack's grip only tightened, his fingers digging into her soft thigh punishing, almost brutal, and, as much as she didn't want to admit it while surrounded by family, highly arousing. His voice deepened. "To your father. Apologise."

Pressing her lips together in a tight line, she glared at Jack and his stupidly handsome face. The way he stared back at her, with one brow cocked and his mouth turned up in one corner, as if he found the whole thing so very amusing, both infuriated her and turned her on, and she didn't know if she wanted to yell at the man or crawl into his lap and snuggle against his chest.

But when he cupped her cheek in his free hand and whispered, "Be a good girl for me, Sophie," she came undone. That dark voice spoke to her on such an intimate level, and as those intense eyes pinned her in place, commanded her to obey his every wish, all resistance melted out of her, and she pressed her cheek into his warm palm.

Her brow smoothed out and her eyes glazed over with need as she stared into her baby daddy's deep blue gaze. Turning to her father, she said, "I'm sorry I snapped at you."

But instead of nodding and silently accepting her apology, as he usually would have, Paul burst out laughing and looked to Jack. "Where the hell were you when she was a teenager?"

She glared at her father, but that only made him laugh more. "I wasn't that bad," she grumbled, stabbing her spoon into the chocolate crème brûlée the waitstaff had placed in front of her. "Considering the circumstances."

Jack's eyes narrowed as he snapped his gaze to hers, but he didn't poke at her wound or comment on the uncomfortable silence that fell between her and her dad. He just squeezed her thigh again, this time in a way that simply told her he was there. There if she needed him.

There for *her*.

She appreciated the gesture more than he knew.

By the time they'd devoured their desserts—and she'd stolen more than half, or even *all* of Jack's—he'd endeared himself to pretty much everyone at the table. Her young cousins were enamoured of him and his extensive knowledge of zombies. Her aunt and uncles spoke to him with genuine warmth in their voices and no longer threatened him with becoming garden mulch. Her grandfather had winked at her from the other end of the table and smiled his signature grin, signalling that he thought she'd done well with this one. Even her father, a man notorious for being succinct at best and downright rude at worst, had carried on a lengthy and congenial conversation with the man about the state of the modelling industry.

As Jane's solution to the wedding cake kerfuffle was served—delicate little cupcakes decorated with bouquets of flowers made from buttercream frosting—Sophie stared at Jack with something akin to awe. Her family were known for many things, their over-protectiveness of each other being one of them. But once that hurdle had been overcome, they were a very accepting bunch of people, something she knew stemmed from other people's unacceptance of their own unconventional upbringings.

So despite the fact that he'd lied to her, and that he was freshly divorced, and that he'd knocked her up, it had apparently taken the Bennett clan less time than it took to hold a wedding to decide he was an acceptable addition to the family.

But that may have also had something to do with the fact that Abby was right, he hadn't exactly lied to her. That had more to do with Sophie's own insecurities flavouring her thought processes. And he wasn't freshly divorced. He'd been trying to finalise those proceedings for years. And he hadn't simply knocked her up. It took two to tango, and she was just as much at fault as he was for her current situation.

Not that she was as upset about that as she'd thought she would be. Sophie had always figured she'd have children one day, and she was thirty years old, not an unacceptable age to pop out a kid. She was financially stable, even without Jack, and she had an amazing support system around her. And her newly minted contract with Martin Cosmetics even included a progressive pregnancy clause, not only assuring her job was safe should she happen to fall pregnant but also providing childcare perks, like an on-set nanny should one be required.

Now actually seemed like the perfect time to have a baby.

Just as the thought made itself comfortable in her mind, there was a yelp from the other end of the table.

"Rafe!" Jane stood there, wide-eyed and white as a sheet, clutching at her very pregnant belly. "I think it's time!"

Her uncle Rafe, one of the most steadfast and sensible men she'd ever known in her life, swallowed hard and looked like he was about to vomit. "But... it's too early."

"Early is normal for twins," Ulysses said. "You were told that." Others at the table nodded in agreement. "I'm actually surprised she's lasted this long."

Rafe stared at his wife like the first-time dad he was—completely clueless. "You're absolutely sure?"

Jane glared at her husband, then grabbed his shoulder and snarled through gritted teeth like only a woman in labour could. "Get me to the hospital *now*, or I swear to all that is holy I will shove your balls so far up your own arse, you'll think you've grown a second pair of tonsils!" Then she doubled over and made a sound like a wounded banshee, obviously in the grips of a contraction.

"It's definitely time," Ulysses said, throwing Jane a sympathetic glance even as he chuckled. "I'll drive."

Suddenly, there was a flurry of action as the bride and groom hurriedly thanked everyone for coming, in particular thanking Jane for the beautiful cakes, before Rafe, Ulysses, and Jane's parents stole her away to the local hospital, a good thirty-minute drive away.

"Do you think they'll be okay?" Jack asked, frowning as they watched the soon-to-be parents being whisked away in her grandfather's Kombi van. "Should I have called for a helicopter or something?"

"A helicopter?" Sophie chuckled, then kissed his cheek, appreciative of his concern for her family. "Do you happen to have a helicopter parked nearby?"

"Not currently."

"Then driving is probably the quicker option. Besides, Jane's dad is a doctor, and Uly drives like a bat outta hell." Jack's eyes widened with concern. "A very safe bat outta hell," she quickly reassured him. "They'll be fine."

Jack slid his arms around her waist and pulled her close,

brushing his nose along the side of hers. "What should we do now?"

A quick glance around her told her Mia and her minions had clean-up well in order, but she'd been raised to offer a helping hand whenever she could. "Mia," she called. "Do you need us for anything?"

"Yeah, nah." The retired Army major smiled wearily but shook her head as she approached, leaning heavily on her walking cane. "It's all under control. Get out of here while you still can," she said.

"And we'll keep you posted about Jane and the babies," Oliver added, joining them. He slid an arm around Mia's shoulders before pressing a kiss to her temple. "It's after ten. You should be resting," he murmured.

"I have a job to do," she protested, stifling a yawn.

"And a bunch of people more than capable of finishing it for you."

Mia scowled at the big man until he caught her up in his arms, cane and all, and wished everyone a good night. After that, her half-hearted protests were silenced by threats of a ruthless tickling.

Sophie laughed at their antics, even as that pang of loneliness flickered behind her ribs again. But then she felt Jack's hand grip hers, felt him intertwine their fingers and the warmth that emanated from him permeate her flesh. Felt that warmth spread higher until it reached that stupid annoying pang and smothered it in hope.

She squeezed his fingers. "Didn't you say something earlier about a hotel?"

He nodded. "I did. I thought it best to get a room for the weekend—" He grinned, and her knees threatened to give out on her right then and there. "—just in case I managed to convince you to give me a second chance."

A small smile tugged at her lips as she slid her hands over his chest and straightened his shirt collar. "Consider me convinced, but we should probably make the rounds and say goodnight to everyone before we make our escape. Goodness knows when we'll all be in the same place at the same time again."

"Then let's go," Jack said, the corner of his mouth kicking up in that sexy half grin that made her panties melt right off her body. "The sooner we say goodnight, the sooner we get to the hotel."

"And the sooner we get to the hotel...?" she whispered, her voice hitching with glee.

Jack slid his hand to the base of her throat and stroked his thumb over her pulse, his playful grin firming into something fiercer, more intense. More... *him*. "The sooner I make you mine."

17

"So... Toby and Lucy are in the lifestyle, huh?"

After nearly half an hour of warm hugs from the women and bone-crushing handshakes from the men, Jack finally stole Sophie away from her family. And if he was being completely honest with himself, he wasn't sure what to do next.

For a man who prided himself on being in control of every aspect of his life, he was feeling a bit lost. When he'd received the call from his solicitor informing him that he was indeed officially divorced, the only thought that had survived the implosion of relief inside his brain had been *Find Sophie*. He'd been running on pure instinct ever since. But now his instincts told him to tread carefully.

Told him the other shoe was yet to drop.

He just wasn't sure why, or how.

He hadn't expected Sophie to welcome him as easily as she had, and he certainly hadn't expected her family to. Not with the disgusting things the tabloid press had been printing about her since New Year's, and especially after discovering she was pregnant.

Pregnant.

With child.

His child.

A smile slowly spread across his face, and whatever Sophie said in reply to his question about her uncle was lost in the ether of his joy. "I'm sorry, I missed that."

"I said, how do you know they're in the lifestyle? They rarely attend the clubs."

Kink clubs, she meant. Jack cleared his throat. "Neither do I." He hadn't attended a club in years, hadn't seen the point. Not when every submissive he crossed paths with saw him as a meal ticket first and a Dom second. "I arrived in time to overhear Lucy's vows. She called your uncle Master. And that kiss at the end, claiming his woman like that...." He blew out an appreciative breath. "Hot as fuck."

Sophie ducked her head and giggled. The sound of it wrapped around his cock and squeezed, teasing him with the memory of the last time he'd heard it, after he'd emptied his balls on her soft thigh and she'd made a mischievous comment about Martin Cosmetics' new skin-care range. He'd enjoyed her wicked sense of humour, but he was also aware that most men detested giggling, seeing it as a sign of immaturity at best, idiocy at worst. But Jack wasn't stupid. He saw it exactly for what it was.

Happiness, pure and simple.

He also knew from experience that when Sophie giggled, she also blushed. A pretty pink stain on her cheeks that spread down her neck to her chest and dusted the tops of her large breasts. His mouth watered at the thought, at the need to strip her bare and taste her flesh. To claim her and make her truly his.

He bit back a grin. Apparently he did know what to do next.

"Yeah, Toby might be a quiet man, but he certainly isn't a shy one," Sophie said. "At least not in front of family. Stick him in a room full of strangers and it's a very different story."

"I know how he feels," Jack said, his mouth twisting to one side. "I'm not a fan of being in a crowd, especially crowds of strangers." Even sitting at a table full of wedding guests he actually liked had stretched his tolerance thin. Being polite and sociable for hours on end was exhausting, and when Sophie had indicated it was time to leave the party, he'd breathed a sigh of relief.

In what he was sure was meant to be a reassuring gesture, she reached over and squeezed his thigh. Unfortunately, his dick didn't get that memo. It completely ignored his steadfast control and jumped to attention at the contact, eager to be the next thing Sophie Bennett got her perfect little hands on.

The woman must have read his mind, because in the next moment, she was sliding her palm higher up this leg, tempting him to drive faster, reach the hotel—the bedroom —as soon as humanly possible.

Speeding fines be damned.

But then the rational part of his brain took over, making Jack rest his hand on top of hers and halting her progress. The last thing he needed was to be pulled over by the cops when all he wanted was to get Sophie alone and naked. He shot her a brief glance—just long enough to see her pretty mouth curve in a cheeky grin—before returning his eyes to the road.

"Brat," he muttered, chuckling. Then, knowing he was probably about to kill the mood, he took a steadying breath. But he had to say what he wanted to say before they reached the hotel. He had to know they were on the same page this time. Had to know she wouldn't run at the first hint of trouble. Jack was in this for the long haul, and he needed to know Sophie was going to be right there with him, every step of the way. "Before we get too deep into this," he said, "I feel like I should warn you of something."

Her hand tightened on his thigh, and her playful expression vanished. "Oh?" she said, her tone forcibly casual. Wary.

He squeezed her fingers, hoping she wouldn't pull away when he admitted his shortcomings. "Yes. The thing is, I kind of suck at relationships."

She surprised him by nodding slowly and asking, "And how many relationships have you been in to come to that conclusion?"

His hand tightened on the steering wheel. "Three so far. Serious ones, at least. Four including you."

"Okay," she said, nodding again. "Well, if it makes you feel any better, my dating track record is kind of sucky too."

That actually did make him feel better, but he kept the comment to himself. "Oh?"

"I've only had two serious relationships myself, and more flings than I care to remember, and I wouldn't consider any of them successful." She snorted derisively. "Apparently men don't like it when you make more money than they do." She flashed him a sudden and welcome grin. "Which I suppose won't be an issue with you, will it?"

Jack chuckled. "It wouldn't have been an issue either way. Unlike some men, I'm not intimidated by successful women," he said. Sophie's smile widened, and she finally relaxed her hand, releasing the death grip she held on his thigh. He lifted it to his mouth and pressed a kiss to the backs of her fingers. "Tell me, how else did these pathetic excuses for manhood prove their worthlessness?"

"Oh, you know, the usual," she said, keeping her voice light. "Lied, cheated, told me I was fat. Stole stuff because they thought I was either too dumb to notice or too rich to care. Called me a bitch when I called them on their bullshit." She paused and swallowed, moistened her lips before continuing. "One of the men I was serious with turned out to be less of a dominant and more of a controlling douchecanoe who did *not* appreciate my inner brat. He—" She cleared her throat and looked out the window. "He hit me. And not in a fun way."

Jack ground his teeth together so hard, he thought they might crack. "Who was it?" he snarled. He was going to track the arsehole down and tear him apart. Piece by fucking piece. And he was going to enjoy every second of it.

Some people didn't deserve the title of *man*.

"No one important," Sophie said, then sighed heavily. "But that's when Dad started teaching me to box."

"I'm sorry you had to go through that, baby," he said, shoving down his fury. He kissed her fingers again and then he sighed, too, remembering what Lisa had told him. "But I should probably mention that one of the reasons my ex gave for leaving me was because she thought I was too controlling."

Sophie ducked her head and glanced away from him again. He didn't like it. He liked it even less when she asked him, "Did you ever... hit her?"

"No," he said darkly. He abhorred men who abused their partners. "Not like that."

"She was submissive? Like me?"

"Not like you," he said. Lisa was a bitch, not a brat. "She only submitted in the bedroom, and even then it was on her terms. Outside of it she was demanding and entitled. She was an unbelievably selfish woman who thought of no one but herself and what *she* wanted." Jack took a moment to breathe deeply, to calm the anger swelling inside him before he let it loose and destroyed any chance he had with Sophie.

He would keep his cool, remain in control.

"She hurt you," she stated plainly.

He didn't deny it. "Yes."

"Because she cheated on you."

He snorted, a wry smile twisting his mouth. "Cheating on me was the least of her crimes."

"Tell me."

"Not tonight."

"Jack—" she started, but he cut her off.

"I promise I will tell you all about it, angel, but not tonight. Tonight is about us. Just us and no one else." He pulled the car into the driveway of the hotel and killed the engine, then turned to face her. "Is that okay?"

Sophie unfastened her seatbelt, then turned towards him, her brow furrowed as she searched his gaze. "Pinkie swear?" she said, holding up one hand, her little finger stuck out towards him.

His eyes widened and his jaw fell slack. "Seriously?"

Her gaze never wavered. "Pinkie swears are always serious."

Jack searched her face and body for cues, but she gave nothing away. She was deadly serious. He stuck out his pinkie. "I promise to tell you anything you want to know," he said, "but you have to do the same for me. No lies, no half-truths. No hiding. Complete honesty. Okay?"

"Say the words, please," she said primly, unrelenting in her mission as she waggled her finger at him. "Say you pinkie swear."

The smile that spread his mouth wide was pure indulgence. *Could she be any cuter?* "You have no idea how much I want to kiss you right now. Yes, I pinkie swear."

"Okay," she said. Hooking her pinkie around his, she tugged him closer, then whispered against his lips, "Thank you."

He was about to slide his hand into the hair at her nape and get that kiss when the car door opened and a valet appeared. "Good evening, Mr Martin. I trust you had a pleasant evening?"

Sophie's shoulders bounced, her silent laughter shaking her whole body, and instead of getting his kiss, he watched, stunned, as she spun away from him, opened her own door, and escaped the car without waiting for him.

Jack ran his tongue over his teeth and exited the car, silencing any more comments from the valet with a glare. His evening had been going great until the little twerp had opened his door and distracted him from his purpose.

Rounding the car, he narrowed his gaze and watched Sophie walking ahead of him, a wicked grin twisting his lips. He could have caught up to her easily enough, but he was enjoying the view too much to want to rush, relishing the sway of her full hips and the way her pretty floral dress clung to her torso and then flared out over her plush arse. And when she glanced back over her shoulder and flashed him a grin of her own, he knew she was enjoying the chase too.

Suddenly, he didn't care that every eye in the hotel foyer was upon them. His woman was there with him, as she always should have been, and he was feeling playful. Catching her gaze and holding it, he uttered one simple word.

"Run."

18

Thank God she'd worn ballet flats to the wedding instead of the heels she'd originally planned on, because the moment Jack uttered his command, Sophie took off for the lift as fast as she dared across the shiny marble floor.

Turned out that wasn't anywhere near fast enough. Jack caught her so easily it was almost laughable. And laugh she did, until he started kissing her. Worshipping her with his mouth, pushing her back against the wall and holding her in place, his muscled thigh smashing the lace of her panties into her clit and making her moan.

"Jack."

"I love it when you say my name like that." His soft chuckle brushed her cheek. "Such a good girl," he murmured as he reached around her to push the call button for the lift. Then he was kissing her again, one hand gripping her waist, his fingers digging into her side in a show of possession, the other gently cupping her face as he kissed a teasing line along her jaw.

Her eyelids fluttered closed and another moan worked

its way up her throat, but then he sank his teeth into her earlobe and she gasped instead. Eyes flying open, her gaze sharpened as it landed on two young women dressed for a night on the town, wide-eyed and grinning at her, their phones in hand. Phones they had pointed directly at her and Jack.

Ducking her head into the crook of his neck, she murmured, "Don't look, but I think we're being photographed again. Possibly filmed."

Of course he chose to ignore her and turned his head to see what she saw. But instead of getting mad as she'd assumed he would, he said, "Have a good evening, ladies." His deep voice echoed across the nearly empty foyer as he nodded politely at the girls. *What the hell?* When he turned back to face her, he wore a broad grin and his eyes twinkled with mischief. "I know I will," he added more softly, for her ears only.

Staring at him like he'd lost his damn mind, Sophie shrank even further behind him. Her gaze darted about, looking to see if anyone else was staring at them as she quietly demanded, "What are you doing?"

But Jack simply smiled at her. "No hiding, remember?"

"With each other," she whispered through gritted teeth. "Not everyone else."

"Why?" he said, one brow cocked in challenge. Then he leaned in close to her ear and she swallowed hard, his heady scent enveloping her whole. It was all she could do to listen to what he said next and not lick his neck or sink her teeth into him. "I don't care if people see us together. Let them take their photos. Let them watch." She opened her mouth to argue, but he silenced her with a kiss, hard and fast and demanding. "We're not doing anything wrong," he whispered against her lips.

Her brain was still adjusting, still processing the transition of his hot, firm mouth artfully commanding hers to the sudden loss of all that heat and authority, so it took her a moment to realise he was right.

They weren't doing anything wrong.

Before she got the chance to respond, the doors to the lift slid quietly open, and Jack manoeuvred her inside. As soon as the lift started moving upward, towards what she assumed was the penthouse, he pinned her to the back wall and stared at her, his hooded gaze slowly devouring every inch of her as it travelled down her body and back again. She'd never seen such hunger in a man's eyes before.

It frightened her.

And excited her.

More than it probably should.

"You look like you want to eat me," she said, her voice breathy, then felt her cheeks heat as she realised how that sounded.

He cocked one brow as he stared at her. "Do I?" His hands clenched on her hips as he thrust forward and let her feel his erection lengthening, thickening as it pushed into the softness of her belly. "Maybe I will." His eyes narrowed. "Or maybe I should punish you instead."

"Punish me?" The words squeaked out of her even as she wriggled against his hard cock, trying to cause friction where she wanted it most. "What did I do?"

"You ate my dessert."

"I only ate half," she said, shrugging, as though it was no big deal. Because it wasn't. Jack was totally overreacting.

"Which half?" he demanded, his sapphire gaze boring into hers.

She tried to look away, but he caught her chin in strong fingers and held her fast. Refused to let her hide from him.

No hiding, remember? "The bottom half," she mumbled, trying to ignore the way his gaze, his touch, his voice made her insides quiver with anticipation.

"And how exactly did you reach the bottom half, hmm?"

Sophie swallowed thickly, but she couldn't bite back her giggles, no matter how hard she tried. Her eyes were wide and focussed solely on Jack's reaction when she said, "By eating through the top half?"

"By eating through the top half," he repeated slowly, shaking his head. "Little brat. I think I will punish you. Teach you not to steal other people's desserts."

"But I'm eating for two," she said, gasping at his threat.

The corners of his mouth tipped up, and she knew he wasn't buying her little innocence act for even a moment. Jack knew as well as she did that the thought of punishing her was making her heart race and her panties wet. He knew how eager she was to feel the sting of his palm on her arse, how much she craved his strength, his dominance.

The lift reached the top floor and the doors slid open. Jack grabbed her wrist in a punishing grip and dragged her behind him as he marched towards the door at the end of the hall. A quick swipe of the room key and they were inside the penthouse. A second later, Sophie found herself pinned against another wall, her wrists secured above her head and her mouth crushed beneath Jack's, his kiss bruising, punishing.

But then he eased himself away and blew out a long breath, dragged a hand through his tousled hair. "As much as I would love to ravish you right now, we should probably talk some more." Stepping back, he swept his arm towards the sitting area and the plush, comfortable-looking sofa. "After you."

Sophie smoothed her hands down her dress, hoping the

action hid the way they shook as she walked past Jack, kicked off her shoes, and took a seat. She didn't feel like talking. She wanted more of his strong hands on her body, more of his hot mouth on her skin. She wanted to feel him inside her again, wanted to hear him moan, wanted him to whisper sweet words in her ear before crying out his pleasure as he wrung orgasm after orgasm out of her.

He sat close beside her. "Come here," he commanded quietly and patted his thigh. "Just because I want to talk doesn't mean I want to stop touching you."

"Oh thank God." A relieved breath escaped her as she scrambled to sit in his lap, and she couldn't help the shy smile that spread her lips wide as she rested her head on his shoulder. "I don't want you to stop touching me either."

Jack chuckled and slid his palm along the length of her leg, shifting the skirt of her dress higher and higher until he could rest his hand on her bare thigh. "I'm glad it's not just me," he said, then began stroking her skin, making her bite her lip to hold in a little hum of appreciation. "It's not just me, right? Tell me you feel this, too, Sophie. This want, this *need* to be with you."

His palm was warm against her skin, his strokes smooth and sure, and as she sat there in his lap, she took her time to look at him before answering. Really look at him. Was he the man she remembered from their one night together, or had she twisted everything around in her mind, made him out to be bigger and better than he actually was?

The longer she stared, the more she realised, nope, she hadn't. Not if dinner was anything to go by. He was still all quiet manners and secret smiles and panty-melting dominance.

Not to mention sexy as fuck.

Unlike Jack's brother, who knew he was drop-dead

gorgeous and unashamedly flaunted it to his advantage, flirting and bantering his way through life, Jack's appeal was less obvious. More unassuming. Almost stealthy.

She bit back a giggle. *Stealthy hotness.*

According to several online sources she just happened to glance at in the last couple of weeks—purely coincidentally, of course, and not at all in an obsessively stalkery kind of way—he was still considered to be very handsome, just not as good-looking as his older brother.

As he returned her stare, unflinching in the face of her inspection, she had to disagree.

It wasn't just his startling blue eyes, or his strong body, or the way his hair flopped over his forehead sometimes, nor was it his expertise in the bedroom, or the many and varied uses he had for his talented tongue. It was the way he carried himself, the way he spoke to those around him, even if he'd only just met them. And the way he'd spoken to her young cousins had been so patient and kind, so... paternal.

Her tummy fluttered and she smiled, nuzzled into the crook of his neck, and kissed his skin. "It's not just you."

"Good," he said, his arm tightening around her, and she could have been mistaken, but he almost sounded relieved. "To be honest, when I crashed the wedding, I thought you'd put up more of a fight."

Sophie snorted. "To be honest, so did I."

Jack's head tilted to one side as he looked down at her and searched her gaze. "Why didn't you?"

Good question. After a moment she shrugged. "Because I'm tired."

"Tired?"

"Yes, tired. In the last month, I've sold my house, moved interstate, started a new job, found out I'm pregnant, *and*

I've had to dodge the paparazzi—who apparently have nothing better to do than call me a gold-digging slut—all while trying to deny how much I've missed you *and* shop for an apartment in Sydney in a housing market that can only be described as hostile. Quite frankly, I'm exhausted." She viciously plucked at the edge of his shirt collar, her irritation palpable as she admitted something to him that she'd barely even acknowledged herself. "I've never wanted someone like this before. Never *needed* like this. And I don't know if I truly feel this way or if it's hormonal or if it's residual romantic energy from the wedding.... It's just—" She screwed up her mouth as she searched for the right word.

"Confusing?" Jack supplied.

"Annoying," she said, then nodded. Yes, that was the right word. Needing someone so much that it physically hurt when they weren't right there with you was *very* annoying. She gritted her teeth. "I don't like needing people." It felt a lot like weakness.

"Neither do I," he said, another small smile tugging at his mouth. "But I meant what I said earlier, Sophie. I have missed you so fucking much. And I know how crazy that sounds, I know we barely know each other, but it's true. I missed you."

Curiosity got the better of her, but she couldn't meet his gaze as she quietly asked, "What did you miss?"

This time he let his smile bloom and spread wide, and her heart skipped a beat at the sight of it. Hooking his knuckle under her chin, he lifted her face higher and pressed a soft kiss to her mouth. "I missed your sass. I missed your big belly laughs and your little giggles. I missed the sound of my name on your tongue when I made you come all over my dick." She sucked down an excited little gasp at his crude remark. Jack laughed and stroked her heated cheek. "And I missed making you blush." The hand still under her skirt slid higher up her thigh, his fingertips brushing against her panties. "I missed falling asleep with you in my arms and your legs tangled with mine, and I missed waking up beside you, making plans with you—" His gaze flicked to her belly and back. "—a future with you." He snorted. "Like I said, crazy."

An overwhelming need to kiss the man tore through Sophie, and she plastered her mouth to his, slammed their lips together and took what she wanted, what she needed from him. It only took Jack a second to respond to her assault, to take control, push her down on the sofa, and pin her hands above her head.

It felt good being spread out beneath him again, feeling the weight of his powerful body pressing her into the plush sofa cushions as he plundered her mouth and kissed the ever-loving life out of her. But then he pulled away, panting hard and shaking his head.

"There's one more thing we need to discuss before we take this any further. Something I should have asked you earlier." He pressed his forehead to hers and she heard him audibly swallow before lifting his head and staring into her eyes, his gaze uncertain. Almost fearful. "Do you even want this baby?"

Sophie stared at Jack like he'd just asked her the most important and at the same time the most ridiculously stupid question in the world, and the answer hit her so hard and fast that she couldn't help but blurt it out. "Yes!"

She'd already decided to keep the baby, had intended to call him first thing Monday morning to inform him of his impending fatherhood, and yet, as if she'd been having even an inkling of a doubt, hearing him ask that question had firmly cemented the decision in place.

She wanted this baby—Jack's baby.

And she wanted Jack too. She'd missed him for all the reasons he'd listed and more. The scent of him on her skin, the feel of his warm hands, his sensual mouth, his silken tongue on her body. The sound of his delicious voice when he called her angel. Listening to the steady beat of his heart when she rested her head on his chest. Even the way he'd spoken to her after sex, the way he'd listened to her, as though what she had to say mattered to him.

As though *she* mattered to him.

She still couldn't believe he hadn't flipped out when she'd told him her news. That wasn't normal, right? Not that she wasn't happy that he was happy, but he was right. The whole situation was *crazy*.

And terrifying. "But I'm scared, Jack. Besides babysitting the twins when I was a teenager, I have zero experience with kids. And my mum...." She laughed bitterly. "Let's just say she wasn't exactly the gold standard of parenthood, you know? And yeah, I'd always thought that one day I'd have a kid of my own, but now one day is right here and—" She moistened her suddenly dry lips and stared at him, knowing her uncertainty, her insecurity was pinging back and forth in her wide eyes, then felt a sharp prickle at the back of her nose, signalling tears were about to fall whether she liked it or not. "What if I can't do this?"

But again Jack surprised her. His expression softened and grew indulgent as he stared down at her. "You talk as though you have to do this alone. But you're not alone, Sophie. You have your family," he said, then pressed his forehead against hers again, "and you have me. And I promise you, angel, I'm not going anywhere."

"You're not alone."

It took a moment for the words to sink in, for the wonder of them to make itself fully known to her. She'd had a similar realisation at the wedding, but somehow, hearing Jack tell her the same thing, knowing what he meant by it and knowing that was something very different to what she'd imagined, made it more tangible. More real.

"You have me."

That felt real too. That felt like the start of something wonderful, something more than just mutual physical satisfaction.

That felt a lot like... *love.*

19

Something shifted in Sophie's expression, something Jack couldn't quite put his finger on. On the one hand, she looked like she'd just won the lottery. On the other hand, she looked damn near terrified.

She's tired. Exhausted. That's what she'd said. On closer inspection, he could see the weariness in her eyes and in the way her shoulders slumped. He had no doubt that her artfully applied make-up was hiding dark rings under her eyes.

She needed sleep.

He needed to make that happen.

Decision made, Jack levered off the sofa, then reached out for Sophie, encouraging her to take his hands. It was time to take care of his girl, to show her he was a man of his word and that she wasn't alone in all of this.

"Let's get you to bed, shall we?"

Her gaze sharpened and flicked to the obvious erection tenting his trousers, and a sultry little smile bloomed on her face as she grabbed his hands. "I'd thought you'd never ask."

Hauling her to her feet, he chuckled and shook his head. "To sleep."

But even exhausted, his girl didn't miss a beat. "It's pronounced *sex*."

He turned her around and swatted her arse, enjoying her little yelp as he urged her towards the bedroom. "We've both had a very long day and could use a good night's rest. It's almost midnight, baby."

"You do remember what we did around midnight the last time we saw each other, right? Besides, I'm not sleepy," she said, pouting before immediately stifling a yawn. He smacked her arse again and cocked one brow in challenge. "Okay, fine, I might be a little bit sleepy," she conceded, "but I sleep so much better after sex." She smiled broadly and batted her eyelashes at him, feigning innocence again, as if she wasn't begging him to fuck her.

Jack bit back a grin and shook his head. "What am I going to do with you?"

"Don't tell me you've run out of ideas already."

"Oh, I have ideas, angel—lots and lots of ideas." He fisted his hand in her hair and tugged her head backwards, leaned into her until his breath brushed over her lips. "But unless you want the first idea to come raining down on your arse until you're a sobbing mess on the floor at my feet, I suggest you be a good little girl and do as you're told."

Sophie's lips parted and she sucked down an almost inaudible breath, causing her chest to heave against his, the unyielding fabric of her dress forcing her breasts to swell above the neckline. Her dark eyes softened, her pupils expanding as she searched his gaze. "Yes, sir," she whispered, then licked her lips, inadvertently brushing the tip of her tongue over his lips in the process.

The urge to kiss her, to take her mouth and dominate

her breath, the very air in her lungs, was almost too much to resist, but he could hardly master his woman if he couldn't master himself.

Pulling away, he released his grip on her hair and stroked his knuckles over her jaw. "Let me take care of you, Sophie."

She leaned into his touch and nodded, a shy smile on her lips. "Okay," she said quietly, quickly adding, "Yes, sir," when he cocked one brow.

"That's my good girl." Jack took Sophie's hand and led her through to the bedroom. "Turn around," he said, then reached for the zipper on her dress.

As he slid it down and helped her step out of the demure garment, revealing the less-than-modest lingerie she wore beneath it, he again took a moment to centre himself, to remind himself that he was supposed to be taking care of his girl's needs, not his own.

Because... *daaamn.*

All that pale pink satin and lace was hugging her curves in all the right ways, especially her luscious arse. His erection had been subsiding, finally agreeing with the more rational part of his brain that he needed to take care of his woman, but at the sight of all that soft flesh, the slight muffin roll spilling over the top of her panties, the way the lace lovingly hugged her hip.... His half-hard cock stood up so fucking fast, it made his head spin.

As if she could read his thoughts—his dick's thoughts, at least—Sophie said, "I wasn't kidding about sex helping me sleep, you know?"

Jack closed his eyes and began counting. He got to three before he realised he needed to put some distance between them. It was either that or throw her on the bed and have his wicked way with her, so he took her dress and hung it up on the other side of the room. "Do you sleep better after sex or after an orgasm?"

By the time he turned back to face her, she'd discarded her bra on the bed and was in the process of slipping her panties down her long legs, exposing her sweet, spankable arse to his hungry gaze, and suddenly his need to master himself didn't seem so important. Not when the woman he'd been fantasising about for weeks—in truth, *years*—was standing at the foot of a large comfortable bed, completely naked and practically vibrating with need.

The urge to do what he'd threatened, to beat that plush arse until she begged for mercy, to force her to her knees and watch her tear-stained face stare up at him as he fed her his cock, almost overwhelmed him.

He stalked towards her.

Sophie made a thoughtful sound. "After an orgasm, I suppose," she said, turning to face him as she tossed her panties on the bed. "Jack?" He heard the frown in her voice. "Are you all right?"

That's when he realised he was staring at her breasts, laser-focussed on her pretty pink nipples as they hardened into taut little peaks, as they begged for his fingers to pluck and pinch them until she cried out, her pain his pleasure. His gaze flicked up to meet hers. "I'm just trying to remember why I wasn't going to have sex with you. I know I had a reason."

"A good one, I'm sure," she said, biting back another grin.

She was teasing him. Women never teased him, even when he was in an obviously good mood. It was like they sensed his dark desires and knew he was not a man to be trifled with, in or out of the bedroom. But Sophie.... Here stood a woman who had experienced his darkness first-hand, who had just caught him staring at her like a man possessed, and her first instinct was to make fun of him. She was brave. Bold.

He liked it.

"A very good one," he said, returning her grin as he slid his hands over her hips and tugged her close, "but now I'm thinking of a much better idea."

Sophie ran her hands over his chest and toyed with his shirt collar, seemingly at ease with the fact that she was completely naked and he was not. "Oh?"

He backed her up against the foot of the bed. "Yes. You're going to get yourself off, and I'm going to watch." Then he lightly shoved her backwards and watched her bounce on the bed, her legs dangling over the edge, her eyes wide and her mouth forming a shocked little O.

"You want me to...."

"Finger your sweet little cunt until you come? Yes, angel, that's exactly what I want."

All humour had fled from her expression the moment he'd pushed her onto the bed, but the look on her face now, the sheer lust glinting in her beautiful eyes as her eyelids shuttered and a sensual smile tugged at her lips, almost made him abandon his plans. Again.

How the hell did she have so much sway over him?

Was it because he'd fantasised about her for so long, built her up in his head to be more than he remembered? Or maybe it was the simple fact that she was carrying his child that rendered him powerless against her. Knowing he would do anything and everything in his power to be at her side, to protect and care for her and their baby.

Knowing his family was right in front of him.

Knowing he'd been given a second chance at happiness.

He wouldn't waste it.

"Touch yourself," he said, his voice so harsh and low, the words were barely audible.

Sophie heard him, though. She squeezed her thighs together and wriggled her arse, then cupped her breast in one hand and slid the other between her legs.

His lustful gaze locked on the apex of her thighs, he said, "Open them. I want to watch."

Pulling her bottom lip between her teeth, she whimpered, but then she nodded, obeyed. Her thighs drifted apart, revealing everything to him as she slipped her fingers between her folds. Spreading her pussy open, she exposed the silky pink heat between her legs, already glistening with wetness, and slid her middle finger in deep.

Jack stared, completely transfixed, watching his girl writhe on the bed, listening to her little moans and hums of pleasure as she plunged her finger in and out, added a second one. Thumbed her clit. Squeezed her tit and pinched her nipple.

His tongue stroked along his lower lip as he unzipped his trousers, and his control was hanging by a thread as he pulled his iron-hard shaft from his boxer briefs and began pumping his fist along his length, his rhythm matching hers.

Neither of them spoke as they worked towards their mutual goal.

No words were needed.

He was entranced by her.

Each time she slid her fingers inside her pussy, her hips would arch off the bed, would roll up to meet the willing intrusion. It was like watching her fuck an invisible lover. And every so often she would withdraw those fingers completely to circle her clit, to spread her moisture around the tiny protruding nub, to tease and tempt and torture it before disappearing back inside her.

But it was the way her expressions changed that truly held his attention. Every little emotion played out across her beautiful face so freely, so openly.

She held nothing back from him.

Jack felt the familiar pull at the base of his spine, knew he wouldn't last much longer. He squeezed the base of his cock to hold back his climax, but when Sophie's hips arched off the bed again, he knew he was done. When her teeth sank into her plush bottom lip and her eyelids shuttered again, a half grin lifted his lips.

He wasn't the only one ready to explode.

"Please," she whimpered, her dark eyes pools of molten need, staring up at him through the curtain of her eyelashes. Staring at him like he was the answer to all her questions, the holder of all her cards. Trusting him not to hurt her as others before him had.

In that moment he knew.

He would do *anything* for her.

His open, honest, trusting girl.

"You want me inside you, baby?"

She nodded so fast, he wasn't sure it was good for his ego. "Yes. *Please*."

He jerked his chin at her. "Move farther back."

She scrambled backwards on her hands, wriggling her arse and digging her heels into the mattress until she rested in the middle of the soft bedding. Her chest rose and fell in quick succession, her silky skin flushed and alluring. Her hands clenched in the blankets around her and her lips parted, the tip of her tongue darting out to moisten the plush little pillows, inviting him, begging him to come closer. So he did.

He quickly followed her onto the bed, so desperate to get inside her that he didn't even bother to shed his clothes. Without a single word, he loomed over her, notched his cock between her thighs, and drove home.

"Jack!" Sophie cried. Her back arched, forcing her breasts against the cotton of his shirt. "Need to touch you," she said between panted breaths, then grabbed at his shirt, tugged it free of his pants, and tore it open.

Jack laughed as buttons flew off in all directions. He couldn't remember the last time he'd felt so fucking happy. Until Sophie pressed her hands against his naked flesh, sending a zing of electricity through every fibre of his being, down to his bones.

Down to his very soul.

Closing his eyes, he shuddered, a physical release of all the tension he'd been carrying around for the last month. All of the longing and lust and frustration he'd felt since Sophie had walked out of that hotel room and left him alone with his anger and regret.

Pushing up on his arms, he slammed his body into hers, drove his cock as deep into her tight, wet pussy as he could get it. "Fuck," he growled. "I have missed you. I have missed this."

"I missed you too," she said, then grinned wickedly up at him. "Now shut up and fuck me."

Jack chuckled but did as she asked, doubling his efforts to bury himself as far inside her as he could. There would be time to paint her arse red later for making the demand. Within moments her muscles fluttered around him, and he saw a telltale redness creep up her neck. Heard the desperation in her panted breaths, but she still hadn't come.

And that was when he realised... she was holding out for him. Waiting for his permission to let herself go. That knowledge alone was almost enough to make him come, but he wouldn't—*couldn't*—not before her.

Then she whispered, "Please, Jack. Sir... *please*."

Leaning down, he pressed his lips to the shell of her ear. "You beg so beautifully," he murmured through gritted teeth, then added, "Come with me, angel. Come. Now."

He bit her earlobe and her whole body tightened around him. Her pussy clenched like a fist around his cock. Her heels dug into his arse, her fingers into his shoulders. Her teeth sank into the muscle between his shoulder and his neck. And then her neck was arching, her head thrown back as a cry of satisfaction escaped her throat.

A cry he echoed seconds later before collapsing on top of her, satiated and content.

They lay like that for a moment, their panted breaths and the pounding of his blood in his ears the only things he could hear. Then he tried to move, tried to shift his weight off her, but her limbs all tensed around him, holding him in place. "Stay inside me," she whispered. "Please."

There was a hitch in her voice that worried him. Lifting his head from the crook of her neck, he stared down at her, watched her tears track silently down her rosied cheeks. "Sophie," he began, but she laid her fingertips over his lips, effectively shutting him up.

"I'm all right," she said, relieving his anxiety when she smiled. "It's just that I haven't come that hard since, well, since the last time I saw you. I'd almost forgotten how good it feels when you're inside me."

Yep. This woman was *waaay* too good for his ego.

He returned her smile and kissed her fingertips. "I guess I'll have to remind you as often as possible, then, won't I?"

"Yes, sir," she said, squeezing her pussy around his dick, urging him back to life. "You will."

20

The next morning, Jack slept in. It was only until seven o'clock, but considering he was usually up before the crack of dawn, it definitely counted. As he stretched his body, he yawned deeply, then rolled to look at Sophie. She was still sound asleep and softly snoring, and not even the bouncing of the bed as he got out of it seemed to bother her, confirming what he'd thought on New Year's morning.

She's a heavy sleeper.

With a final glance at his lover, he made his way to the bathroom and climbed into the shower. Standing under the spray of hot water, he let it soak his hair and soothe his tired muscles as he allowed his mind to wander. He was exhausted, but it was a good exhaustion. The type of full-body tiredness that came from doing a good day's—or night's—work.

His angel had worn him out.

In his defence, he had been on the go since 4:00 a.m. the previous day, and as tired as Sophie had been when he got her back to the hotel, he hadn't expected her to catch a second wind. He certainly hadn't expected the third. Jack chuckled as he washed himself. He'd been with women who had high libidos before, but never one as adventurous or as enthusiastic as Sophie.

Nor as strong.

Physically, Sophie was a large woman. She was as tall as him, standing at six feet, maybe even a fraction taller, and she had at least ten kilos on him in weight, possibly fifteen.

No wonder she was such a brat.

She probably hadn't met a man yet who knew how to properly control her, knew how to give her that thing she craved most, but she would learn. Jack would teach her. She didn't have to be strong with him, not if she didn't want to be.

He would take care of her, protect her.

He would do whatever necessary to keep her by his side.

Turning off the water, he stepped out of the shower and quickly dried himself, then wrapped the towel around his hips. Exiting the bathroom, he looked to the bed. Sophie was still sprawled across the mattress, her hair a wild tangle strewn about her head, her large breasts exposed above the cotton sheet and her pretty pink nipples peaked in the cool climate-controlled air.

The urge to wake her up and fuck her all over again was intense, but she needed her sleep and he—unfortunately— had work to do.

A couple of hours, a few phone calls, and several emails later, Jack approached the bed and gently shook his lover's shoulder. "Sophie, it's time to wake up, angel." Her only response was a dismissive grunting sound, followed by rolling over and facing away from him. His mouth quirked into a pinched smile as he held back his laughter and tried again, shaking her more forcibly. "Sophie," he said, injecting his voice with a level of command he knew she usually responded to. "It's time to get up. Now."

She groaned, then whined, "But it's so early. Why are you so mean?"

No longer able to restrain his humour, Jack chuckled. He'd never considered dating a brat before, had always seen them as a lot of work for very little payoff, but he was man enough to admit when he was wrong. Having a brat like Sophie, a mature woman whose brattiness leaned more towards sarcasm and teasing and less towards tantrums and testing of his patience, was turning out to be a lot of fun. And that was something he hadn't had enough of in a long, long time.

"It's after nine, baby. We have to check out soon. Time to get up, get dressed, and get going."

That got her attention. Rolling towards him, she shielded her eyes from the light with her forearm but lifted it high enough to peek out at him. "Go where?"

"Home," he said, sitting beside her on the edge of the bed. He rested his hand on her hip, ensuring he could stop her from rolling away again. "I have to get back to Sydney, and you're coming with me."

She didn't even blink at his boldness, just stared at him for a moment, silent, before her lips thinned in a devious smile and she said in a calm voice, "Oh? And why will I be doing that?"

"Three reasons," he replied, taking her wrist in a firm grip and shifting her arm away from her face. He wanted her full attention for this conversation. "One, you need to be back in Sydney tomorrow morning for your hair and makeup test. Two, you're moving in with me."

"Excuse me?"

"My people will have all of your belongings moved into

my apartment by the time we get home tonight. And three—"

"Hang on a sec," she blurted, sitting up and shoving her hair out of her eyes. "What do you mean, I'm moving in with you? And your people are touching my stuff? What people? How do they even know where to find my stuff? It's *my* stuff."

"You are currently between places, correct?"

He waited for her to nod. Her eyes narrowed. "Yes."

"And you've been crashing on Anna's couch for how long now?"

Her mouth twisted to one side. "About a week. And how did you even know about that?" He raised one brow and grinned. Sophie closed her eyes and growled. "Anna told you, didn't she? Presumably when she gave you a list of all my favourite things and told you where to find me this weekend."

"She did."

Sophie crossed her arms over her chest and harrumphed. "She's dead to me."

"She's a good friend who cares very deeply for you," Jack said. "And if it matters, she also told me she would remove my testicles and turn them into a coin purse if I did anything to hurt you."

Her lips pinched together, but that didn't stop her tiny snort of laughter. "It does matter," she said, her tone begrudging, before growing serious again. "But it's also completely beside the point."

"And what is the point?"

"That you can't just decide I'm moving in with you without discussing it with me first. That's not how this works."

He was enjoying her ire more than he should, the

redness creeping up her neck like she was a living ther-
mometer about to explode. "Oh? And how does *this* work,
then?"

"You *ask* me to move in with you like a *civilised* human
being."

He cocked one brow and grinned at her. "You didn't
mind my lack of civility last night."

She stared at him like he'd just said the dumbest thing
in the world. "You were eating me out like the blue ribbon
winner at a pie-eating contest. No woman on the planet is
going to complain about that. But again, that's not how this
works. You can't tongue-fuck me into submission. That's
not how grown-ups communicate."

"It is if they're any fun."

"And that sounds like something your brother would
say to avoid talking to me."

Jack sobered immediately.

No one had ever compared him to Ethan in that way
before, and he found it unsettling. Ethan did use sex to
avoid conversations—to avoid connections—especially
intimate ones. It was one of the myriad of reasons why his
brother had never had a serious relationship. Jack, on the
other hand, liked tackling things head-on. It was one of the
reasons he was so successful in business.

It was also one of the reasons his love life was so
woefully crap.

Besides his ex-wife accusing him of being too controlling, previous girlfriends had told him he was bossy, arro-
gant, and a humourless, cold-hearted prick. Personality
flaws that apparently stemmed from asking blatantly
pointed questions.

Questions he generally knew the answers to before
asking them.

His mouth thinned into a tight smile as he contemplated admitting to something he normally wouldn't. He'd found himself doing that a lot recently, but he needed this relationship to work, and if that meant changing the way he did things, admitting his flaws publicly, then so be it.

His brother was right. He'd fallen for Sophie Bennett—*hard*—and failure was not an option.

Not this time.

"I don't usually ask questions I don't already know the answer to," he said. "And sometimes it's better to ask for forgiveness than permission."

Sophie's eyes narrowed. "First of all," she said, pointing a finger in his face, "where my body, mind, and soul are concerned, you will *always* ask permission. I learned the hard way what asking for forgiveness looks like, and I won't go through that again."

She waited for him to agree, which he did without hesitation, before continuing.

"Second, asking questions you already know the answer to is cheating. But...." She shifted, her whole body fidgeting as though she was fighting against it, trying to contain whatever was dying to spill out of her, like a laugh at a funeral. "If you really need to know, my answer is yes." She shrugged one shoulder, as if she hadn't just handed him the world on a silver platter. "There. Now you know the answer, you have no excuse not to be civil."

His smile spread slow and wide, and his shoulders bounced with laughter. He didn't know whether to kiss the woman for taking the lead or spank her for handling him. He settled for telling her, "You're incredible."

"I know," she said, as if he'd just stated the obvious. And in what he was coming to realise was a very Sophie thing to do, she raised her brow and added, "But I didn't hear a question in there."

This woman—*his* woman—was not going to let him rest on his laurels. "You're not going to give me an inch, are you?"

Her sudden grin was spectacular. "Where's the fun in that?"

He laughed again. "Come here."

Obeying his command, she leaned towards him immediately and captured his lips in a sweet but fleeting kiss. "Ask me," she whispered.

He smoothed her hair back from her face, then gathered the voluminous strands in his fist and held her fast, made sure she couldn't look away from him. "Sophie Bennett."

"Yes, Jack Martin?"

"Will you please, with cherries on top, move in with me?"

Her expression grew overly thoughtful as she made him sweat for a moment. "Well, I do like cherries," she said.

"Is that a yes?"

"Don't rush me," she scolded lightly, frowning at him. "This is a big decision."

"Sophie," he growled, his fist tightening in her hair. Her gasp of pain was followed by a sultry little moan, making his dick jump to attention and hammer against the zipper of his shorts. "Say it."

Jack was usually a very patient man, but this question —and more to the point, this *woman*— had every scrap of poise he possessed ready to mutiny. He wanted her answer, and he wanted it now. Even if he already knew what it was.

He wanted to know she was his. Wanted *her* to know she was his. He needed to hear her say it. Needed to know those words were out in the universe weaving their magic for all to see.

"Okay. Yes, I'll move in with you."

Jack let go of Sophie's hair and cupped her cheek, but before he could get a single word out, her phone rang. She grabbed the device off the bedside table, and in a gesture he liked way more than he probably should have, her sass gave way to submission as she looked to him for permission before answering it. "May I? It's Diana."

Jack nodded. "Of course." He would never come between her and her family.

Sophie answered the call and spoke to her young cousin. She was so patient with the girl, so caring, and despite her concerns the night before, Jack had a hunch she was going to be a great mum.

"She did?" She looked to him, her whole face lit up with excitement as she laughed happily. "Jane had the babies early this morning. Boys! She had twin boys. Oh my God. How did Uly take it?" The conversation continued for another few minutes before she looked to him again, her brows raised in question. "Dad wants to know if we'll be at The Forge for lunch," she said, then added, shrugging, "I need to pick up the rest of my things anyway."

"Lunch sounds great. Do they want us to bring anything?" he asked, earning him a smile.

Sophie repeated the question to her cousin, then looked at him and shook her head. "Okay, we'll see you in a couple of hours. Bye." She put the phone aside. "Twin boys," she said excitedly. "Uly is beside himself, first grandsons and all that." Then she sniffed herself. "Oof," she said, wrinkling her nose. "I need a shower." Then she groaned and let her head fall back against the headboard. "But I don't have any clean clothes to put on. Or underwear."

"Yes, you do. Clean underwear, at least." Sophie frowned at him, her confusion clear. "I washed them after you fell asleep. They should be dry by now."

She blinked at him. "You washed my undies?"

"Yes. I realised you didn't have any others to wear, so—"

Holding up a hand, she stopped him. "I'm sorry, I'm still stuck on the fact that you hand-washed my delicates. Without being asked to." Her eyes widened. "Do you cook? Because I suck at cooking. Seriously. Dad used to joke that I could burn water and boil toast, except that it's not a joke because I really do just suck at cooking."

Jack chuckled. *Could she be any cuter?* "I'm sure you can't be that bad," he said, to which she threw him a look that said he was very wrong. "But yes, I can cook. And do the washing, and vacuum, and change the sheets, and I even hang up my towel after I shower."

Sophie stared at him the same way she'd stared at his dessert at the wedding reception, with a hungry and covetous gaze. "Tell me how you load a dishwasher."

His grin was slow and deliberate. "Like a Scandinavian architect."

Sophie whimpered and pressed her thighs together. "That is so hot."

"If you think that's hot," Jack said, grabbing the sheet still covering Sophie and slowly dragging it down her body, exposing her sexy curves one inch at a time, "wait until you see me fold a fitted sheet."

She bit her bottom lip, and a sweet blush stained her perfect cheeks. "When do we have to check out?"

"Not for another hour." He cocked one brow. He knew what she was getting at but wanted to hear her say it. "Why?"

"Because if you don't get inside me *now*," she said, getting on her knees before him, "I'm going to be a very bad girl."

"How bad?"

Taking him by surprise, she leapt at him and used her weight to pin him to the bed. "Very, very bad."

Jack tucked his hands behind his head and grinned up at her. "Do your worst, angel."

21

Sophie relaxed back in the luxurious leather car seat and watched the scenery whizzing past her window, one hand in her lap and the other resting on Jack's thigh, their fingers intertwined as he drove them back to Melville's Cross for lunch.

Her entire body felt limp and languorous as she sat there with a small yet persistent smile on her face, as she contemplated whether or not her legs would never hold her up again. She felt almost boneless after Jack had put her in her place.

Knocking him over and straddling him on the bed, challenging him, goading him into fucking her, had been an impulsive action on her part. And a foolhardy one.

"Do your worst, angel."

His reaction to her behaviour had been unexpected, less dominant than she'd anticipated. She'd hesitated, and in her hesitation, he'd seized the opportunity to flip her onto her stomach and spank her arse raw.

His nonchalance had lulled her into a false sense of security, a trick he'd learned in high school apparently, when he'd been captain of the wrestling team, a skill he said he'd recently rediscovered a passion for, now that his submissive was a tall, curvy brat.

In all honesty, it had been a relief to know he had not only the physical strength but the mental wherewithal to handle her plus-sized arse. She'd discovered over the years that not many men shared the ability. Most gave up, either unable or unwilling to indulge her fantasies, as if they weren't getting something out of it too. And the few who did stick it out only did so to satisfy their own twisted needs, caring little—if at all—for her wellbeing.

Jack was a different breed of man.

He seemed more than willing to indulge her, almost to the point of spoiling her, and her wellbeing always seemed to be at the forefront of his mind. Something he'd proven on multiple occasions when he'd soothed her hot skin with gentle kisses, followed by massaging her arse with a special after-spanking cream that took the sting right out of her aching flesh.

He squeezed her fingers. "What are you thinking about?"

She turned her head to look at him, that small smile refusing to leave her lips as she took in his handsome and powerful profile. "I was thinking you're off to a good start," she said, her smile widening into a grin.

Jack shot her a brief glance before refocussing on the road. "If I recall correctly—and I usually do—the last time you said I was off to a good start, you scolded me for calling you beautiful."

Sophie chuckled and held up her hands. "No scolding this time, I promise."

"Okay, then how am I off to a good start this time?"

"Well, mostly it's because you treat me—and my bratty

side—with respect," she said, ducking her head slightly before adding, "It's nice not being told I'm *too much* all the time."

Jack frowned. "What do you mean by too much?"

"You know," she said with a small sigh and let her head fall back against the headrest. "I'm too tall, or too big, or I have too much attitude, or I'm too aggressive, or I'm too loud." Her mouth twisted with irritation. "I can't help being this big. You've met my family. We're all big, and with a few notable exceptions, most of us are loud. Maybe not all the time, but Bennett family get-togethers are often an eye-opening affair for the uninitiated."

Jack chuckled, then lifted her hand to his mouth and kissed her knuckles. "Last night was definitely eye-opening," he agreed. "But it was also a lot of fun."

She wanted to believe him, she really did, but experience had taught her to be wary. Sure, things were going well so far, but how long would it last? Even with a baby in the mix—*especially* with a baby in the mix—how long would it be before Jack started wanting her to change, to be more demure, more ladylike?

Less bratty.

Not that she was much of a brat to begin with. She definitely leaned more towards the tongue-in-cheek, sass-and-tease, earn-herself-some-funishment variety. She wasn't a hard-core attention seeker like some of the brats she'd met over the years. She liked her independence too much for that.

"Look at me, Sophie."

"I don't want to," she replied, steadfastly avoiding his gaze.

The next thing she heard was a car horn wailing at them, and then she was bracing her hands on the dash as

Jack suddenly pulled the car off the road and onto the shoulder. "Dickhead," he muttered under his voice, then cut the engine and turned to face her.

"What are you doing?" she demanded. "We'll be late for lunch."

"Fuck lunch. Look at me."

She looked at him all right. She looked at him like the crazy person he was, only the expression that met her gaze was not the scowl she'd anticipated but his usual patient stare. He stroked her cheek. "Talk to me, angel. What's bothering you?" When she opened her mouth, ready to dismiss his concerns, he added, "And don't even think about lying to me."

Pressing her lips into a thin line, she took a moment to think about her answer. "I know you said you had fun last night, but...."

"You're wondering how long it will last," he said, as if he could see her thoughts. But when he continued, she realised he'd been thinking the same thing. The thoughts of someone who had been hurt more than once. "You're wondering how long it will be before you're forced to change, forced to become what they want you to be. What they expect you to be."

"Exactly," she said quietly, then shook her head. "I don't usually introduce guys to my family because I know they're not planning on sticking around. And the ones who I thought might be different, the few I did take along to family get-togethers—" She huffed a dissatisfied breath and stared at her hands in her lap, twisted her fingers together. "Well, they either ran for the hills the moment they figured out that what you see is what you get—a big, loud brat from a family of big, loud bastards—or they went out of their way to make me feel small, to cram me into some preconceived pigeonhole. The model. The fat chick. The party girl." She chanced a glance at Jack and frowned at what she found. He was smirking at her, as if it was all a big joke to him. She folded her arms and looked away. "Forget it. Let's just go to lunch."

But Jack gripped her jaw in his warm hand and gently turned her face towards his. "We're not going anywhere until we discuss this," he said. "Because you seem to be forgetting what I told you last night, that I also come from a big, loud family." Grinning, he slid his hand to her nape and fisted it in her hair. "I'm not afraid of you, Sophie Bennett, and I don't need to make you feel small just to prove how big my dick is. Hearing you scream my name as I plough your sweet pussy is all the affirmation I need."

The unexpected comment made Sophie laugh out loud, made her body relax and release the tension she hadn't realised she'd been carrying. "You're weird. I like that."

Jack shifted his grip from her hair to her neck and dragged her closer, met her over the gear stick, and brought his mouth within a hair's breadth of hers. "I'm glad to hear it," he murmured, then kissed her soundly, tightening his grip on her nape so she had no way of escaping him, even if she'd wanted to. When he pulled back, he gentled his hold on her and stroked her cheek. "I don't expect you to be anything other than what or who you are, as long as you extend me the same courtesy. So be as loud as you want, take up as much space as you want, because I'm not going anywhere."

Sophie bit her lip as she absorbed Jack's words, leaned into the warm feeling they caused to bloom in her chest. They were so different from the ones she'd heard from other men in her life. So different even from the ones she'd heard growing up with her mother. Was he really saying he accepted her? As is? Even though he himself was quiet and private and shy? Maybe that was why she felt the need to reassure him, to tell him, "You know I'm not loud all the time, though, right? I like peace and quiet too." She tucked a loose strand of hair behind her ear. "I'm actually pretty tame compared to my late teen years."

Losing her mother to drugs had been a wake-up call no one should ever need, had stopped her party-train ways in their tracks and set her on a new path, one with some direction. Who knew that direction would point her towards Martin Cosmetics, and ultimately Jack?

"I know," he said, aiming that indulgent smile at her again. "And I look forward to spending many quiet evenings with you curled up in my lap, all naked and warm. But I don't ever want you to feel like you need to be something you're not, and if I do ever make you feel that way, you call me on it, okay?"

"Yes," she said. "Okay."

"Good," he said, turning his attention to getting the car back on the road.

As Jack accelerated, Sophie reached over and laid her hand on his thigh, smiling when she felt the muscles twitch and flex. "Thank you for saying what you did. You don't know how much I appreciate it. And thank you for agreeing to lunch. I know you wanted to get back to Sydney as soon as possible, but I don't get to hang out with my family as much as I'd like to. I appreciate you changing your plans for me."

Jack lifted her hand and pressed a kiss to the backs of her fingers. "Sydney will still be there tonight," he said. "We'll have lunch and visit for a while."

And that's exactly what they did. They ate, they talked,

they laughed, they oohed and ahhed over the endless stream of baby photos Ulysses spammed their family chat group with. Elijah Ulysses Rafael Bennett and Evan Alec Rafael Bennett had to be two of the cutest babies Sophie had ever laid eyes on, and all reports from the hospital—where her proud grandfather had apparently set up camp indefinitely—confirmed that Jane and the babies were all doing well. The last photo they'd received showed Rafe sound asleep in a chair beside Jane's bed, with one of the babies cradled against his chest, one tiny fist shoved in his mouth.

It was adorable.

As the afternoon passed, Sophie watched Jack interact with her family as if he'd known them for years, not hours. He blended in perfectly, proving again that he really was a weirdo, and again she felt that little flutter around her heart. That sense that something special was happening right in front of her. Happening to her. Something new. Something she'd never felt before.

Something she felt totally unprepared for.

"What are you thinking about, angel?"

Jack's question startled her. She hadn't even realised the room had gone quiet until he'd turned his attention to her. Pasting on a picture-perfect smile, as if he hadn't just caught her in the throes of an emotional revelation—or crisis—she said, "Not much. Why? What are you thinking about?"

Jack smiled but there was an edge to it, an almost feral deviousness that made her lady parts perk up and pay attention, which was damned inconvenient considering where they were.

Until he dumped a bucket of cold water on her head. "I was thinking we should get married."

Sophie blinked at him for a moment, unsure she'd heard him correctly. "I'm sorry, what did you say?"

His grin broadened. "I said, we should get married."

For the second time that day, she stared at him like the crazy person he obviously was. "But you just got divorced."

He shrugged. "So?"

Not to be left out of the absurdity, her family chimed in. "Ooh, do you think you'll take Jack's surname or keep your own?" Oliver asked.

"Or hyphenate like Jane did," Abby added.

"Sophie Bennett-Martin," Crispin mused. "Has a nice ring to it."

"Speaking of rings," Avery added, grinning.

"I haven't said yes yet," Sophie blurted, her eyes wide and her voice higher than usual.

"Yet," Jack repeated, surprising her with a quick kiss. "My favourite word." When Sophie continued staring at him, he added, "I bet you ten dollars you say yes within a month."

"I'll take some of that action," Charlie said. "Anyone else?"

Sophie's gaze sharpened, narrowed as she glared at her uncle taking bets from everyone in the room. Jack thought he was so clever, getting her family on side. But he would learn. Sophie Bennett was not to be underestimated. She wasn't just a brat. She was a stubborn brat.

Folding her arms cross her chest, she stuck out her chin and said, "Easiest ten dollars I'll ever make."

22

J ack had always been a nervous flyer—turbulence was not his friend—but this time he had Sophie with him, and when he'd mentioned his long-term aversion to aviation, she'd suggested that all he needed was a distraction. So after taking off and after the seatbelt sign went out, long before there had been any turbulence to worry about, she'd dropped to her knees and begun distracting the hell out of him.

"Angel," he groaned, fisting his hands in her hair and thrusting into her welcoming mouth. Oh yeah, turbulence was the last thing on his mind.

With a wet pop, Sophie lifted her head from his lap but kept a firm grip on his cock. "More?" she asked, that cheeky glint he was coming to appreciate more and more in her deliciously dark eyes.

He cocked one brow at her. "Did I tell you to stop?"

She sucked back a sharp breath, causing her breasts to heave and her pupils to dilate. "No, sir," she whispered, then licked him from root to tip before taking him back in her mouth.

"*Faaark.*" He groaned again, his head tipping back against the headrest, then tightened his grip in her hair, tugging the thick strands until he heard her whimper. "That's my good girl. Take me to the back of your throat."

Sophie shuffled closer, took him deeper, whimpered louder and wriggled her arse.

Jack chuckled. "You horny, baby? You need me to take care of my girl?"

She tried nodding—which he imagined was not an easy feat with his cock in her throat—and then she hummed, sending the most exhilarating vibrations through his shaft and along every thread of nerves he owned. The sensation was sublime, and his body tightened in response causing his hips to thrust up sharply and make Sophie gag.

Spluttering and coughing, she eased herself off his cock and glared at him.

He caught her chin in his hand. "I'm sorry, baby," he apologised, then ran his thumb over her mouth, smearing the wetness that clung to her lips. "Are you okay?" She tried to bite him and it made him laugh. "Now, now. That's no way for my girl to behave," he said, tightening his grip on her chin. "Only good girls get rewards, and you want your reward, don't you, Sophie?"

She tried nodding again, but he squeezed her chin, his desire ratcheting higher when her eyelids shuttered and she sucked down ragged little breaths.

"Use your words."

In an instant her demeanour changed, and she narrowed her eyes and glared at him. He'd noticed that she didn't like it when he made her say things, speak her desires out loud. She had zero qualms about acting on those desires, but if he had to guess, he'd say someone—probably someone influential—had made her feel ashamed of voicing her needs, made her mind question what her body knew to be true. She was a sexual submissive and a masochist. A curious, adventurous, sensual woman who enjoyed a bite of pain with her pleasure.

There was nothing shameful in that.

He stared her down, silently watching her with a stern brow until she relented and dropped her gaze, until she admitted what he already knew.

"Yes, sir. I want my reward," she said quietly, her cheeks darkening to a gorgeous pink.

"Then stand up," he said, getting to his feet and holding out his hand to help her up. As soon as she complied, he tightened his grip around her fingers and dragged her to the back of the plane, to the plush leather couch that sat along one wall. "Bend over and spread your legs."

Again, she did as she was told, bending over the couch and resting her hands flat against the cushions, her feet shoulder width apart. Sophie had changed her clothes as soon as they'd reached The Forge for lunch, ditching the pretty floral dress she'd worn to her uncle's wedding in favour of a pink denim skirt and white T-shirt. Bent over as she was, the denim stretched taut across her ample arse and his need to spank her made his palms itch.

"Pull up your skirt," he demanded, his voice lower than usual, rougher, his lust riding him hard.

She did so without a word, reaching back to tug the skirt up over her hips until the fabric bunched around her waist and revealed her simple white cotton panties. Jack licked his lips at the sight, especially the darkened spot of fabric between her thighs.

She was wet for him.

So wet she was making a mess of her underwear.

"Good girl," he purred, then hooked his thumbs inside

the waistband of her panties and slowly dragged them down her long legs. He wanted to savour the moment but knew they didn't have long. The flight between the Sunshine Coast and Sydney was only a short hop, and they were running out of time.

As Sophie's underwear reached her ankles, Jack abandoned all pretence of decorum and knelt behind her, then leaned forward and pressed his face against her pussy. He loved her sharp little intake of breath as he swiped his tongue along her slit and nuzzled against her dampness, his fingers digging into her hips to prevent her escape as he inhaled her sweet scent.

"Jack." She whimpered and squirmed against him and tried to close her legs, but a quick slap against her inner thigh made her still, made her muscles tighten and quiver. "Sir."

"Are you ready for your reward, baby?"

She audibly swallowed and her voice quavered as she said, "Depends on what it is."

"Don't you trust me?" he asked, his grin evident in his voice.

He didn't know how he thought she would answer that, but he hadn't expected her to look over her shoulder at him and smile shyly. "Yes, sir. I *do* trust you."

The way she said it made him think she'd only just realised that fact herself—Sophie *trusted* him—and he wondered if her heart was beating as fast as his, wondered if maybe he wasn't alone in the way he felt.

Maybe she was falling in love with him too.

The thought made his cock twitch and flex where it sat in his open fly, eager to seat itself inside her hot, tight pussy, but first he needed to taste her. Needed the scent of her on his skin, the taste of her on his tongue.

He needed to devour and consume her.

Without another thought he shoved his face between her thighs and ate her cunt like a man possessed. Sophie cried out at his ferocity, and he heard the leather cushions squeak and squeal as her fingers scrunched against them. Pulling her folds wider apart, he slipped his tongue deeper. He loved her squeal of shock, loved the way she pushed back against his face, urging him to delve deeper. Loved hearing her breathing grow ragged, hearing her curse him to hell and back for the things he did to her. Loved hearing her snarl in frustration when he pulled away and levered to his feet.

Shoving his shorts down and out of his way, Jack lined their bodies up and eased himself between Sophie's soft folds. His lover let out one long groan as he entered her and he grinned, imagining her eyes rolling back in her head. He had seen it happen often enough when he'd fucked her face to face.

He moved inside her slowly at first, pulling back and pushing forwards in an easy, gentle rhythm. But she was so wet for him, so hot and tight and soft that he couldn't resist the urge to truly fuck her for long, especially when she demanded more from him.

When she begged for it.

"Please, sir," she panted. "Harder. Please."

Who the fuck was he to deny his woman what she wanted?

What she needed.

"Okay, baby. Hold on tight."

The only hint she gave that she'd heard him at all was a muttered "Uh-huh". But then she shifted her hands to the back of the couch instead of the seat and gripped those leather cushions so tightly he thought her perfectly manicured nails might tear through the soft hide.

"Ready?"

"Yes, sir."

"Good." Because he was done holding back. Gripping her hips tightly, he slammed their bodies together with such force that Sophie's knees buckled and she scrambled to kneel on the couch before she collapsed on the floor instead.

"Oh, God!" she screamed as he continued thrusting, her spine bowing and her head thrown back. "Yes!"

Jack released her hip and stroked his fingers up her spine, enjoying the sight of goosebumps appearing in their wake and watching her whole body shiver and shake with the added sensation. Then he drew that hand back and let it fly, smacking her arse with enough force to elicit another scream from his girl, another moan, another enthusiastic "Yes."

Another desperate "Please."

He spanked her again. And again and again, adding to the faded welts he'd left her with after their morning romp. Alternating which cheek he hit and with how much force, he spanked her until her arse was as pink as her pretty little pussy, her cheeks were soaked with tears and Sophie was a sobbing, shaking mess of arousal and need.

"Tell me you're my girl," he demanded.

"Yes, sir," she sobbed. "I am your girl."

He spanked her again, the brutal slap landing with a sharp crack of skin on skin. Her body jolted forwards, like she was trying to escape the pain but the moan that fell from her lips silenced the doubts in his mind. Still, he needed to be sure he wasn't pushing her too hard, pushing her beyond her limits. "Tell me to stop," he said through gritted teeth.

She glanced back at him again, her eyes soft even though they were wet, her smile wide and reassuring. "Never."

He returned her smile and slowed his thrusts. "Then tell me you'll marry me."

Her smile sharpened into a vicious grin and she shook her head. "No."

Jack reached into her ponytail and fisted his hand in the dark strands. "You *will* marry me, Sophie."

His girl laughed and fought against his grip. "Maybe I will," she said, "but not until I win my ten dollars."

Jack laughed out loud before he released her hair and spanked her again. "Then I hope you enjoy not sitting down for the next month," he said. "Because I'm going to spank this arse raw every day until you agree to marry me."

"Bring it," she said, wriggling her arse as if begging for more. "*Sir.*" She was taunting him, baiting him.

Enthralling him.

And he was loving every moment of it.

Sophie had sparked something inside him the moment they'd met, like the lightning bolt that had reignited Frankenstein's monster's heart. He felt alive again. Felt worthy again. And he was going to do everything in his power to prove to her that they should be together. Always.

It made no sense to him logically. He barely knew the woman, the mother of his unborn child. Sure, he knew all the details of her public life, all the stuff she put out there via social media, and while that was what had initially attracted him to her, that wasn't the whole picture of who she was. And Jack wanted to get to know that person, not just the parts everyone knew but the ones only a select few ever got to see.

He wanted all of her, wanted to consume every part of her. Every tear, every breath, every sigh, every thought, every scream was his for the taking.

Pregnant or not, Sophie was *his* woman and he would not take no for an answer.

Not for long, anyway.

Reaching under her, he stroked his fingers through her wetness and over her clit, chuckling when she shivered against his hand. "You're so wet, baby. So sensitive." He flicked her clit again and grinned as she moaned. She was so close to coming. And if they'd been in bed, he would have drawn out her release, edged her over and over again until she begged him to let her come. But time was running short —they'd be landing soon—so he gave her want she needed. Gave his girl her reward.

Gripping her hips in both hands again, he increased his pace and thrust into her tight embrace until his own release threatened to push him over the edge. "Come for me, baby," he said, his voice ragged and low. "Come with me."

"Yes!" Sophie threw back her head and screamed as she came, her slick wetness coating his cock and dripping down his thighs as he pounded into her from behind.

"That's my good girl," Jack growled through gritted teeth, the force of Sophie's pussy clenching around him as exhilarating as it had been the first time he'd taken her to bed.

It only took one more thrust before he was right there with her, spilling his come inside her and cursing softly at the feeling of ecstasy that rocketed up his spine and ricocheted through his limbs, electrifying every cell in his body. An orgasm so powerful he was sure it would have knocked him off his feet if he hadn't been clinging to Sophie like a life buoy.

He stayed inside her until the blood pounding in his ears quietened to a dull roar, and his breathing evened out. "You still with me, angel?" he asked, reluctant to pull out of her wet heat while he could still feel her pussy fluttering around his cock. She didn't answer him in words, merely moaned, lifted her hand and gave him a thumbs up. Chuckling, he stroked his hands over her back again, felt her lungs expanding and contracting as she sucked in breath after breath.

Eventually, Sophie's breathing evened out, too, and Jack slowly eased out of her and took a step back, inspecting his handiwork. Her arse was gloriously red, a patchwork of old and new welts, but not damaged enough to leave a bruise. Even so, he made a mental note to massage a soothing salve into her skin before going to bed, something to lessen the ache a little faster and ensure her skin was protected.

As he continued inspecting her reddened flesh, he watched his come drip from her pussy and stick to her thighs. The sight of it ignited something in his lizard brain, and even though she was already pregnant with his child, he couldn't help himself. He gently gathered his come on his fingers, collecting it from where it clung to her thighs and pushed it back inside her, eliciting another moan from her, another "oh, God" as his fingers slid deep.

"Perfect," he murmured, more to himself than Sophie. She looked over her shoulder at him then, a small, tired smile on her lips. A smile he returned as he helped her stand, gathered her into his arms and kissed her softly. "We'll be landing soon. Get dressed and I'll fetch you some water."

"Thank you," she said quietly, then bent down to drag her panties back up and straighten her clothes.

Jack returned with a bottle of water and a light cotton blanket. He took a seat on the couch and coaxed Sophie into his lap, draping the blanket over their legs before unscrewing the cap on the water. "Small sips," he said, holding the bottle to her lips.

"I can manage," she said, a small frown bending her brow as she stared at him.

"I know you can, but I need to do this. I need to take care of you." He felt awkward telling her that but he'd promised to be honest. "It calms me."

"Calms you how?"

He locked his gaze to hers expecting to find censure at his admission, at his apparent weakness, but there was only curiosity in her dark brown depths. "I just beat your arse raw for the second time today *and* had one of the most intense orgasms I've ever experienced while doing so. I'm perverted, Sophie. Depraved. If you knew half the things I've fantasised about doing to you, even before I met you—" He closed his eyes and took a breath, then opened them and met her gaze once more. "As much as I enjoy decorating your flesh, it is never—*will* never—be my intention to actually hurt you." He held the bottle to her lips and let her drink. A few droplets of water dribbled down her chin, making her giggle when he leaned in and kissed them away. "Aftercare is just as important for me as it is for you, okay?"

"Okay," she said, that sure smile spreading her lips again. "But just so you know, you didn't hurt me, Jack. I enjoyed what we did. All of it. And I look forward to learning all about your perverted fantasies. Very much." Her gaze dipped, submissive again, and her chest heaved just a little bit as she shrugged one shoulder. "Maybe I'll even share some of my own."

Besides binding her wrists, a little breath play and the spankings, Jack hadn't even tried to push Sophie's limits. They hadn't had that discussion yet, hadn't listed their preferences and kinks, and he wouldn't do anything more without negotiating with her first, but knowing she'd enjoyed the rougher sex, enjoyed the harsher spanking, settled something inside him. Something he hadn't even known was off kilter until she'd spoken up.

Previous partners had always found his brand of dominance too severe, almost cruel, sadistic, but Sophie's revelation made him want to laugh out loud. He settled for snuggling his angel close and grinning like a loon.

"What are you so happy about?" she asked him, one brow cocked as she stared at him.

"You," he said, his laughter breaking free. He *was* happy. "You're just as depraved as me."

23

Sophie clung to Jack's hand as he led her out of the lift and into the foyer of his penthouse. She was tired—exhausted, actually—and in dire need of a snack and a long, hot bath, so she didn't immediately notice the oddly familiar décor. But as Jack settled his large hand against the small of her back and directed her into the lounge room, she would have to have been a complete idiot not to see her floral couch, her overstuffed armchairs, her faux zebra rug and pink-painted cabinets, her Art Deco coffee table, her books, her knick-knacks, her artworks... just her *stuff* everywhere she looked, only arranged much nicer than she'd ever managed.

Jack's lounge room looked like the sumptuous maximalism photographs on Pinterest she'd tried to emulate instead of the hot mess she usually lived with, and she loved it.

"Well, this is... unexpected," she said, dropping her overnight bag on the floor by the couch. "When you said you were moving my stuff in, I assumed it was being shoved in a spare bedroom somewhere."

Jack stood behind her, slid his arms around her waist and rested his chin on her shoulder. "I asked my designer to meld your belongings with mine. I wanted you to feel at home here." He chuckled. "Obviously Layla thinks your stuff is nicer than mine, because I don't think there's anything of mine left."

"And the wallpaper?" she asked, nodding at the dark teal walls that set off her collection of artworks, photographs and an ornate gilt-framed mirror perfectly.

"It wasn't here when I left," he said, then moved towards a large raw timber cabinet that definitely wasn't hers and read the note that was sticky taped to the front of it.

"And you're okay with that?" she asked, following him to the mystery cabinet.

Jack chuckled and held up the note for her to read. There was a colour chart stapled to the back of it.

> I know you can't live without your stupid TV, so I had this made to blend in with Sophie's superior style aesthetic. Ask her to pick a colour and text it to me. I'll be back next week to paint it. You're welcome, L xoxo

"I gave Layla carte blanche, told her to go nuts," he said, carefully folding the note and colour chart in half and slipping them inside his back pocket. Then he opened the cabinet, revealing a massive television. His shoulders bounced with laughter and he shook his head. "She literally squealed with joy when I called her this morning, even though it was only five o'clock. She's been at me for years to change my décor."

"Let me guess," Sophie said. "A black leather couch, a glass coffee table and a... hmm, I want to say *grey* rug?"

"The rug was white, actually," Jack replied, looking sheepish, "but the rest is spot on. How did you know?"

"I have seven uncles, many of whom are not that much older than me. They all went through the 'leather couch, glass table' bachelor phase, but they all grew out of it by the time they hit thirty."

"I must be a late bloomer, then," Jack said, closing the cabinet. "I'm thirty-five. Although, in my defence," he continued, "I don't actually spend that much time here, so I've never cared what it looked like, only that it functioned."

Sophie frowned. "Where do you spend your downtime, if not here?"

Jack shrugged. "The gym, mostly. I'm a gym junkie, remember?"

"And a workaholic, by the sounds of it."

"I haven't had a reason not to be." His tone was very matter-of-fact.

A sudden feeling of discomfort made Sophie take a step back, which in turn made Jack frown. She glanced around the room at all of her belongings, at all of the things that usually made her feel calm and embraced her in soothing memories, and then she looked at Jack. She stared at this man who had taken her into his life and was obviously making an effort to make her feel as welcome as he possibly could, and she clenched her jaw against the anxiety clawing its way through her veins. Her hands tightened into fists.

As annoyed as she was at first with his heavy-handed insistence that she move in with him, she did appreciate that he was trying to do what he thought was best. He was trying to take care of her, trying to provide for their child in the only way he knew how.

But she needed more than that.

More than shelter, more than money, more than material *stuff*—all of which she could provide without his help—she needed *him*.

All of him.

"Jack, I just...." She swallowed hard, then took a moment to simply breathe. She'd been in similar situations before with varying results. Never with a baby, though, which made her even more hesitant to broach the subject at hand. But as she stared into Jack's piercing gaze she knew she had to step up, knew she had to be brave and make the choice to not be submissive, to not be a brat, and to put voice to her very valid concerns.

No matter the end result of doing so.

She wouldn't let herself—or her baby—be mistreated again.

"What is it, Soph?" His frown softened, and he reached out for her. "What's wrong?"

She took another step back. "Can we sit?"

"Of course," Jack said, his tone cautious, but he took a seat, his narrowed gaze curious as he watched her sit at the opposite end of the couch.

Tucking one foot under her arse, Sophie dragged a cushion into her lap and held it to her chest like a decorative, foam-filled barrier. A piss-poor excuse for a shield against what may or may not be a revealing moment in their burgeoning relationship, but one that made her feel slightly more secure, just like a nice thick blanket pulled up to her chin was the perfect protection against the monsters who lived under her bed when she was a kid.

She took a deep breath. "I just need to know that you're here with me, here for this. All of this." When Jack's frown deepened, she charged on, needing to be as open as possible and hoping he'd understand. "You said it yourself, you're a gym junkie and a workaholic, and—"

"Sophie—"

"Please let me finish," she said, refusing to drop her gaze, even though it went against every submissive bone in her body. "I need to get this out or I may never say what I have to." Jack closed his mouth and a muscle ticked in his jaw, but he nodded and waited for her to speak. "I know you're a busy man, Jack, an important man, and I know that sometimes the company will come first. Shit happens, and as CEO, it's your job to fix it. I get that. But as the child of two workaholics, one a gym junkie and one a, well, regular junkie, I need to know you'll put me and our kids first as much as humanly possible."

She hugged the cushion tighter. "I'm already rich, so I couldn't give less of a shit about your money and all the things it can do," she said, gesturing at the freshly decorated room, "but I do care about you showing up for things. Showing up for us. Not just physically but mentally and emotionally too. I need to know that you're all in with this, with us. Because I am, Jack. I am so here for this. All of this. With you."

Her heartbeat raced, and she clenched her jaw as she willed back the prickle of tears brewing behind her eyes. Jack's continued silence as his eyes narrowed under a stern brow was unsettling, but she forced herself to stay in her seat and not flinch away, even as his beautiful blue gaze bored into hers as though he could see right down to her very soul.

When he finally spoke, she almost jumped out of her skin, the depth of emotion in his voice like a wave crashing over her, deep and dark and threatening to drown her. "Real question time," Jack said, his voice like gravel, his hand gripping the back of the couch so tightly, his knuckles blanched. "Would you still want to be with me if you weren't pregnant?"

The unexpected question sent a surge of relief through Sophie, forcing her to release the breath she hadn't realised she'd been holding and smashing through the dam keeping her tears at bay. It seemed she wasn't the only one feeling insecure. Nodding, she answered eagerly, "Yes!"

Suddenly her lovely embroidered barrier was gone, the cushion discarded on the floor, and Jack was dragging her into his lap, wrapping her up in his strong arms, and whispering gentle words of reassurance in her ear as she sobbed on his shoulder. "I've got you, baby. Hush now."

Lifting her head from the crook of Jack's neck, Sophie sniffed loudly. "I haven't stopped thinking about you since we met," she said, swiping her hands across her cheeks to stem the flow of waterworks. "Even when I was furious with you for not telling me the whole truth about your situation, I couldn't get you out of my head. And I tried so hard to forget you, I really did, but then you sent me my favourite roses, and chocolates, and *cheese*, and the more I thought about you, the more I missed you. And the more I missed you...."

Jack stroked her hair away from her face, his perceptive gaze darting back and forth as he searched her own, humour evident in his velvety voice, "Yes? The more you missed me...?"

She half snorted, half laughed at his egotistical preening. "The more I missed you, the more I regretted walking out of that stupid hotel room. I wanted to call you. Talk to you. Hear your voice."

"Oh?" His grin was slow and downright evil but so

damn sexy. "And what would you have said to me if you *had* called?"

The last of her tears dried up as her confidence returned. Sliding one hand down Jack's chest, she toyed with the button on his shorts and popped it open. "I would have said that I finally understood why Ethan never introduced us when we were dating. That he was right when he said you and I were much better suited to each other than he and I ever were."

Slipping his hand to her nape, Jack pulled her closer and whispered across her lips, "I usually hate it when he's right, but I'm willing to concede defeat and agree with him, just this once." Then he kissed her quick and hard. "Now, tell me what you'd hoped to hear me say."

The feel of Jack's hand on her neck, the warmth of his palm pressed against her flesh, the strength of his fingers gripping her, anchoring her to him, aided the sense of calm that slipped through her bloodstream and flooded her brain with a natural high. Time slowed, her heart did, too, and the last of her anxiety melted away as she moistened her lips and told him the truth. "I wanted to hear the command in your voice," she said. "I wanted you to tell me you missed me as much as I missed you, that you were sorry, that you forgave me, that you still wanted me. That I was your girl. Your good girl."

"You are my good girl, Sophie. And I did miss you. More than I thought possible."

Sophie rested her head on Jack's shoulder and snuggled against his chest, toying with the buttons on his shirt. "I like the way I feel when I'm with you. Like I can just be myself and not some impossible version of myself that other people want me to be. And I know what I'm about to admit is quite possibly the least sexy thing I can say to a man, but when I'm with you, Jack, I feel... safe."

His arms tightened around her and he pressed his lips against her hair. "As a dominant man, knowing my girl feels safe in my care is the best compliment you could give me. Thank you, angel."

She smiled against his chest. "You're welcome."

"And like I said before, I never had a reason not to be a workaholic, but I do now. I'm all in, Soph. I am here for this, for us. For you."

She lifted her head and met his gaze, matched his smile. "You are?"

"I am. And you know what else?"

"What?"

"You said you needed to know that I'd be there for our *kids*, plural," he said, his own smile softening, growing more indulgent as he brushed a stray hair from her face. "I love that you're anticipating more than one."

She had said that, hadn't she? A subconscious slip of the tongue because, just maybe, some of those daydreams she'd been having about Jack had involved a baby or two, three at the most. "How many kids do you want?"

"Hmm... at least two," Jack said. "No more than five. Maybe six."

Her eyes widened, and she swallowed hard. "*Six* kids?" Her pussy ached just thinking about pushing out that many babies.

Jack laughed at the obvious horror written across her face. "Relax, I'm kidding," he said, then kissed her again, even as she slapped her hand against his shoulder. "I'm happy with however many you want to give me."

Eyeing him dubiously, she rubbed her belly. "Well, let's just get through this one first and see how we go, okay?"

"Okay," he said, then checked his watch. "It's getting late. Are you hungry?"

Her stomach revolted at the mere mention of food, but she hadn't eaten anything since lunch. "I could eat."

"What are you in the mood for? There's a great Thai place nearby that delivers late, or we could get a pizza."

"Pizza please, Pepperoni with extra cheese."

"What is it with you and cheese?"

She grabbed her belly and gave it a wobble, immediately regretting the decision as her stomach roiled, but she ignored the sensation, and said, "Hey, these curves don't happen by chance, you know?"

"Oh, so I have cheese to thank for this beautiful body?" he asked, grabbing her arse and making her yelp, the flesh still tender from the spanking he'd given her on the plane. At least it distracted her from her stomach.

"Cheese," she said, then winked as she added, "and always skipping leg day."

"Brat." Her lover chuckled and shook his head, then pointed a finger in her face in mock seriousness. "Never skip leg day."

Sophie lurched forward and took his finger into her mouth, sucking it deep. He groaned and shook his head and pretended to glare at her. "Don't distract me when I'm scolding you."

"No promises."

A few minutes later Jack had ordered their pizza and Sophie had taken another antinausea pill. Then he took her on a quick tour of her new home. Four bedrooms, all with ensuite bathrooms, an additional guest bathroom off the lobby, a gourmet kitchen with a fully stocked butler's pantry, a full-sized dining room and a large entertaining area with views over Sydney Harbour that were to die for.

"What do you think?" he asked, standing beside her on the balcony.

"I think Layla and I have a lot of work to do," she said, watching the lights of the city twinkle brightly, like a million earthborn stars. "Who knew there were so many different shades of beige?"

Jack's laughter wrapped around her. "I believe it's called a neutral palette."

She turned to face him, throwing him a pitying look. "I believe it's called boring as fuck."

"Come here." His smile was broad as he tugged her closer, gripping her upper arm in one hand and wrapping the other around her throat.

A shiver ran up Sophie's spine, and she melted into his hold. Her eyelids dipped and her lips parted, her pulse racing, and her breath ragged. "Sir," she whispered.

"Look at me." His voice was deeper, more growly than usual, and when she lifted her gaze to his, she understood why. His eyes were blue fire, and the way he stared at her, devoured her whole with his brilliant stare, made her mouth dry and her pussy wet. He leaned close, his lips hovering over hers, and lightly squeezed her neck, but before he kissed her long and deep, he said the last thing she'd expected to hear. "I fucking love you."

24

"I'm sorry, he said what?"

Sophie screwed up her nose at Anna's question and poured freshly boiled water over the teabags in the waiting mugs. "He said 'I fucking love you.'"

After an early start to the day, followed by an awkward exchange with Jack, then a long day of hair and make-up tests for the upcoming ad campaign, Sophie had been looking forward to a quiet afternoon. Alone. Some time to gather her thoughts and sort through her feelings, analyse everything that had happened in the past forty-eight hours. But Anna had ambushed those plans with a batch of freshly baked blueberry muffins and a packet of Sophie's favourite tea. A housewarming gift, she'd said. And an excuse to snoop and stick her nose into Sophie's business. It was a good thing she loved the woman like a big sister.

"Okay," Anna said, shoving a morsel of muffin in her mouth. "And you're absolutely certain he didn't say 'I love fucking you'?"

She rolled her eyes. "Yes, I'm sure. I mean, he said that

later in bed when we were actually fucking, but out on the balcony, he definitely said the other thing."

"Oh my God." Anna paused to absorb that information, then demanded, "And... so? What did you say? Details, woman! You can't drop a bomb like that and then stop."

"I didn't say anything." She yanked the teabags out and tossed them in the bin, then added milk and sugar to her mug. Anna took hers black. "I just stared at him with my mouth hanging open and no sound coming out of it like a fucking idiot."

"Did he say anything else?"

"He was going to, but then the pizza arrived and it all sorta got shunted to the side while we ate. And then it got *really* awkward, because every time I tried to say something, he changed the subject, like he was embarrassed. Or worse, regretted saying it at all."

"Well, that sucks."

Sophie bit her lip as the urge to cry welled up inside her. "Did I fuck this up already?"

Anna was off her stool and had Sophie in her arms in an instant, hugging her so tightly she could barely breathe. "Hey, of course not. You haven't fucked anything up."

"But I didn't say it back, and I know that hurt him." She stepped back, shook her head and sniffed back her tears. "The look in his eyes, Anna. You should have seen how sad he looked."

"First of all, you are under no obligation to tell someone you love them just to spare their feelings. Especially if you *don't* love them. And second...." Her friend took a breath, clasped her hands on Sophie's shoulders and stared her down. "*Do* you love him?"

"I don't know. I know I have a lot of very big feelings about him, but I don't know if it's love."

"Okay, big feelings is a good start. Tell me about them."

"What is this, the Dr. Anna show?"

"My surname *is* Valentine."

"That doesn't make you an expert on love, you know?"

"No, but I've been in therapy long enough to know that talking shit through really does help. And it's possible I feel *slightly* responsible for your current situation," she said, holding up her finger and thumb to pinch the air.

"Slightly? If you and Ethan hadn't set us up, none of this would be happening."

"And you wouldn't have met a great guy who you now have very big feelings for."

Sophie opened her mouth to argue further but couldn't. Anna was right. About all of it. Instead, she gulped down half her tea, then grabbed a muffin and began dissecting it, pulling out the blueberries and eating them one by one. "Is it normal to feel so... desperate?"

Anna frowned. "Explain," she said, taking her seat again on the other side of the kitchen island.

"I don't really know how else to describe it. Maybe *crave* is a good word? Like, I *crave* his touch. His skin is soft but his hands are so strong, and when he touches me it's absolutely electric. Geez, just thinking about his hand around my throat is making me horny."

A spluttering sound dragged her attention back to Anna, who was wiping her mouth with the back of her hand. "So Ethan was right, huh? Jack is into all that kinky stuff, like you?"

"Hey, Ethan is no angel in the bedroom either, you know, but yes, Jack is into all that kinky stuff." Heat bloomed in her cheeks even as she smiled. "And he's really, *really* good at it." She poked at the remains of her muffin. "Actually, he's pretty great in general."

"For example?"

"You've seen the lounge room, right? He made that happen because he wanted me to feel welcome here. He paid his decorator to have her team up at the butt crack of dawn to make sure it was finished by the time we got home. On a Sunday. *And* he's letting me choose how to redecorate the entire apartment. I have a meeting with Layla next week." She shook her head and chuckled. "And as annoying as it was that he asked you about my favourite things, at least he took the time to ask and didn't just send the usual clichéd crap men think women want."

"He literally sent you roses and chocolates. How is that not clichéd?"

"Twilight Zone roses, Anna. Do you know how rare it is for a florist to carry Twilight Zone roses? God only knows where he found them."

"And then you chopped their heads off and sent back the stems."

"Well, duh. I wasn't going to send back the pretty bits."

"And the chocolates?"

"You mean the artisanal chocolates with the seasonal fillings that they only make at certain times of the year? The ones he got them to make specifically for me even though they're currently out of season? Not exactly clichéd."

"And the cheese basket? You didn't eat that."

"Only because my refrigerator had already gone into storage, and there was no way I could have eaten that much cheese before it went bad. I mean, really. Unrefrigerated dairy in Queensland in summer? I don't think so."

Anna chuckled. "Good point."

"And it's not as if I didn't eat any of it. When I gave it to my neighbours, they invited me in for fivesies, and that blue vein camembert—" She lifted her fingers to her mouth and kissed their tips. "—to die for." A small smile tugged at her lips as she remembered how she'd felt when she'd received the gifts. Irritated, yes, but the consideration Jack had put into his gift-giving game made her feel as if he knew her, saw her. Understood her. "I will admit though, as bossy as Jack is, he's very sweet, and I've never been with a man who's sweet before. Or thoughtful. Or just so damn *nice*."

"You say that like it's a bad thing."

"It's not a bad thing," she said defensively. "It's an unexpected thing, but it's definitely not a bad thing. And to be honest, I could use a little more nice in my life. My romantic partners, as you know, have not always been very nice."

Anna raised her mug in salute. "You and me both, sister."

"I don't know. Maybe—" She sighed heavily and rubbed at the sudden tension squeezing her forehead. "Maybe I'm just so used to dating shitheads that I can't recognise what love is supposed to look like. It's not like I had a great role model in that regard. My mother changed her boyfriends more often than her underwear. And dad was no better. At least he was discreet about it."

Anna blinked, her mouth open. "Hang on a sec. Paul was a hound? *Paul.* Straight-laced, quiet, snobby Paul."

Chuckling at her friend's surprise, she nodded. "After he and mum broke up, yeah. He dated *a lot*. But he stopped when mum sent me to live with him."

"When your mum kicked you out, you mean," Anna said, her mouth twisting in disgust. "Let's not sugarcoat it. The woman openly admitted to being jealous of you—her own daughter—because the arseholes *she* brought home started hitting on you."

Sophie twitched her shoulder in a half-shrug,

pretending to not be as upset at the memory as she really was. The men her mother dated had been the lowest of the low. Monied, drugged-up playboys with morals as loose as their purse-strings. As much as it had hurt at the time, Sophie had come to realise her mother sending her away was a good thing. And as much of a hard time as she'd given her father, his rules and rigidity had saved her life.

"Yes, well, after I moved in, he spent all of his free time dealing with my angsty teenaged arse. Apparently I put quite the dent in his dating history."

"Mum says love looks different with different people, and at different ages," Anna said, staring into her mug. "Like when I was seventeen, love looked like wearing a boy's footy jersey and making out behind the cricket nets. And in my early twenties, it looked like me finally figuring out that I didn't like men in their early twenties."

"When I was seventeen it looked like making out in the back row at the movies where his mates couldn't see him snogging the fat girl."

"Teenage boys are idiots."

"And in *my* early twenties, love looked like fringe gallery openings, seedy clubs, too much cheap wine, bruised ribs, and a concussion because he didn't like my brattitude."

Anna reached across the island and grabbed Sophie's hand. "You know that wasn't your fault. That guy was a walking red flag."

"It didn't look red up close," she said, savagely dumping the rest of her tea in the sink. "Not until it was too late." She scowled at the memories assaulting her brain, at the harsh realities of then and now and the realisation they brought with them. "And what I felt for that jerk pales in comparison to how I feel about Jack, so why couldn't I tell him I love him? Because... I do. I *love* Jack. Which I know is insane because I barely know the man." She cast an anxious glance at Anna, the ache in her head increasing to a steady pounding rhythm. "Or maybe it's just baby hormones."

"Or maybe we should get to know each other better and find out."

Sophie spun towards the kitchen door and saw Jack leaning against the doorjamb, his arms folded, one foot crossed over the other, and a lopsided grin decorating his handsome face. "You're home," she said, his presence sucking all the air out of the room and leaving her breathless.

"How long have you been standing there?" Anna asked, her eyes narrowed.

His grin widened. "Long enough." And then to Sophie, he said, "Come here."

Without hesitation, she walked towards him, his command like an invisible string pulling her into his orbit, and the closer she got, the more she noticed the heat burning in his sapphire eyes. A heat that threatened to engulf her in flames and eat her alive.

Behind her, Anna cleared her throat. "I think that's my cue to leave."

Sophie barely even registered her friend slipping past them and uttering her goodbyes as she disappeared from view, but she noticed Jack's hands on her body well enough, pulling her close as he enveloped her in his warmth and stole a kiss.

"Are you feeling okay?" he asked, the heat in his gaze cooling into concern as he focussed on her face. "Are you nauseous again?"

Choosing to ignore the insecurities at the back of her mind telling her she looked like shit—why else would Jack assume she felt ill—she decided to lean into foreign territory and trust he was being sincere. "A little bit," she said. "And I have a headache."

Jack kissed her forehead. "Okay, first we take care of you," he said, directing her through to the lounge room and seating her on the couch. "A little food, a lot of fluids, and maybe a foot rub?" His eyebrows rose. When she smiled and nodded, he continued. "Good, because then we're gunna play twenty questions." The smile fell from his face. "And you can bet your spectacular arse one of those questions will be the name of the fucker who hit you."

25

I *love Jack.*

  He'd heard her say it, clear as day. Sophie Bennett, the woman Jack had fantasised about for longer than he was willing to admit, loved him.

Now he just needed her to say it to his face.

He hadn't meant to eavesdrop on her conversation with Anna, but when she'd mentioned the arsehole giving her a concussion, fury had consumed him, and he'd needed a moment to calm himself before going to her. But then she'd admitted her feelings for him. And then she'd tried to pass it off as baby brain.

No. He wasn't settling for that.

She had made a good point, though, when she'd said she barely knew him. They had skipped most of the "getting to know each other" part of dating in favour of falling into bed and getting lost in their pleasure. From personal experience, he knew a lot about what turned her on and what made her come apart in his arms. From her friends and family he'd learned about her favourite flowers and treats, and he knew she had a serviceable escape plan in case of the zombie apocalypse. And from her social media he knew which charities she supported and why, knew her favourite colour was pink, that she preferred Coke over Pepsi, and sunsets over sunrise.

But she knew very little about him. He hadn't even shared his Instagram profile with her.

Jack hoped he had showed her at least some of his true self, besides the fact he was a gym junkie and workaholic. He knew those weren't his best qualities, and hadn't lied when he'd told her he would change. He'd never had a reason to skip leg day, or go home on time, let alone early, which was how he'd come to be in the apartment at four in the afternoon and hear Sophie say she loved him.

After settling her on the couch, he retreated to the kitchen, prepared her a light meal, and poured her a glass of ginger and lemon iced tea. When he returned to the lounge room with the food and drink, he found her reading a parenting book, and marking passages with a bright yellow highlighter.

"Studying up?" he joked and placed the food tray on the coffee table. He waited for her to put the book down before handing her one of her antinausea tablets and some parac-etamol for her headache.

Sophie swallowed the pills and sipped her drink, then nodded, and said, "Yes. I brought it back from the library at The Forge. I remember reading it when the twins were born and being completely grossed out by it, but it doesn't seem quite so gross now."

Jack sat beside her. "Eat," he said, taking her glass and picking up the plate.

She shook her head. "I'm really not hungry."

A slight frown pulled at his brow as he studied her face. "A little food will help your nausea, as will the tea." When she still looked hesitant, he added, "Just two bites of anything on the plate, and then I won't say another word about it, okay?"

She eyed the selection of shredded chicken breast, dry crackers and apple slices, and chose to pick at the chicken.

"Good girl," he purred, then revelled in the way she immediately ducked her gaze and a shy smile played on her perfect lips. Fuck, she was beautiful.

"I thought we were going to play twenty questions," she said, grabbing the apple slices next. "And when do I get my foot rub?"

"Brat." Jack chuckled. "Is that your first question?" When she narrowed her eyes at him, he laughed harder. "Get comfy, angel. We might be here a while."

Sophie grinned at him and shifted to the far end of the couch, then stretched her legs out towards him and eagerly placed her feet in his lap. He took one foot in his hands and began rubbing it, pressing his thumbs deep into the tissue of her sole. He loved the groan that escaped her as he massaged her arch and worked her toes. Loved seeing the tension bleed out of her body. Loved watching her eyes close and her smile soften as she relaxed into the comfort of the couch.

Loved her.

"Do you want to go first?" he asked.

Sophie blinked her eyes open and tilted her head to one side as she watched him rub her feet. She took her time before asking her first question, as if mulling over every possibility, but when she finally settled on one, it was not what he'd expected. "What's one thing that scares you that no one else one knows about?"

"You mean besides the possibility of screwing up my

mother's company in the first year I'm in charge, or impending fatherhood?"

Sophie thought about that for a second before nodding. "Yes, besides those."

Jack snorted a laugh, but he didn't have to think about his answer. He'd been terrified of one thing more than any other since he was seven. "Crocodiles in swimming pools."

"That's very specific. Why crocodiles in swimming pools?"

Jack felt his face flush as he admitted to Sophie what no one else knew. "My mum watched this Aussie miniseries on tele when I was a kid. I don't remember what it was called, but some people tried to kill a woman by putting a saltwater crocodile in her swimming pool, knowing she swam laps every morning. So of course, the lady went for her usual swim and the croc attacked. I had nightmares for a week." He paused to take in Sophie's horrified expression. "Even now, I check the pool for crocodiles before jumping in."

"Wow," she said, wide eyed and slack jawed. "That was not what I expected you to say."

He cocked one brow. "What *did* you expect?"

"I thought you'd say you were afraid of heights or something, like a normal person."

He chuckled again. "I guess I'm not normal."

"Crocodiles in swimming pools? Definitely not normal. Your turn."

"Okay." He thought for a moment. "Why can't you cook?"

Ducking her gaze again, Sophie shrugged. "Because my parents hired people to do that for them. And the one time my mother took me to Italy when I was a kid, my nonna rapped me over the knuckles with a wooden spoon and banned me from her kitchen."

Anger spewed up inside him again. Why were people always hurting Sophie? Her own grandmother hit her, too? What the fuck? "Why would she do that?"

He saw the hurt flicker in her dark eyes. "She said I was the reason my mother was so miserable. That I was to blame for her addictions. Told me I was *marcia*. Rotten."

"Jesus. How old were you?"

"Ten. Mum had taken me to meet her family for my tenth birthday."

"And that's how they treated you? You were a kid."

"A kid born out of wedlock. They were very religious, and I was a walking, talking reminder of my mother's sin. To her credit, when Mum found out what Nonna did, she packed us up and we came straight home to Sydney." She smiled, but it was small and sad. "She wasn't the greatest mum, but she stood up for me when it mattered. At least she did when I was little." Again, she cast her gaze down and shrugged, something he noticed she did a lot when she felt uncomfortable. "Anyway, after that I had no interest in learning how to cook. Now I get my meals delivered in bulk every week. Pretty hard to screw up pre-made lasagne and a salad."

Jack stopped rubbing her feet and stared her down. "Oh, baby, no. You won't be eating that shit anymore."

"Well, I'm not eating dry chicken breast and raw broccoli for the rest of my life either. You said you knew how to cook, but I've seen the inside of your fridge, Jack. It's not pretty."

"I promise I will cook you something better when you stop feeling nauseous all the time. According to all of my female relatives with kids, bland food is best right now. But

I will make all the lasagne you want when your tummy settles."

She narrowed her gaze and watched him for a moment, then leaned forwards and stuck out her little finger. "Pinkie swear?"

He grinned and hooked his finger around hers. "Pinkie swear." When she sat back again, he added, "Your turn."

That went on for well over an hour, asking questions back and forth. Some serious, some not so much.

He was surprised to discover her favourite movie genre was action films, and agreed with him that, yes, actually, *Die Hard* was a Christmas movie.

She'd snorted at his Instagram handle—@jonny-get-your-fleek-on—the one Ethan had come up with and Jack had never bothered to change. And she'd laughed her arse off at him for admitting to streaking naked across his family's estate when he was sixteen and telling everyone it was his brother.

"To this day, mum still thinks it was Ethan," he said, laughing along with her.

"Ethan naked in public isn't exactly a stretch of the imagination," she said, grinning. "Your turn."

As promised, he asked her for the name of the man who had abused her, the one who should have protected and cherished her.

She tried to pull her feet back, to pull away from him and curl in on herself, but he wouldn't relent and held them firmly in his lap. She scowled and crossed her arms. "Why do you want to know?"

"Because he hurt you, and I'd like to repay the favour."

She thought about that for a moment, then said, "Fine. I'll tell you his name if you tell me what your ex did that was worse than cheating."

Jack sighed quietly but nodded. He had to tell her some-time, and there was no time like the present. "She broke my heart. But not because she cheated on me." He shoved his hand through his hair as if that could shove out the ache from his chest. "Lisa and I got married because she was pregnant."

"So, this is a hobby for you? Knocking women up and marrying them?"

"No, it's not." He scrubbed a hand over his stubble. "Our situation is very different."

Her eyebrows shot into her hairline, scepticism drip-ping from every word. "Oh, how so?"

"Because unlike you, Lisa got pregnant on purpose. She knew it was the easiest way to get me to marry her. She knew I wanted to start a family and used that against me."

Sophie's expression grew cautious, more concerned. "What happened? What did she do?"

"As soon as she got access to my expense account—" He gritted his teeth and fought down his pain and anger, but couldn't stop it from flavouring his words. "—she had an abortion."

His sweet girl looked mortified, her hand flying to her mouth to contain her gasp.

Jack continued. "For months I believed her lies, believed she'd miscarried, but then Ethan organised for a private detective to follow her, and we found out the truth. She had lovers all over Sydney, men she could control with *my* money."

"But didn't she come from a wealthy family?"

"Yes. But her father controlled everything. She was desperate to get away from him and did what she thought she had to."

Sophie plucked at the edge of a cushion and didn't quite meet his gaze. "Did you... love her?"

He shook his head. "No," he said, pleased to see the relief in her eyes when she lifted her head and looked at him again. "Ours was not a loving relationship. She was into kink, and I appreciated her discretion in that regard. And she wanted a new life, freedom from her father's control. I can't fault her for that. But I can't forgive what she did either."

Sophie scrambled across the couch and climbed into his lap, rested her head on his shoulder, and placed his hands over her belly, wrapped herself up in him. "His name is Trevor Moran, and he's a photographer. I never reported him because he threatened to release nude photos of me. Said he'd put them up on all the porn sites and ruin my career."

Jack's fingers curled against her belly as he resisted the urge to form them into fists. "Fucking sonofabitch."

Before he could ask for more details, she added, "I say we forget them both. Good riddance to bad rubbish."

Putting a leash on his rage, he agreed. "Good idea," he said. "Good riddance." But he would avenge his angel. Somehow, someday, Trevor Moran the photographer would learn a valuable lesson about how to treat a woman.

Hooking a knuckle under her chin, he lifted her face and stared down at her. The colour had returned to her cheeks and she didn't seem as anxious as she had earlier. "How are you feeling now?"

"Better. You were right," she muttered, her mouth a mulish line. "Eating did help."

He tried not to gloat... and failed miserably. "I'm sorry, can you say that again? I was... what?"

"Make me say it again and I'll make you eat my cooking."

"I'll risk it." Sophie pursed her lips, refusing to speak. "Come on, say it. I was...?"

"Right," she grumbled.

"Good girl," he said, stroking her hair. "And good girls get rewards."

That caught her attention. "What kind of reward?"

Jack slid his hand from her belly to her breast, then higher, clasping his hand around her neck. "What does my girl want?"

Sophie leaned into his grasp and wriggled against his hardening cock, her pretty pink tongue darting out to moisten her lips. "You."

26

Sophie had never been an early riser—a morning person she wasn't—but she was so excited about the principal photo shoot for the campaign finally coming together that she found herself awake at the ungodly hour of 6 a.m. But at least Jack was with her, snuggled up to her, one arm slung over her hips and his thick cock poking against her back.

For the past week he'd stuck to his word and cut back on hitting the gym every morning. He'd also made an effort to finish work at the same time every day so they could continue spending time together, getting to know each other. The previous night had been spent watching one of Jack's favourite crime dramas on his big-screen TV and discussing baby names.

She'd explained to him the Bennett family tradition of giving all children their father's name as their middle name, even the girls, and that, yes, her middle name was Paul, Sally's middle name was Henry, and Abby's middle name was Ulysses.

"Abigail Ulysses? Seriously?" He'd laughed.

She'd scowled. "Like you can talk, Jonathon Aloysius."

"Good point."

She'd also explained that her uncle Charlie had been somewhat kinder to the twins, gifting Josie and Diana with the name Charlotte instead.

"So we have a middle name all picked out," Jack had said. "I have to admit, I actually kinda like Jack as a girl's middle name. Not Jackie, not Jacqueline, just Jack."

Sophie had smiled at his willingness to embrace her family's quirks. It boded well for their future. "Agreed. Now we just need a first name. Any thoughts?"

"I had a great-aunt who was very special to me growing up," he'd said. "Her name was Evelyn. I've always thought it a pretty name."

"Evelyn." Sophie had repeated the name twice more, getting a feel for it. "Evie for short?"

Jack nodded. "Evelyn 'Evie' Jack. I like it." He'd pressed a kiss to her temple. "What about a boy's name?"

"I've always liked Liam as a name," she'd said. "And Aiden. Something traditional like that. But I'm not against going full celebrity with names like London or Paris either."

"Hmm... London Jack sounds a little too serial killer for my liking."

Sophie had chuckled. "Good point."

"I do like Aiden, though. Aiden Jack. AJ for short."

"Evie and AJ." She'd lifted her head from his shoulder and stared at him, the moment feeling suddenly momentous, yet surprisingly *not* overwhelming. She'd felt calm, at peace with her herself, content. "Did we just name our kids?"

"I think we did." He'd nuzzled against her cheek before nibbling along her jaw and tonguing the shell of her ear, then pinned her to the couch, her wrists in his steely grasp and his rock-hard thigh shoved between her own. "And I'm still loving the fact you're planning on more than one. It makes me so fucking horny."

"You're so weird," she'd said, laughing and shaking her head at him. "How are you not freaking out about this? Hell, I'm still freaking out about this."

"I guess I've just never been one to freak out over things, especially something I've wanted for a long time."

"You realise you're proving my point, right?"

"Which point?" he'd asked, grinning down at her, one brow cocked. "That I'm weird?"

"Yes. I've never met a man who actively wants kids. It's... I don't know."

He'd laughed, obviously entertained by her disbelief. "Weird?"

"Yeah." She'd giggled, his humour infectious. "But a good weird, you know?"

"I do," he'd said, then kissed her slow and deep, stripped her naked, and had his wicked way with her.

The memory of Jack's hands on her body, of his mouth on her skin, coupled with the thick erection currently pressed against her arse—and the knowledge of what that beast could do—was making her pussy very wet, and her inner brat wanted to play.

Morning sickness be damned.

She wanted Jack inside her, and she wanted him now.

Reaching behind her, she took his cock in hand and lightly stroked him from root to tip, stilling when she heard him chuckle.

"Someone's awake early." His voice was thick with sleep, deep and sexy and warm.

She wriggled her arse and glanced over her shoulder, grinned at him. "What are you going to do about it?"

His chuckle grew sinister as his grip tightened on her hip. "I'm going to fuck my brat into submission," he growled, then notched himself between her legs, the smooth tip of his cock nudging inside her. "Are you wet for me, baby? I know you are," he whispered by her ear, his dark velvet voice wrapping itself around her, holding her enthralled. "I can feel you, all silky soft and dripping wet."

Sophie bit her lip to hold back her whimper, but she wriggled her arse again, encouraging him to do as he wished. To push deeper.

"You want me inside you, angel? You want sir's thick cock filling you up?"

She desperately wanted to scream at him for teasing her, especially when the hand that had been gripping her hip slid between her legs and found her clit with pinpoint accuracy. She wanted to play, wanted to taunt, wanted to drag it out for as long as she possibly could, but there was that desperation again creeping through her, holding her captive. That *craving*. That need to have him take her and love her and make her completely and utterly his.

"Yes, sir. I want that very much."

"Then be a good little girl and beg me for it," he snarled. "Beg for my cock."

Jack slid in a fraction deeper, just enough for her pussy to stretch around him, to ignite those nerve endings and shoot paroxysms of pleasure deep into her core. She shivered all over and this time her whimpers would not be restrained.

"Jack, sir. Please. Please fill me with your cock. I want to be your good girl. I want to be yours."

A week had passed since she'd admitted to Anna in the kitchen that she loved Jack, but she still hadn't gathered the courage to say it to his face. She still held back just that little bit, afraid it was all a beautiful dream and she was going to wake up at any moment and find herself right back where she'd started, scared and alone.

An outsider, unwanted and unloved.

But this she could do.

Sex was easy.

Sex was the common denominator of all things.

At least she could trick herself into believing that for as long as Jack was inside her. Which he wasn't. Not yet. She hadn't begged enough.

"Please," she said again, surprised by the catch in her voice. "Please fuck me into submission. Please hold me. Please take me. Please... love me."

Jack slammed his hips forward, seating himself deep inside her and held her so tightly she thought her ribs might crack. "I do love you, angel. I will always love you." He held out his little finger. "I pinkie swear it."

Sophie hiccoughed a laugh and joined her pinkie with his, the gesture, as childish as it was, meaning more to her than he knew. Then a sudden burst of brattitude made her push away from her lover and turn to face him.

Ripping back the covers, she exposed his glorious body to her hungry gaze and took a moment to admire and ogle him, from his broad shoulders, to his washboard abs, to his long, thick cock, still glistening with her juices.

"Like what you see?" he said, humour dancing in his perfect blue eyes.

"Yep." Sophie laughed happily and straddled his hips, then grabbed his erection and guided it back inside her. Where it belonged. "I wanted to see your face," she said, slowly sinking down on him as she drank in his handsome features. "I needed to see what you looked like when I—" The feel of his erection hitting deep stole the breath from her lungs and all thought from her mind, the sensation sublime.

"When you what, angel?"

Coming back to her senses, she licked her lips and rocked her hips, eliciting a satisfying moan from her lover. A confidence boosting moan that encouraged her to be brave. To be vulnerable. "When I tell you, sir, Jack... I love you."

"Sophie." Jack whispered her name through smiling lips. She'd made him happy, and she hadn't done it just to spare his feelings but because she had finally taken charge of her own.

Gripping her arse in one hand and her throat in the other, Jack took control and did as promised. He fucked her into submission.

Sophie rode out her first orgasm within minutes, the position she was in and the angle of their bodies ensuring Jack's cock filled her to the point of being almost painful. A delicious pain that fuelled her pleasure and took her higher, carried her away on wave after wave of ecstasy. And his clever fingers worked her clit like no man ever had, adding another layer to the blissful sensations crashing through her body and mind.

Honestly, if she ever found out who taught him how to do that, she was sending them a well-earned thank-you card.

Her second orgasm was slower to arrive. Jack rocked their bodies together, like the roll of the ocean, serene and constant and full of unfathomable depths. He pulled her closer, down to his chest, and wrapped his arms around her.

"I love my girl," he whispered in her ear. "My beautiful brat. My angel."

"And I love my sir," she whispered back. "I love you,

Jack."

When they came, they came together, and Sophie felt a fullness of body, mind, and soul, a sense of togetherness and rightness. A love she'd never experienced before, but one she was already addicted to.

One she craved more of.

More than was probably healthy.

Jack held her afterwards, cradled her against his chest and stroked her hair, soothed her with gentle, constant touches, but it didn't last.

Her nausea was back.

Sitting up, she pressed her hands against his chest and lifted herself off him. But she didn't go far before realising something was very wrong.

A sharp, gut-wrenching pain sliced through her abdomen.

She gasped at the sensation, realising it was one she was all too familiar with. But no, that couldn't be right. She was pregnant. She shouldn't be having those pains.

"Baby, what's wrong?"

In an instant, Jack was out of bed and helping her to stand, holding her up as she doubled over in agony. "Jack." His name was barely even a whisper.

Fear had stolen her voice.

Rushing to the bathroom, she grabbed a hand towel and stuffed it between her legs. A moment later she heard Jack speak, but not to her.

"I need an ambulance," he said, his voice eerily calm. "I think my girlfriend is having a miscarriage."

Locking eyes with Jack, she saw the tears tracking down his face, and when she pulled the towel away, she knew he was right. Her dream was shattering apart.

The towel was soaked in blood.

27

J ack paced beside Sophie's hospital bed, a thin blue curtain the only thing shielding them from the noise and the chaos of the emergency room.

A nurse had ushered them in there over thirty minutes earlier, but they were yet to see a doctor.

"Jack." Sophie's strained voice made him stop.

"What is it, baby?" he asked, taking her hand in his.

"I'm sorry," she whispered before another onslaught of tears flooded down her cheeks.

Gathering her into his arms, he sat on the edge of her bed and held her, stroked her hair and reassured her. She'd done nothing wrong.

As heartbroken as he was to lose another child, he was more concerned with Sophie's wellbeing. He needed to know she was going to be okay. He needed her to know it too.

Where is the fucking doctor?

Another forty minutes passed before the curtain drew back and a doctor appeared. An older-looking man with greying hair and a clean-shaven face. A stern-looking man with hard features and a distant gaze. Old school. "My apologies for the wait," he said, his tone short and to the point. "We're short-staffed today." He flipped open the folder in his hands. "Now, Miss Bennett, can you tell me what happened?"

Jack tried to move away and give Sophie space, but she refused to let him go, her grip tightening on his shirt. "After we had sex this morning, I started feeling nauseous again. I thought it was morning sickness until the pain hit me and I started to bleed."

"And why do you think it's a miscarriage and not your period?" he asked, not even looking up from the file. "The symptoms can be very similar."

Sophie shook her head. "I took a bunch of pregnancy tests when the nausea first started."

"And when was that?"

"A little over a week ago. They all came back positive." After a beat of silence, she added, "My cycle has always been irregular, and it's always heavy and painful, but it's been over two months since my last period. I've never gone that long without bleeding before."

The doctor took notes as Sophie talked, his pen flying across the page, but he didn't look up at her even once, and his tone remained cold and unaffected. Jack knew the reason for it—professional distance, don't get involved—but it didn't stop him from wanting to shake the man and make him look at the woman in front of him. Make him acknowledge her pain.

"And how far along do you think you were?"

Jack squeezed Sophie's hand and took over answering. Maybe Dr Douchecanoe would respond better if a man was doing the talking. "About five weeks," he said. "New Year's Eve."

"You're sure of your dates?"

"I am."

The doctor nodded and made more notes. Then, as expected, he looked to Jack and not Sophie. "Unfortunately, with such an early state pregnancy, there's little we can do but wait for the body to expel the tissue on its own." He scribbled more notes. "I will ask your girlfriend to take another pregnancy test, though. The hormones required for a positive test will still be present in her system, so this will tell us if she was actually pregnant or if this is just her irregular menstrual cycle at work."

"I'm sitting right here," Sophie muttered, but the doctor ignored the comment.

"A nurse will be back shortly with the test," he said, then pulled the curtain back. "How's your pain?"

"Painful," Sophie said, not quite snapping the word at the doctor.

"I'll order you some pain relief too."

And with that, he was gone again, and the curtain fell back into place.

"How do you really feel?" Jack asked. "I know you can handle a decent amount of pain but I need to know if you're truly hurting."

"Jack, I'm fine," she sniped, then winced and bit her lip, indicating she was anything but. *Stubborn brat.* "I'd kill for my heat pack though," she added through gritted teeth. "And a brick of chocolate."

Jack scrubbed his hand across his jaw. "Is he right, do you think? Could this just be your period?"

"You both seem to be forgetting about the pregnancy tests I took. Three of them. All positive." She folded her arms and scowled. "If you don't believe me, ask Abby or Lucy. They were there when I took them. In fact, it was their suggestion to do all three just in case the first one was wrong, mostly because none of us believed I could be pregnant since we'd used protection for all but our last time together that night, and even then, you didn't come inside me."

"Yes, I spoke to someone about that too. Our family doctor, my cousin Matt. He said it was possible to become pregnant even when using condoms, and that *where* I came on you was more than sufficient to knock you up. It's not common but it does happen."

"I'm not your ex," Sophie said, her voice so quiet that Jack almost didn't hear her.

"I know you're not her, Soph."

"Do you?" she demanded. "You obviously don't trust me or you wouldn't have asked your cousin if it was possible." She swiped at her tears. "I would have shown you the tests if you'd asked. Hell, I would have taken another one if you'd wanted me to."

"Soph—"

"Maybe I should have," she whispered, more to herself than him. "Then we would have known for sure." She stared at him, searched his gaze with wild eyes. "Do you even want to be with me if I'm not pregnant?"

"Of course I do."

He stared at his lover, returned her fierce expression, the shock of her words momentarily clouding his brain from the truth of them. She was anxious, scared. Terrified he only wanted her for the baby, that he would now reject her and send her away as he had with Lisa.

But Sophie was *not* Lisa.

She wasn't vindictive and cruel.

She wasn't selfish and entitled.

Sophie Bennett had a beautiful soul with a kind heart, a

wicked sense of humour, and an arse that just wouldn't quit. He'd been half in love with her before they'd even met, and meeting her had been the best moment of his life.

"I sent you gifts without knowing you were pregnant," he said, gripping her chin and making her look at him. "I came looking for you at your uncle's wedding without knowing you were pregnant. It's *you* I want, Sophie. I fell head over heels in love with you the night we met, and baby or not, I will continue loving you until my dying breath."

Rich brown eyes blinked up at him, less wild than they were before, and her voice softened, lost its troubled edge. "Jack."

"You're mine, Sophie, and you mean so much more to me than whether or not you can give me kids. I love all of you, every part of you." He placed his hand over her belly. "Not just this. Understand?"

She opened her mouth to respond, but a nurse pulled back the curtain. An older woman this time, kindly looking with laugh lines around her eyes and mouth. "Knock, knock," she said. "I'm Marina. I have some pain relief for you, Sophie, and then we're taking a walk to the bathroom, okay?"

Sophie nodded, and Jack moved out of the way to let the nurse do her thing. "Do you want me to come with you, baby?"

She shook her head and got to her feet. "I'm fine."

She didn't sound fine, but he said, "Okay," and let her do what she had to.

When they returned fifteen minutes later, Sophie was visibly upset. Her eyes were red again, like she'd just had a good cry, and she was sniffing. "We can go home," she said, picking up her handbag. "I'm not pregnant." Her voice caught on the words. "I never was. The test was negative."

Jack looked to the nurse and furrowed his brow. "If this test was negative, then how did she get three positive tests a week ago?"

The nurse stuffed her hands in her pockets and frowned. "I'm assuming they were they all out of the same box?"

Sophie nodded. "Yes."

"Do you remember the brand name?"

"No. Why?"

"There was a product recall recently for two different types of tests, made by the same manufacturer. Several batches were contaminated, causing the tests to show a positive result even when it was negative."

"What?" Jack couldn't hide his anger. "You'd think something like that would be in the news."

The nurse lifted her shoulder in a half shrug, her expression one of pity, of apology. "It probably was, tucked away somewhere in one tiny corner of the internet." When Sophie started crying again, the older woman wrapped her arm around her shoulders and gave her a reassuring hug. "Oh, honey, these things happen sometimes. Personally, I'd be thankful it was just a faulty test and *not* a miscarriage. Not every woman is as lucky." She looked to Jack, and added quietly, "But if you know which brand it was, maybe check online to see if any batches have been recently recalled. You might be eligible for compensation."

Jack shook his head, even more confused. "If the tests were faulty, why did she have all the symptoms of pregnancy? She's had constant nausea, headaches, food sensitivity, she's fatigued."

"And my boobs hurt," Sophie added, sniffing back tears. "And I need to pee twenty times a day. What else could it have been?"

"Have you been under any stress recently?"

"No," she said at the same time Jack said, "Yes."

Sophie glared at him, but he stared her down, one brow raised, until she dropped her gaze, until she submitted. "She's sold her house, moved interstate, and started both a new job and a new relationship all in the span of a few weeks." Not to mention still being harassed in the media by his ex-wife, even though he'd warned her not to.

"Well, that sounds pretty stressful to me," the nurse said. "And stress often presents with similar symptoms to pregnancy, including disrupting your menstrual cycle."

"You have got to be kidding me," Sophie muttered, her anger momentarily overriding her grief. She barked an incredulous laugh. "So all of this basically boils down to faulty pee sticks and stress? I got my hopes up—*we* got our hopes up—for nothing."

His girl looked up at him, her lovely face red and blotchy from crying, her lips pale and her hair limp, and still as beautiful to him as the night they met. "Not for nothing, angel," Jack said, cupping her cheeks, refusing to let her look away. He needed her to see the sincerity in his eyes, hear it in his voice. "We're together now. That's all that matters."

"But you wanted this baby so badly," she whispered. "So did I."

"Then we'll try again. And again and again. And if it doesn't take, then we'll look at IVF or adoption. And if that doesn't work then... fuck it. I'll buy us a baby." He paused to register the smile spreading slowly across her face. "But you need to know, Sophie, you need to understand that even if we don't have any kids at all, I am happy, I am content, and I am in love with *you*. The whole woman, remember?"

She pressed her hand against her belly. "Not just this."

Silent tears streamed down Sophie's cheeks, only this time she didn't look sad. She looked at him the way she had when they'd made love that morning, when she'd finally said the words he'd been dying to hear. "I love you, too," she whispered. "So much."

A soft sob came from near the curtain, and they turned to see Marina wiping her nose with a tissue, a watery smile on her face as she stared at them. Jack hadn't realised she was still there. "I'm sorry. But you two are so freaking cute together. Take it from me, honey, he's a keeper." She handed Jack a clipboard. "If you'll sign the form, you're all good to go."

An hour later they were back in their apartment, Sophie with her heat pack strapped to her belly and Jack on his laptop, working from home, keeping an eye on his angel.

They'd decided to hold off on telling everyone what had happened, beyond saying Sophie was unwell. But just for a day. Just until they had both wrapped their heads around it and accepted it as truth.

Until then, they would carry on as usual, would continue getting to know each other. They would laugh and cry, hug and kiss, cook and eat. But most importantly, they would build a life together. A life others envied.

A life—a *love*—to last forever.

EPILOGUE

S ophie's feet hurt. And the bridesmaid dress she'd squeezed her slowly expanding body into that morning wasn't doing the rest of her any favours either. Not that Jack seemed to care about her extra weight. He hadn't kept his hands off her in days.

Not since they had discovered she was pregnant.

For real this time.

They'd used six different pregnancy tests from three different companies over two days just to be sure.

But just the same as last time, finding out she was pregnant seemed to flick the caveman switch in Jack's brain, and he'd fucked her every which way come Sunday ever since, like a never-ending victory lap of sex. A celebration of his virility.

She was exhausted.

Not that she was complaining. Jack Martin was the best lover she'd ever had or could ever want. Attentive, caring, creative, dominant as fuck, and the things that man could do with his tongue should be illegal.

And he was all hers.

Ours, she thought as she slid one hand over her belly.

Hers and their baby's.

As they swayed in time to the music, Jack hooked a knuckle under her chin and lifted her face to his, making sure she couldn't turn away, then pressed a kiss to her lips. "I love you, Sophie," he said, moving his hand to cup her cheek, his fingertips soft and warm against her skin.

"I love you too."

"And I can't wait to have this baby with you, to start a family with you, grow old with you." He pulled away and reached inside his jacket pocket, then went down on one knee.

In the middle of the freaking dance floor.

"What are you doing?" she whispered through gritted teeth, nervously glancing around her to see if anyone else was watching the insanity going on right in front of her. "Are you crazy?"

He grinned. "I thought I was weird."

"You're both. You can't propose at someone else's wedding. It's rude. Stand up before someone sees you."

She didn't care how much she loved the man, she would not allow him to ruin Abby's big day, but it was too late. People had already begun to stare. Worse, they were leaving the dance floor, leaving her alone with her lunatic boyfriend who apparently thought it was perfectly fine to make a scene at someone else's wedding.

Ready to disabuse of him of that notion, she opened her mouth… only to snap it shut without a word when she realised the music had stopped. Glancing around them again, she became very aware of the fact that she was standing in the middle of the church hall, Jack on one knee in front of her with a ring box in his hand and every person in the room watching them, including Abby and Wolf, who rather suspiciously did not look particularly upset—or even surprised—by what was happening.

She stared at the grinning newlyweds, confusion knitting her brow. "What the—"

"Eyes on me, angel."

As always, Jack's delicious voice drew her attention back to him, the rich, deep timbre holding sway over her, and when she stared down into his gorgeous blue eyes, his indulgent gaze told her she was his world.

God knew he was hers.

"Sophie, I have adored you from the moment I saw your first make-up tutorial blooper reel on Instagram." A twittering of laughter echoed around the hall. "And I have loved you from the moment we first met on that hotel balcony on New Year's Eve. I can't imagine a life without you in it. I refuse to imagine a life without you by my side. Say you'll marry me, angel. Say you'll be my wife."

The urge to cry, to throw herself at him and scream yes was narrowly averted when she realised he hadn't actually asked her to marry him. Cocking one brow at his thinly veiled command, she planted her hands on her hips and said, "I didn't hear a question in there."

Jack bowed his head and chuckled, along with everyone else in attendance. "It's never the easy way with you, is it?"

She returned his grin and shrugged. "Where's the fun in that?"

Jack lifted his head and stared at her, his shoulders bouncing with laughter. "All right, baby. You win." He took a breath and shook his head at her, his wicked smile promising her arse was in for a world of hurt when they got home. "Sophie Bennett, will you marry me?"

"See?" she said, needing to push him further, needing to

know he was there for all of it, all of her. Brattiness included. "That wasn't so hard, was it?"

"Sophie," he growled, his warning clear as he took her hand in his. "Don't make me put you over my knee in front of all these people, baby."

He'd said the same thing to her at the last wedding they'd attended. The first time she'd thought she was having his baby.

The night he'd truly claimed her as his.

"Okay, fine," she said, giggling when he huffed a muffled "Brat" at her. "Yes, I'll marry you."

As soon as Sophie said the words, the room exploded with cheering and streamers and music. But she didn't hear any of it. She was too focussed on the man sliding the most beautiful—and enormous—diamond ring she'd ever seen onto her finger.

"Wow," she said, her vocabulary failing her as she took in what had to be at least five carats of emerald-cut perfection now weighing down her left hand. "That is so heavy."

Jack levered to his feet and inspected the ring. "Do you want me to buy you something smaller?"

"Don't you dare!" she replied, feigning horror as she snatched her hand back and hid it from him, making him laugh. God, she loved his laugh. "I'll just have to get stronger, that's all. Learn how to carry the weight of it."

Jack pulled her into his arms and pressed his forehead against hers. "You're already one of the strongest women I know, and I'll help you carry whatever weighs you down for as long as you let me."

She smiled. "That's not even remotely what I meant," she said, knowing full well he knew that but loving that he'd said it anyway.

"But it's the truth nonetheless," he said. "You're my

woman, Sophie. My baby, my good girl, my brat. You're my angel, and while I can't promise you that every day will be sunshine and roses, I will spend the rest of my life reminding you that you are loved, you are cherished, and you are not alone."

The urge to throw herself at him was clawing at her again, but she wasn't ready to submit to him just yet. Pushing his buttons, on the other hand, was always a good idea. "So what you're really saying is I'm stuck with you."

He pursed his lips, but not before another laugh slipped out. "Yep." He wasn't taking the bait.

Dropping her gaze, she toyed with the buttons on his shirt. "You know you're stuck with me, too, right? Fat arse, bratty attitude, and all?"

Jack smacked her arse and hauled her closer, pushed his thickening cock against the apex of her thighs. "Never forget, I have an abiding love for this arse of yours, especially when your bratty attitude gives me an excuse to paint it red."

She bit back a fresh grin and popped the top button open. "Should I give you an excuse right now?"

He cocked one brow and stared at her in that bossy way she loved that made her heart race and her panties wet. "Are you that eager for a spanking?" he murmured, looking around at the other wedding guests as they filled the dance floor again.

"I'm eager to get off my feet," she clarified. "But I wouldn't say no to a nice spanking."

"A nice spanking," he repeated, shaking his head, then laughed. "Little brat. When I get you home, the spanking you get will be anything but *nice*."

She grabbed his wrist and checked his watch for the time. "And when will that be exactly?"

"When I say so," he said, leading her away from the crowd and towards a table and chairs.

"You're going to make me wait, aren't you?"

Jack sat her down and removed her shoes. "Yep."

"I hate waiting," she said, folding her arms and pouting.

He grinned at her again. "I know." He began rubbing her feet. "But I'll make it worth the wait."

Sophie moaned as Jack dug his thumbs into a particularly sore spot on the ball of one foot, then leaned forward and pressed a kiss to his sensual mouth. "You always do," she said softly, remembering how he'd taken care of her needs over the past few months. How nothing was ever too much trouble or an inconvenience. How he'd made her feel so welcome in his life, so necessary.

Before she could retreat, he wrapped his hand around her nape and dragged her back for another kiss. Harder than the last, deeper, longer. Possessive and dominant yet sweet and reassuring. "I always will," he said, stroking his knuckles over her cheek.

"I love you, Jack," she murmured against his mouth.

"I love you, too, baby."

"And Jack?"

"Yes, angel?"

"You owe me ten dollars."

Jack burst out laughing, the sound one of joy and love and acceptance. A sound that filled her heart and soul with the same emotions and wrapped her up in the comfort of them, the comfort of *him*. "Brat."

"Hey, a bet's a bet, and you lost fair and square."

Her fiancé kissed her again, still chuckling all the while. "I might have lost the bet," he said, resting his hand over her stomach, "but I won something 100 percent better."

"A baby?" she whispered.

He shook his head. "A family."

And that was the moment when her inner brat sat the fuck down and shut the fuck up and let Sophie submit to the torrent of feelings pouring through her. That was the moment she gave in and threw herself at him, climbed into his lap, and settled in against those tree trunks he called thighs, knowing he had the strength to carry her home if he had to. Knowing he had the strength to handle her with ease, that she wasn't too much or too big or too loud.

Knowing he thought she was his perfect fit.

Before Jack came along, Sophie had always felt so awkward and out of place, but he'd given her his love so freely, so absolutely, had made room for her in his heart, room to move and grow right along with him. Room to be a family.

Her heart swelled and filled to overflowing with her love for him.

As she snuggled against Jack's chest and rested her head on his shoulder, she felt the steady beat of his heart thumping in time with her own. The strong heart of a powerful man. Her man. Her heart.

Her family.

THE END

MORE FROM JENNIE KEW

Battery Operated Boyfriend

Tying The Knot

Quirky: The Complete Q Collection

ACKNOWLEDGEMENTS

To my family for all their encouragement, their love and understanding, thank you for being you and for putting up with me being me, especially when deadlines are involved.

To my editor, Kristin Scearce, who accepts my weird writing style and quirky humour as canon and is still willing to work with me, you rock!

And finally to my readers, thank you for taking this journey with me, and for allowing me to share with you all the people and places who occupy my head and my heart. I hope you enjoy reading about them as much as I enjoy writing about them.

MEET THE AUTHOR

Jennie has always enjoyed reading but never had aspirations of becoming a published author. At least not until a dance with death made her ask herself what she really wanted out of life, and she's been writing ever since.

When not writing stories about her imaginary friends, Jennie can usually be found reading a book, watching a movie or building stuff out of Lego. She lives in regional New South Wales with her husband, her husband's magnificent beard, and their small menagerie of furry companions.

www.jenniekew.com

GLOSSARY

As all of my books are set in Australia and use a lot of Australian terms and slang, I've created this guide for my readers to keep you on track when you come across any Aussie-isms in my books.

A bit of all right: If someone is 'a bit of all right' they're considered to be very attractive.

Ambo: Short for ambulance, the term has come to mean anyone associated with any of the public or private ambulance services, their drivers and paramedics.

Arse: Aussie spelling of ass, aka buttocks, bottom, booty and bum.

Arvo and *Sarvo*: 'Afternoon' and 'this afternoon'.

Copper: Police, cops.

Cricket nets: batting practice cages for the Australian summer sport of cricket.

Fashion Rag/Local Rag: Fashion magazine, any locally produced magazines or newspapers.

Fierie/s: Firefighter/s.

Fivesies: Pre-dinner drinks and snacks, usually consisting of wine, and cheese, served around 5 p.m.

Fuck-knuckle: An idiot.

G'day: Pronounced 'gidday', this official Australian greeting is a contraction of the words 'good' and 'day'.

G-string: Thong underwear

Kiwi: Pronounced 'kee-wee', anyone born in New Zealand.

Larrikin: An unruly, boisterous but generally good natured person, usually male.

Mate: Unlike paranormal or sci-fi erotic romances where your 'mate' is the person you're fated to be with for the rest of your life, in Australian culture 'mate' could mean anyone from your best friend to some random bloke you just met.

Pav: Pavlova, a dessert made from baked meringue, topped with cream and fresh fruit, particularly popular around Christmas. We nicked it from the Kiwis.

Phwoar: An estimation of the sound one makes when a bit of all right enters your vicinity. See also, 'panting' and 'drooling'.

RFS: Rural Fire Service.

Sanga: Sandwich.

She'll be right, mate: Usually given as a response when someone is offering aid of some kind, it means 'Everything will be fine but thanks for asking'.

Thongs: Flip-flops/footwear

Togs: A swimsuit.

Tradie: Any tradesman.

Uni: Pronounced 'you-nee', University aka College.

Yeah, nah and *Nah, yeah*: Whichever word the phrase ends on, is the affirmative answer, therefore 'Yeah, nah' means 'No', and 'Nah, yeah' means 'Yes'.